T0197131

The Tortoise Shell Comb

English Translation by Jean-Pierre Angel

Jean-Pierre Angel

authorHOUSE®

AuthorHouse™
1663 Liberty Drive
Bloomington, IN 47403
www.authorhouse.com
Phone: 1 (800) 839-8640

Published by AuthorHouse   10/28/2015

ISBN: 978-1-5049-2434-4 (sc)
ISBN: 978-1-5049-2433-7 (e)

Library of Congress Control Number: 2015911916

To Andrea Leers whose support unleashed my inspiration

CHAPTER 1

May 1941

8 p.m. My mother is anxious. At 23 rue des Écouffes in the heart of the Marais in Paris, my father hasn't returned from work. He usually arrives around 7:30 p.m. and he's never very late. My mother and I walk down the street, pass by the grocery store, enter the pharmacy, then the café. Each time my mother asks the same question.

"Have you seen my husband? He hasn't come home yet."

Each time they shake their heads "no." We walk as far as the Métro hoping to meet him on the way. Perhaps there was a breakdown on the line but everything seems normal. We cross the rue du Roi de Sicile, walk alongside the rue Saint Antoine, and come back by the rue des Franc-Bourgeois. Maman walks fast.

"Hurry up, Simon."

We return to the apartment. Hearing our footsteps, my sister Élise opens the door. She was worried as she waited for us. My mother's face is pale.

10 o'clock then 11 o'clock. Still no news. Maman knocks on our neighbors' door. They come out on the landing in their pajamas. They were asleep and feel sorry for my mother. They try to appease her, but it's no use. Maman comes back inside.

She can't sleep but Élise and I doze off next to her on the sofa. I wake up with a start when maman bursts out crying. She gets up, goes to the bedroom, passes by the kitchen, and returns to the bedroom before coming back to the living room and slumping in an armchair. She cries quietly. She doesn't know what to do.

Maman is back on the street with the first light of dawn. The café owner on Rue des Rosiers waves at her. "Ah, Madame Crespi! I was about to come for you. I just hung up. Someone called and a man left you a message."

"Who was it? Did he give his name?"

"No. He said he was relaying a message from Victor Crespi."

The café owner hesitates before continuing. "Your husband was arrested. He wants you to know he will write as soon as he can to let you know where he is." My mother is in shock.

"Is that all?" she asks.

"That's all."

My father was picked up in a round-up on his way home from work. Police officers were hiding in the hallways of the Saint Paul subway station. They were everywhere. Some wore uniforms, others were in civilian clothes. It was impossible to escape the trap. The police stopped the men and asked to see their papers. They arrested all foreign Jews. It wasn't difficult to identify my father. The word "**JUIF**" was stamped in red on his ID card as it was on that of the others arrested. They took him to the police station and from there transported him to a center where hundreds of men were already assembled—all in the same situation. Papa talked to a police officer who seemed more understanding than the others. He asked the officer to call the café on rue des Rosiers and leave a message for his wife, Fanny Crespi. After my father slipped him a 50-franc banknote to emphasize his request, the officer agreed. Luckily my father had just received his paycheck that day.

Coming out of the café, maman rushes to the police station looking for information. An officer gives in to her persistence and makes two or three phone calls to find out the status of those arrested.

"All foreign Jews taken in custody yesterday are to be transferred to a camp," he reports.

"Where?" She asks.

"In the region of the Loiret."

Her reaction is to leave immediately to visit her husband. She has one idea in mind: find out how he is and how to free him. The officer says it is still too early. "You must be patient, Madame. No list is yet available. Come back in a few days."

"In a few days!"

"After the men have been transferred."

Three days later a letter from papa appears at our house. There is no stamp on the envelope. Someone must have slipped it discreetly into the mailbox.

Camp of Beaune-la-Rolande

May 19, 1941

My dear Fanny, my dear children,

I was caught in a round-up on my way home from work. The police were hiding in the subway corridors checking IDs. I was transferred to a camp for immigrants in Beaune-la-Rolande, in the Loiret, some three hours south of Paris. Our barracks look like stables. We lack everything, including food. We sleep on triple bunks, just straw covered boards. There are 150 men in my barrack.

They say visits may eventually be permitted and I will send you the date when you will be allowed to come.

I need clothes. They said you'd be able to take away my dirty laundry and send it back clean through the mail. There is no risk in coming to visit. They only arrest men. Please bring me some soap, a razor, sheets, a needle and thread, and above all some food. They feed us very little. In the morning we get a weak bitter tea, at noon a turnip and potato soup, and at night a small piece of bread with a little margarine.

Élise, your mother will need your help. And you, Simon, try to behave. I kiss all three of you.

Victor

PS. Simonet owes me the last 100 francs on three suits he ordered for Mode Parisienne. Please go and ask him for payment.

When the authorization to visit finally arrives, maman rises early to organize the trip to Beaune-la-Rolande for that Sunday morning. She is taking us with her, hoping it will cheer papa. The three of us push and shove to get on a packed train at the Austerlitz station. Although Mother carries a big bundle with food and clothes, we have to stand in the coach corridor.

The group getting off the train is composed mostly of women. Together we walk the three kilometers to the camp that is surrounded by fields. The camp itself is ringed by a high barbed wire fence punctuated every 100 meters by a wooden lookout tower. Facing the camp's gate on the opposite side of the road, a tall round tower adjoins a corrugated roof shed. It's a silo for storing wheat. We go through the camp's entrance gate, a large wooden frame laced with barbed wire. Beyond the entry we find a vast courtyard leading to two long rows of barracks. There are 14 of them in all. French gendarmes—a military police force—administer the camp.

The men confined here are assembled in the courtyard awaiting visitors. Hundred of eyes search for a familiar face. Voices call out names. But we are lead directly towards a large shed near the entrance. Gendarmes open all packages to check their contents before hand-searching each visitor. At last they let us into the courtyard where the prisoners immediately surround us.

"Fanny!" shouts a voice on the outside edge of the assembly.

Maman takes my hand and advances towards the voice. Élise follows with anticipation. Maman throws herself into papa's arms. They hold each other tightly for a long while. He then kisses Élise and me.

Papa signals us to follow him away from the commotion. The four of us take a place on a grassy mound and maman hands the package to papa.

"Things to eat," she says. "And clothes. Just as you asked."

He looks through the bundle. "I will give you my dirty laundry before you leave... Ah! Books, Thank you!"

He describes life in the camp. "Many of us work in a nearby sugar beet factory. The work is hard, but at least we can get out. The gendarmes escort us to the factory and keep watch on us until we return to camp. Some of the factory workers are nice to us and I made friends with one of them. From time to time he slips me a chunk of bread or a fruit. It helps a lot because here they don't give us much to eat," he adds sadly.

"But what are they going to do with you?" asks maman.

"I think they will keep us here until the end of harvest. Then, for sure, they will send us back home." What papa purposely omits is that there are rumors in the camp that they will likely be sent to Germany to work in factories.

Papa and maman move further away sitting close to each other on the grass, holding hands. Élise and I remain quiet. Restless, I tear blades of grass, and watch my parents surreptitiously.

They stay a long while without moving; expressing in silence what cannot be expressed in words. Then they resume their intimate conversation. Time passes and at around 4 o'clock, women start moving towards the gate. They prepare to leave, anxious not to miss the last returning train of the day.

We stand up while papa goes to the barracks and comes back with his laundry. Then he hugs maman one last time and they hold each other a long time. Papa whispers in her ear. She cries and nods in silence.

"No te preocupes, hanoun, en la vida, todo tiene fin."

"Don't worry, darling, in life, there is an end to everything." He pronounces each word tenderly, in Ladino, the language of Sephardic Jews, our language. Papa kisses us and gives us his last instructions. He tells us to listen to our mother and to help make her life easier. We walk slowly toward the camp exit. I would have liked so much more…I turn and wave a last good-bye. Tears run down maman's cheeks.

*

My father writes as often as he is allowed to and maman answers every letter. Each time he sends her a package voucher she prepares a bundle. There are many regulations about the mail and only correspondence on camp forms is authorized. Letters are limited in number and are subject to censorship. Whenever possible, maman and papa use other means to correspond privately and more frequently. Some letters are handed to visitors, others are hidden in dirty laundry, or in the lining of a garment to be washed.

Élise and I write too. I fill in the official cards authorized by the camp administration.

Hier abtrennent!

Diese Seite ist fur die de Angehorigen Deutlich auf die Zeilen schreiben !

....

This side reserved for family members of the prisoners of war.

Write only on the lines and legibly. Detach along the dotted line.

....

Dear papa,

We miss you an awful lot. The house is so odd without you. I hope they will let you come home soon and I think of you all the time. Élise and maman, too. I told maman that I was thinking of you each night before going to sleep. So I came up with a thought, which I told maman. She thinks it's a good idea: All three of us together will think of you every night at 9 p.m., before we go to bed. I thought that if you could think of us at the same time, we would be thinking about each other together. Isn't that a good idea? Maman is busy making a food package. 'Til next time, my dear papa. Your son who loves you,

Simon

A few weeks later, maman receives permission to return to the camp. Once more, I go with her. Life there is getting increasingly difficult. New arrivals flood the camp. Papa has lost a lot of weight and his face is pale; he is depressed and dejected. The men are still poorly nourished and lack all basic things. They are still sleeping on straw.

Maman smiles and tries to appear strong. Although the purpose of the visit is to cheer papa, maman cannot help herself and bursts out crying during the visit. By the time we return to Paris she is exhausted. Her eyes are red and swollen. The next morning she finds the energy to tell Élise about daddy's health, his depressed mood, his courage, and the conditions of his detention.

Camp of Beaune-la-Rolande

Tuesday June 3 1941

My darling wife,

Your last visit gave me such pleasure, but I don't want you to worry so much for me. Your packages really sustain me. So much sugar beet and wheat grows around the camp. You would think it could help feed us. But no!

Here, boredom is our enemy. People organize lectures and concerts in the barracks. Some of the prisoners arrived here with violins, flutes, or other instruments. There is a very good violinist in my barrack.

The latrines are almost 200 meters from the barracks and there is mud everywhere when it rains. It clings to our feet and we drag it back inside.

I know how difficult life has become for you. Responsibility for the whole family has fallen on your shoulders until I return, and it is hard to handle it alone. You are very courageous, Fanica querida, and I know you take good care of the children.

Be courageous too, my dear children and do all you can to help your mother until my return.

Simon: I also think of the three of you every night at nine p.m.. It gives me the feeling we are together, at least in thought.

Fanny, answer me as soon as you can, and each time you send a package remember to slip in a well-hidden letter to avoid censorship.

I kiss you very tenderly, my darling wife,

Victor

PS. I had ordered a roll of fabric from Aignan's, for which I have already given him a down payment. You must go and see him. Explain the circumstances and ask him to return the down payment.

*

We have been living off our savings for the past few weeks. Maman sometimes manages to bring in small sewing jobs that she works on at home, as she did before Élise was born. It doesn't pay enough but it helps a bit. Maman has a reserve of money she keeps separate and she tells us one evening, "I want you to know that we have a little money put aside for emergencies. I hid it in the sugar jar in the kitchen."

*

In August, Hitler breaks the non-aggression pact concluded three years earlier with Russia. Launching a vast offensive, the Germans invade Russia and many people see a glimmer of hope in this sudden change. Fighting now on two fronts, the Germans might put less pressure on us, but these considerations are not enough to raise the morale of foreign Jews trapped in Paris.

Nothing changes for my father in Beaune-la-Rolande. He works either at the sugar factory or inside the camp. Maman continues to visit him whenever she can. New restrictions in Paris forbid Jews from owning a telephone. The French administration sends someone around to cut the lines. Maman bursts out angrily, "We never had a phone on rue des Écouffes anyway!"

The round-ups continue. Jews think twice before going outside their houses. When they do, they try to stay out of sight and breathe a sigh of relief when they return home safely.

At the end of August a rumor reaches the café: the 11ᵗʰ arrondissement is swarming with police. They pick up men walking on the street, coming out of the subway, and even in their own homes. They round up a great many Jews. The 11ᵗʰ is not far from us, just on the other side of Place de la Bastille! We soon hear that during a massive three-day round-up, thousand of men fall victim, and for the first time French born Jewish men are included.

Although the school year starts as usual, I notice that a number of Jewish students are missing. No one can explain why or where they went.

I steer clear of political discussions between students during breaks in the courtyard, where debates mirror the opinions and positions of each one's family. On one side are those for Pétain: They applaud the decisions of the old marshal and curse the British who bomb French factories. On the other side are those for De Gaulle: They support the British and call Petain's sympathizers: *collabos.*

Sometimes the two sides clash and they don't spare each other. The teachers have to intervene. Several on both sides use anti-Semitic clichés commonly heard among a good many French people (as well as read in the press).

Fortunately, there are exceptions. Papazian is one of them. He remains my good friend. Although we never discuss events that affect and frighten the Jews, I sense he does not share the feelings and ideas of other students.

CHAPTER 2

My father, Victor Crespi, was 19 in 1924, when he decided to immigrate to France to seek a better life. Born in Salonika, Greece, of Turkish parents, he was five when his family returned to Smyrna in Turkey, where he attended the school of the *Alliance Israelite Universelle*. Besides learning fluent French, he also learned that professions such as medicine or law were reserved solely for Muslims. Although Turkey displayed no resentment towards its Jews, the minorities, including Greeks, Armenians, and Jews were confined to business professions.

When he turned 14, Victor began an apprenticeship with a tailor, which the local rabbi had recommended. The tailor worked and lived in an apartment he shared with his wife and two children. At the beginning of his apprenticeship, Victor swept the workshop, ran errands and took out the garbage. He even went, on occasion, to fetch the children at school when their mother was busy. After a while, Victor's boss decided it was time to teach him to sew. The lessons took place in the afternoon, after his chores were completed. The tailor sat Victor on a stool near the woman doing finishing work. He taught him one stitch one day, another the next, then buttonholes, and so on. Later, the young man learned to work on the sewing machine, and eventually discovered the pleasure of ironing. In three years, he became proficient at construction and pattern making. It is around this time that he began to think of leaving Turkey.

As a Jew, he felt no patriotic attachment towards Turkey. He shared the common bias of the Jews of his country: Muslim culture was primitive and outdated and had not much to offer for the future of a young Jew. France, however, attracted him. No matter how painful the separation, he was ready to leave his family and move to Paris. He accepted that loneliness might be the price of leaving the pleasant life whose sweetness had filled each moment of his youth.

Life in Turkey hindered his thirst for independence and freedom. In France, he thought dreamily, all is possible.

"How do you know?" friends asked.

"I read it."

"How do you know it's not a pipe dream?"

"Nothing ventured, nothing gained," Victor replied. He didn't have enough education to try medicine or law, but he could succeed as a tailor.

Maurice Benaroya, a cousin two years older had immigrated to Argentina, a country he thought would be even more open than France, with numerous opportunities for success. Maurice sent glowing letters to his family. Argentina, he reported, is a paradise for those who want to succeed! He described in detail an attractive and easy life. He hoped to inspire young Jews from his native Smyrna to follow his example.

But Victor had chosen France, and had no interest in changing his mind. He thought himself just as ambitious as Maurice Benaroya but following a different route. He had learned about France at the *Alliance* and had no doubt it would fulfill his expectations. His family shared his high regard for the country.

Those Jews who had traveled the world thought of France as the *country of the rights of man.* They saw France as an enlightened and cultured nation on whose buildings were carved a universal ideal: *Liberté, Égalité, Fraternité.* Isn't a nation founded on the principles of tolerance the ideal place to build one's future? Victor was full of hope and ready to face the toughest obstacles in order to succeed.

Immediately upon arriving in Marseille, he took the evening train for Paris. He carried reference letters from family friends, from various businessmen, from his old boss, and from the community rabbi. He also carried addresses of Jews who had preceded him in Paris.

A young family established a few years earlier in the 3rd arrondissement welcomed him. They offered him a place to stay and helped him find a job as a presser with Isaac Abramowitz, a coat manufacturer on rues de Turenne. After a few months, Victor was able to rent a furnished room on boulevard Voltaire. He got along well with Abramowitz, tackling more responsibility each week. Soon he was doing finishing, then construction work and tailoring.

*

Mediterranean Jews are called *Sefarads*, which, in Hebrew, means from Spain. They are distinct from Jews of central Europe called *Ashkenazi*, which means German. While Ashkenazi Jews speak *Yiddish*, Sephardic Jews speak *Ladino* also known as *Djudio*. When the inquisition drove Sephardic Jews out of Spain, they spread throughout Italy and other Mediterranean countries, to Greece, Lebanon, Morocco, and of course Turkey where the emir *Bayazid II* generously opened the doors of his country. There, they flourished for centuries as they had in Andalusia before, under Muslim leadership.

Ladino is the language Sefarads carried in their luggage. Over time, words in Hebrew, Greek, Arabic, or Turkish became inserted in the language, which, however, retained its basic medieval Spanish vocabulary and grammar. Mediterranean Jews also spoke French, which in the Middle East had become the expression of high culture.

The workshop where my father was employed was a tower of Babel where Greek, Turkish, Ladino, and Yiddish were all spoken.

Victor was one of the youngest workers and although less experienced than most, he was happy to learn, and he applied himself with fervor. He gained the respect of his co-workers who knew they could count on him. These were happy times for the young man. Work was hard but Victor liked to push himself. He dreamed of one day working on his own. He enjoyed living in a modern, free country and did not regret coming to France.

Isaac Abramowitz closed the workshop on Saturday to observe Shabbat and Victor attended the Sephardic synagogue on rue Saint Lazare. There, surrounded by the familiar atmosphere of Jews from Turkey, he let nostalgia take hold of him. He made friends with a group of young men who spent Sundays bicycling around the surrounding countryside.

The synagogue on rue Saint Lazare was the breeding ground of matchmakers, mature women who thrived on arranging nuptial encounters. It didn't take long before they spotted the new arrival. Their approach was generally to introduce the two families to each other. Once they had given their approval, the young man and woman were permitted to meet. Sarah Nahmias approached Victor one day as he was talking to friends in front of the synagogue. She was a matchmaker known as Madame Sarah.

"Ven aqui, mancevico!" Come here young man, she called out to Victor while her hands searched the folds of her skirt for her notebook.

"I bet you are looking for a fiancée."

She leafed through her notes, wetting the lead of her pencil with her tongue and bombarding Victor with questions. She wanted to know the name of his mother, his father, and the occupations of each of the members of his family. Did Victor have relatives in France? In Istanbul, perhaps? In Athens? She dutifully wrote down the answers given while looking out of the corner of her eye at Victor Crespi who answered with an amused look.

Madame Sarah felt confident she would eventually interest the young man in one or another of the available young women she knew. As for my father, he put the cross-examination out of his mind. He did not feel he needed the services of a matchmaker. The furtive looks he exchanged with young girls leaving synagogue after Kiddush sufficed for now. When, sometime later, he again met Madame Sarah, he was the one who discreetly pointed out the young woman who had caught his eye at the Saturday morning service. In time, Madame Sarah accompanied him for tea one Sunday on a visit to a family living on rue du Chemin Vert.

The young woman's name was Fanny Mechulam. She was born in Istanbul and now lived with her mother. She looked smart and pretty with a temperament that could easily bristle when frustrated. The afternoon passed quickly in pleasant company. For Victor, it felt as though he was back in Turkey, sitting in this little Parisian living room; drinking tea, eating sweets, and stealing glances at the young woman without ever interrupting the flow of his conversation.

Before Victor's departure, Esther Mechulam, Fanny's mother, invited him for diner the following week. It then became routine for my father to attend the Shabbat lunch each Saturday on rue du Chemin Vert.

There he met Fanny's sister, Fortunée Carasso and her husband Salvatore. Fortunée had married two years earlier to the relief of her family and friends; for she was about to turn 24 and all were concerned she might remain an old maid. Although his parents were from Istanbul, Salvatore was born in France. Fortunée had therefore acquired the French citizenship by marriage. The couple had a little girl named Sarah. Salvatore had started his own watch business on Place La Fayette.

When Victor invited Fanny to the movies, Esther accepted for her daughter and specified that she would also come along. Taking Victor's arm, she said in Ladino, *"Ayde mancevo, dame tu brasso para caminar."* Give me your arm, young man so we can walk properly. Victor understood he would have to wait many weeks before gaining permission to go out alone with Fanny.

His patience—and Fanny's—were eventually rewarded. The two young people met regularly on Sundays for a walk in the Bois de Boulogne. They announced their engagement in the first days of March 1926.

The wedding celebration took place eight months later at the synagogue on rue Saint Lazare, where it had all started. Madame Sarah was among the guests. She looked at the couple with the satisfied and remote gaze of a painter contemplating her work, and wished them all the happiness in the world.

Victor and Fanny's three-room lodging was on rue des Écouffes in the heart of the Marais, the old Jewish district of Paris. They lived on the fourth floor, across a courtyard of an apartment house. On the front of the building that faced the street: were two enamel plaques: one read "Running Water" and the other *"Gas on every floor"*.

One reached the apartment via an old spiral staircase with shaky, worn steps that climbed along a wall of peeling paint. The apartment door opened onto a tiny vestibule. To the left was a long narrow kitchen. Beyond, a corridor led to the living room, then to one of the bedrooms. The other bedroom, on the opposite side of the corridor would soon become a sewing workshop. All the rooms were a bit dark, since the windows faced into the courtyard.

Communal squat toilets were located on each floor landing; tiny and smelly spaces equipped with what people called *alaturka*—a Turkish toilet appointed with foot rests around a drain. Victor's friends never failed to point the irony of the name.

Each floor landing was also fitted with a faucet above a cracked enamel sink. That constituted the running water. Fanny took their laundry to the public washhouse every other week.

*

The day after the wedding, Victor and Fanny received the family. Esther arrived with two women friends. Salvatore's sister Louise accompanied her brother, as well as Fortunée and little Sarah.

Fanny followed the Turkish custom of offering visitors a jar of rose preserve and a glass of water. After swallowing a spoonful of the jam, one of Esther's friends raised her glass and toasted, *"Bendicha esta casa y los que viven en eya!"* May god bless this house and those who live in it.

"May their life be good and happy," added another friend.

Victor served Turkish coffee in small cups. One of Esther's friends left the room and discreetly entered the newlywed's bedroom. She soon returned to show all a towel stained with blood, while Fanny disappeared in the kitchen to hide her blushing face.

"Mazal Tov!" The assembled group exclaimed before they began singing in Ladino.

*

Victor Crespi stopped in regularly at the café on rue des Rosiers after work for a glass of *raki,* to meet acquaintances, and to make a few phone calls. He sometimes lingered to play a game of domino until dinnertime. He counted both Sephardim and Ashkenazim among his friends. They came from Istanbul, from Athens, or from some tiny *shtetl* deep inside Poland. Many had entered France illegally and their papers were not in order.

On Saturday, Victor and Fanny went to rue du Chemin Vert where Esther prepared a Shabbat lunch for her daughters and sons-in-law. Some of Esther Mechulam's friends occasionally also joined them.

When Victor and Fanny showed up around noon the table was already set, covered with a white tablecloth and two candlesticks in the center. The arriving guests went straight to the kitchen to marvel at the array of Turkish dishes to which Esther was putting the final touches. Once everything was ready, Esther would take off her apron and cover her head with a scarf. Joining her guest in the dining room, she lit the candles and said the prayer with her hands circling the flames. Then, hands covering her eyes, with only her lips still moving, she silently continued to pray.

The ritual was part of the Friday night ceremony, but Esther enjoyed repeating it on Saturday while her entire family was present. Never mind if it stretched religious traditions. When Esther was done, one of the men followed with the Kiddush, then another with the blessing of the bread. Each of the guests standing around the table received a piece of braided challah, according to tradition.

The two sisters went to the kitchen to fetch platters full of stuffed tomatoes and zucchini, meatballs called *kufté*, a mixture of meat with leeks and bread. There was also spinach mixed with white beans, and *borécas*, and olives they called *azetounas* and then, delicious little cookies called *biscotchos*. To finish, Esther would take the *soutlache* out of the oven: a caramelized cream dessert made with sweetened milk and rice flour.

Mixing French and Ladino, the conversation stretched until late in the afternoon, when Esther prepared herself to return to synagogue for the last service of Shabbat.

*

Fanny gave birth to Élise ten months after the wedding. Proud as a peacock, Victor went to the 4th Arrondissement City Hall to register her birth. On the way back, he stopped at the café on rue des Rosiers to show off the official family booklet he had just received.

"She, at least, is French!" Exclaimed the father proudly.

He and Fanny had already filled out endless forms to become French citizens. Buried in red tape, the case—so far—remained inconclusive. Is not the first duty of an emigrant to learn patience?

When Victor felt ready, he set out to realize the ambition he had nurtured ever since he left Turkey. He bought a used sewing machine and a second-hand Stockman mannequin, and he opened his own shop. From then on, he could be seen climbing the spiral staircase with a role of fabric on one shoulder; descending a few days later with a number of suits and dresses on his arm. Fanny stitched the linings and did the finishing work while her baby was asleep.

Clients often climbed the four stories for a fitting. When Victor had too much work, he hired Maurice Adler as a daily worker, to do the pressing. Maurice took off his jacket and started to work as soon as he arrived. But he always kept his hat on, and never uttered a word. Each time he heard footsteps outside, he would put his jacket back on and go to the window looking anxiously, ready for any trouble that might be coming up the stairs. He had no immigration papers.

Soon Élise was old enough to be registered in the nursery school on rue des Hospitalières Saint Gervais. The building, once a slaughterhouse, still displayed two bronze bovine heads on each side of the entrance, like some pagan symbol.

Victor launched his own business manufacturing men's shirts. He borrowed money from Salvatore to rent a space and equip it with sewing machines. Fanny supervised the cutting of the fabric and the assembly of the pieces while her husband ran around Paris taking orders and delivering the finished goods. Victor was about to discover the hazards of running one's own business: competition, slow periods, shrinking profit margins during the off season, employees to let go, and unsold stocks to liquidate on the public markets around Paris.

*

In April 1931, Fanny headed for the Hôpital Rothschild in the 12th Arrondissement to give birth to a son. Most of the Marais was invited to celebrate the *brit mila*, the circumcision performed on the eighth day. They decided to call me Simon, in memory of my father's father who had passed away in Turkey two years earlier. Ashkenazim and Sephardim crowded into the small apartment on rue des Écouffes. They dressed me in a satin dress–the very one my mother's father had worn for the same event, and that my grandmother had packed when she left Turkey. They placed a drop of wine on my tongue, they sung blessings, and when I started to cry, the guests shouted, *"Mazal Tov!"*

While my mother put me back to bed, glasses were filled with raki, quantities of hot and cold *mézés* were passed around: cheese, tomatoes, eggplant, stuffed grape leaves, olives. The ceremony had lasted a few minutes but the guests lingered on until night.

*

I was a nervous and sensitive baby with a worried expression. The least noise woke me up and I cried for hours. The only person able to soothe my anxious nature was my mother, and she never spared her efforts to comfort me. As I grew up I loved to be around her. I followed her with my eyes as she went about the house or sat at her sewing machine, and whenever our eyes met, she rewarded me with her beautiful smile. She took me with her on errands in the neighborhood. The same ritual always preceded leaving the house. Sitting in front of her mirror, maman combed her hair and finished by holding it back with a tortoise shell comb. At night, in the room I shared with my sister, she sang lullabies to send me to sleep. The song I preferred was that of a girl in the South American pampas called the *"Negrita"*, admired for her black eyes and copper skin.

My nervous temperament persisted as I grew up. I stuttered and refused to speak for hours. I stayed away from other children in the sand box of the Place des Vosges. I had few friends and preferred to play alone at home with simple toys. My favorite was a box of old buttons. In my imagination, they became marching soldiers, the largest one, golden colored, I imagined to be a marshal on a horse. My father was not sympathetic to a sensitive and withdrawn son. I realized he would have preferred me to be like those boys who are always making noise and having fights.

One of my fondest memories was watching my mother smoke a cigarette after dinner. It enchanted me. She came to the darkened children's room and she smoked leaning on the threshold. She slowly brought the cigarette to her lips, sent out a puff with a smile before leaving without a word.

*

"Your file is being normally processed, Monsieur Crespi."

The response never varied when my father went to inquire about the progress of his application for French citizenship.

The civil servant sighed with a sorry look. "We are flooded with requests, you know."

"But it has been a long time..."

"Patience, monsieur Crespi, patience."

Would the family forever be confined to the limited world of the foreign Jews? Nevertheless, Jews had been established in France for generations, among them those from Alsace. They considered themselves one hundred percent French. Many who fought in World War I were proud to display their medals.

My father liked to follow political affairs and was frustrated to remain confined to the role of spectator. What could he do? How could a foreigner make his voice heard? Meanwhile, newspapers carried threatening messages. Editorials vilified communists and the foreigners who abused their welcome in a France that was generous. Jews were singled out as profiteers.

The tirades increased when the leftist *Front Populaire* movement brought Léon Blum to power. For anti-Semites as well as the average French people, it was too much! Jews looked at the standing of Blum with a mixture of pride and anguish, as always when one of their own became highly visible.

A turbulent period followed: strikes, and factories occupied by workers; anti-Semitic press campaigns of the *Action Française*; profuse insults poured on Léon Blum. Jews were blamed for the insurrection of Franco in Spain supported by Hitler and Mussolini. Gathered in the cafés of the Marais, people argued endlessly, expressed opinions about how to get Europe out of the crisis, and searched the papers in vain for reassuring news.

"Jews are fleeing from Germany selling everything for nothing! They line up for hours to get visas!"

"Visas? To go where?"

"To come to France, of course! They know here they will find protection."

"How do you know, Attali? Why would Jews find protection here?"

"Because this is the country of the declaration of rights of man and of the citizen! Equality, liberty, the protection of citizens against their own government. Jews recognize nothing can happen to them here."

In fact, anti-Semitism spread, bringing waves of troubled waters to the beaches of peaceful exile. Nothing seemed able to stop it. Everywhere in Central Europe Jews were attacked in the street, their windows broken, and their shops set on fire. They were harassed and beaten black and blue.

One had to be blind not to notice that the curse was drawing closer. During Passover, my sister Élise related to us what happened to her in school. Two girls eyed her snack and asked, "What are you eating? It looks so good!"

"It's called matzos. Do you want to try it?"

"Oh no!" One girl answered. "My mother says you make it with the blood of Christian babies."

Élise ran home to the rue des Écouffes, all the way down the rue des Rosiers, as if responding to a century old fear.

Papa sighed deeply. "Élise you must try not to appear different from the others."

I understood what my father's remark meant—his desire to protect us as we were, combined with his uneasiness at the thought of our being different. He was a foreigner and he was Jewish. In spite of his efforts to speak good French his accent betrayed him. He was further branded by his Middle Eastern customs. His children were suffering the consequences of his decision to start a new life in France. At the same time, he recognized his own dissatisfaction. My father's overall disappointment increased as the atmosphere in the country deteriorated.

"As for you, Simon, you must apply yourself in school."

Truthfully, I was not a great success in school. I needed help and would easily get confused without reason, and that irritated my father. He thought I was too shy, not assertive enough. Providentially, my mother protected me from his impatience.

Maman had resumed working, now that both Élise and I were in school. Financially, my parents were doing better. During the summer of 1938, papa closed the workshop and the family took its first vacation. We spent a week in Trouville where we swam in the sea and ate lots of fish. We left behind the family worries, the trouble of the Jews, and the insanity taking hold of Europe.

In September, however, the situation had worsened. The unfortunate French were looking for scapegoats. Newspapers such as *Je Suis Partout* incited people to point a finger at international finance and corrupt intellectuals—meaning once again the Jews.

*

Papa came back one day with a tabletop radio, which he proudly placed on the mantle in the living room. The set was encased in a rectangular cabinet of varnished wood. Its face was equipped with a loud speaker covered with fabric, and a dial with numbers above four black Bakelite knobs. Papa turned one of the knobs and we waited until the vacuum tubes in the back warmed up. Then a round green eye lit up on the dial. Turning another knob, my father moved a red hand on the face along a list of faraway cities printed below the numbers: Strasbourg, Stuttgart, Marseille, London, and Brussels. The hand stopped on *Radio-Paris* and the set started broadcasting music. Élise and I jumped with joy.

"Now we can hear the news directly at home," papa said with a satisfied look.

The radio did not stop him from reading the daily newspapers, however, among which was the *Petit Parisien*.

"Can we still trust France?" My worried mother asked as my father closed his paper.

"France is a tolerant country," he answered thoughtfully. The anti-Semites make a lot of noise but one day we too will be French and proud of it. In the meanwhile, I grant you we should not forget that the Jews were chased out of Spain in 1492; adding, "We are still the scapegoats of others, and it has been so for two thousand years."

"And so?" maman would impatiently ask.

"Then it is best to keep a suitcase packed at all times."

*

In the spring of 1939, the government prepared the 150th celebration of the French Revolution. What we heard over *Radio-Paris* and all we read in the *Petit Parisien* were long discussions about the declaration of the Rights of Man and the abolition of aristocracy's privileges. Yet the revolution had also led to the emancipation of Jews, but the press failed to mention it.

My parents decided to send me to a summer camp organized by the City Hall of the 4th Arrondissement. Maman and Élise saw me off at the Austerlitz train station, where I cried at the separation.

"You're only going for two weeks," reminded my mother to console me, while Élise was getting annoyed.

"Don't make such a fuss! One would think you're leaving for America!"

I was sad to leave my mother and anxious finding myself among a group of strangers. The rowdiness of some of the boys frightened me. Furthermore, I knew I was different because I was Jewish. I worried what other boys would think of me and I kept away from them. However, I confided I was Jewish to the few other Jewish boys in the group who, in fact, were as secretive as I was. I worried a lot about what would happen when I found myself naked in the shower, my circumcision under the glares of the non-Jews, some of which might come from anti-Semite families.

**

When Germany recovered the Sarre territory on its border, it immediately applied its discriminatory laws to the region. Jews had to flee. Families, established in Saarbrucken since the 14th century, were compelled to pack and take refuge in France or Belgium. In spite of all that happened around us, papa remained confident.

"Don't forget the Maginot line!" People said at the café on rue des Rosiers; they will never be able to cross it.

We did the right thing choosing France, thought my father walking home. At least the children are French. He paused and smiled as he remembered Élise reciting her first history lesson, a few years ago which began: "Our ancestors the Gauls…"

CHAPTER 3

September 1939

The news that Hitler and Stalin signed a pact of mutual non-aggression hits us like a thunderbolt. The cards were suddenly reshuffled.

One day in September, my father arrives home climbing the stairs two steps at a time, and catching his breath he shouts:

- Quick, Élise! Turn on the radio!

Élise hurries and turns the Bakelite knobs. After the usual static while the tubes are warming up, the monotonous voice of the Radio-Paris announcer comes out of the speaker. It shows no emotion, as was then the custom.

- German troops have entered Polish territory... Warsaw is bombed.

Maman stands in the kitchen doorway drying her hands with a dishtowel before placing her fingers over her mouth. She is at once stupefied and anxious.

In Paris, continues the announcer, *the council of ministers has taken three emergency measures. General mobilization has been approved and becomes effective today at midnight. A state of siege is declared on French and Algerian soil. Finally, the chambers of the National Assembly are convened for an exceptional session tomorrow, Saturday September 2nd.*

An elbow on the chimney, papa listens carefully. He has not yet taken the time to take off his coat. When the broadcast is over, he straightens up with a deep sigh.

- What are they saying at the café? Fanny asks.

- Men talk of volunteering...

- Even foreigners?

- Yes, even foreign Jews.

Husband and wife exchange a glance, laden with unspoken fear. Although my mother doubts any implied sacrifice is warranted, she keeps her thoughts to herself. She doesn't want to further alarm her husband.

The following day England, then France, declare war on Germany. In great numbers, men walk towards the Boulevard Sebastopol, and from their, towards the Gare du Nord or Gare de l'Est train stations. Every family is affected. In just a few days, Paris is emptied of all able-bodied men. A group of young Polish Jews decides to go to the Mobilization Center on rue de *Rivoli* and to volunteer for the Foreign Legion. Everywhere in the Marais district, men are seen walking towards the subway, a suitcase in hand. Only women, children, and the elderly remain in the *Pletzl*, as the Askenazim call our neighborhood. Foreign men still incapable of deciding which side to take discuss endlessly in the cafés.

- France is the strongest! Assert newspapers. We have the best army in the world! They claim.

Transportation systems are overwhelmed. Requisitioned buses, trucks, and horses are put at the disposal of men attempting to reach their units.

- The war will not last! Some say with courage or candor. We are going to give Hitler the kick in the ass he deserves. Then we will come back home and return to work!

I wonder what thoughts my father harbors under his wrinkled forehead. He turns his Middle-Eastern worry beads between his fingers, an old habit from Turkey. I hear him saying with a harsh voice to my mother:

- Didn't we decide to become French citizens?

She looks annoyed and frustrated but does not answer.

- We must behave like French people, continues Victor. I want to do my duty. I must volunteer. This country welcomed us…

- And the workshop? Who is going to take care of the workshop?

--You, of course!

- And the children?

A heavy silence falls between them, before Victor picks up again with a calmer voice:

- It will not be easy. I know.

Holding back tears, Fanny listens.

The war will not last; he goes on to reassure her. It will be over by the end of the year, and then life will pick up where we left it.

- *Si quiere l'Dio*, sighs maman.

God willing.

*

Papa kisses all three of us before leaving. It's his turn to take his little suitcase and to cross the *Pletzl* towards the rue de *Rivoli*. He reaches the recruiting center and registers as an enlisted volunteer in the Foreign Legion. Soon after, he let us know they handed him a uniform and sent him with others to the military camp of *Septfonds*, near *Montauban*, where he will receive basic training.

In Paris, maman organizes our new routine. Élise and I do our best to help – or at least not to further complicate our mother's life. In spite of her efforts to appear optimistic, sadness is all over maman's face and we know she cries when she is alone.

When she sends me out for food, I listen to the conversations of people waiting in lines. The mood is sour. According to the news, the Germans have annexed the Sudetenland.

- What is the Sudetenland? I ask Élise when I get home.

- It's near Czechoslovakia, why don't you study geography?

I frown, attempting to get my thoughts together, but end up looking at a map of Europe.

I follow the progression of the Wehrmacht across Poland day by day. An army can go so fast! Don't the Poles have any soldiers? Or are they inferior to the Germans? Like my father, I read the newspapers, looking for answers to questions that worry me. They call Polish soldiers heroes, yet they are always facing an army superior in men and equipment, and they always end up surrendering. By the end of October, they are defeated. Germany and Russia divide the country. Some people on rue des Rosiers read the news with strong pessimism while other voices remain optimistic:

- Wait until the British and French get in, the Germans will not go further.

In fact, our troops are massed along the Rhine. The well-known Maginot line has been reinforced. The population of the towns between the line and the Rhine is evacuated towards the South West... Isn't the southwest where my father is billeted? What will happen to him? Why are we without news from him? Will he be sent to the front? What will happen to all of us left here? We live in anticipation reminiscent of a lull before the storm.

News from *Septfonds* at last! In a brief note papa asserts:

- It's a mess, here. Everything is disorganized. The soldiers are left waiting and watching a beautiful autumn slowly unfold.

To lift the spirit of their listeners, radio stations play trendy music. The newspapers begin to use the expression *"the phony war"*. Those, in fact, who saw the trenches and battles of WWI can't believe it. The war, for them, is not to sit waiting; it is to shell the enemy and machine gun men and grounds. An old man on rue de Rivoli, his chest covered with decorations, cries out:

- I don't call that a war! As he goes on his way grumbling and cursing at modern times.

But slowly, anguish encompasses us. The word "bombardment" keeps returning to everyone's lips.

Car headlights are painted blue to allow only a thin beam of light. Antiaircraft shelters are set up in cellars of buildings and in subway stations. The authorities recommend protecting against broken glass by applying bands of adhesive paper to the windows. Parisians come and go normally in the streets, but storekeepers faced with an uncertain future hesitate to renew their stock. The school year starts normally, and I note that maman manages the workshop rather well, although only a limited number of seamstresses come to work now. At night, maman does the bookkeeping under a lamp, its lampshade covered with a dishtowel.

Before leaving for the army, papa withdrew his meager savings from the bank. The money is now kept in the kitchen sugar jar together with a few gold coins and American dollars. Fearing enemy bombs, those Parisians who can afford it have sent their children to the country. Others have closed their apartment altogether and relocated in the country until the storm passes. But maman must stay to earn the little money she can. Besides, she feels more secure in the old Jewish quarter. The Jews help each other, while the French often look at us with suspicion, or make unsavory remarks as we walk by, particularly when we go food shopping on rue Saint Antoine.

*

The winter is harsh. In the east, the temperature drops to 20 below zero centigrade. Women everywhere knit balaclavas, gloves and scarves for the men who freeze in drafty blockhouses on the front. Metal for the manufacture of armament is collected.

- With your scrap metal, asserts the announcer of Radio-Paris, we will forge the victorious steel of tomorrow!

In February, papa comes home on leave. Beyond the joy of seeing us, anxiety is visible in his gaze. He looks tired and has lost weight. He considers the unknown turns of event with confusion. No one in the Marais is surprised to see him going about in his Legion uniform. But on rue Saint Antoine, covert remarks imply that he, and other Jews, volunteered to receive free food and lodging.

Because my father understands Spanish, he has been named interpreter, at the *Septfonds* military camp. No one notices that his Spanish is in fact Ladino – a medieval Castilian! He manages well and takes his duties very seriously.

- Being interpreter could help you avoid going to the front, ventures maman.

- I will go where they tell me to go, retorts Victor.

The discussion makes him nervous and irritable. Maman lowers her head, without a word.

One evening near the end of his leave, papa takes me aside and says with a serious look on his face:

- Tell me Simon, how is school? Are you doing well?

- It's OK. The teacher is nice.

- Listen… You are going to have to be careful, from now on. Don't tell anyone you are Jewish. Not even to adults. It's important. If you are asked, say you are Catholic…

- But…

- There is no but. Do you understand?

I have always been embarrassed to hear my parents speak Ladino. It brands them as different, as Jews, just as Yiddish does. I would be so happy if the only language they spoke was French! When they are in private or in the company of other Sephardim, they return to the language they learned as children. They cannot help it, although they can control that it never happens in front of non-Jews. That behavior contributes to my feeling different from others.

Spring arrives. I keep looking at my map of Europe and reading headlines at the newspaper stand on rue des Rosiers. "Hitler attacks Denmark and Norway." In vain, the allies send a Franco-British commando of paratroopers to Norway,

Rotterdam is bombed, then Brussels. The Germans go around the Maginot line to avoid its defenses! They are now in Belgium, on France's doorstep. Extra French units are sent to protect the border. Paul Reynaud, the chief of the government, tries to reassure the people that their army is the strongest. Yet everyone senses that day by day, the Teutonic grip is closing in. In the schoolyard, discussions move at a fast pace. Returning home, I announce:

- Everyone says our Curtiss perform better than the Messerschmitt!

- The Curtiss? Élise asks with a frown, while listening to the radio.

- They are modern fighter aircrafts, I explain.

She shrugs and returns to listening to the music. She shows little concern about the war. Like many teenage girls, she keeps humming popular tunes of *Charles Trenet*:

Y a d'la joie, partout, y'a d'la joie! At other times, she and her friends listen to songs of *Tino Rossi*:

Oh ! Catarinetta bella, tchi, tchi…

My sister's frivolous behavior gets on maman's nerves. She calls her brainless. In fact, worries pile up at home. The workshop must frequently close for lack of work. Money is getting short. Are we going to have to dig into our savings? Maman takes piecework home and sits at the sewing machine.

At the age of nine, I have not lost any of my shyness. I am still a lonely and melancholy boy. Our teacher suggested we write a diary, and I start filling the pages of a notebook. It soon becomes my way of distancing myself from fears brought on by the war, from the anti-Semitic insults of kids at school, from the absence of papa and from maman' worries.

*

Diary of Simon Crespi

Papa is in the army. Maman does not know when he will return, however she believes that it won't be long. I wonder if that is true.

The other day during the break in the schoolyard, two guys were saying that the Jews caused the war. I know it's false. But I did not respond. Although I don't like that we are different from other people, I also don't like that people stick all that's wrong on the Jews. My father is just a tailor, after all. What's wrong with that? Madame Boisseau, our teacher, wants us to write to soldiers at the front, who are away from their families. They need to receive news, she says. So in class we write letters together.

I listen to the radio. The Germans advance so quickly!

One of my friends is named Rigaud. He likes to tell me what he does on Sundays. He says he goes to movies near Place de la République. Last Sunday he saw a cartoon: Snow White and the Seven Dwarfs. His father is a waiter in a café on rue de Bretagne. He must be a nice father to take him to movies. I would love to be in the same situation as Rigaud. I would not mind if my father was not Jewish, even if he was only a waiter in a café.

This will be all for today.

*

At the café rue des Rosiers, people gather around the radio to hear the news. The Germans pursue their advance on the western front.

Battles are taking place in the area of Saint Quentin, says the announcer of Radio-Paris.

- Saint Quentin! Exclaims a stupefied customer, but that's very close!

It is in fact, and Belgians as well as residents of the north of France have already taken to the roads to escape bombings. The exodus has started and the Germans advance towards Paris. The French government decides to move south to the city of *Tour* on the Loire River, then almost immediately to *Bordeaux*. Soon, Parisians will also want to escape south with their luggage; and refugees will form long lines of cars covered with mattresses, their sole protection against the Stukas.

Radio-Paris precedes its news reports with the first notes of *"la Marseillaise."* Announcers now talk of strategic withdrawal. It appears French troops have decided to fall back. In school, teachers try to reassure their pupils.

- Kids, the counter attack is about to start.

- We're going to give the *Boches* a beating, right Sir? Asks a student.

- They are not going to show off much longer and threaten us. You'll see. In the meantime, open your notebooks while I write the exercise on the blackboard.

As soon as his pupils bend over their work, the teacher goes in the corridor to engage in feverish discussion with his colleagues.

The next stage is the closing of all the schools. A headline announces on the newspaper front page: *We will defend Paris one house at a time!* They might as well admit that the Wehrmacht is at the gates of the capital. In just a few days the Marais is deserted, all our neighbors have left.

- How about us? Aren't we leaving too? Asks Élise, coming down from the clouds after a long absence.

Maman is disconcerted. My aunt *Fortunée* and her husband Salvatore who took refuge in the Provinces with their children and my grandmother Esther wrote a few days ago. They beg us to join them. But maman does not think it is such a good idea. Worried about money, she does not know what kind of work she is likely to find. She knows no one outside Paris. More than anything, she is afraid to lose contact with papa.

At the end of May, Belgium capitulates, and Paris is declared an *open city*, abandoning all defensive efforts. On June 3rd the papers announce bombardments. Then, Italy enters the war, on the German side.

*

Finally, maman resolves we had better leave. She quickly prepares a suitcase and hides the money from the sugar canister in a pouch under her clothes. The three of us get underway: Rue des *Rosiers*; rue *Pavée* and its handsome synagogue, the rue de *Rivoli* deserted today. We stumble down the stairs of the Saint Paul subway station. After the Bastille subway stop, we arrive at the *Gare de Lyon*. A dense crowd, flustered and pressed together, stands on the subway platform and makes it hard for us to get off. All these would-be travelers are also laden with suitcases and packages. They drag along sniffling and stunned children clutching their toys. Maman unfastens the belt of her raincoat and ties my sister and me at one end so we don't get separated. She will lead us in that way: Her heavy suitcase in one hand and us in the other as if on a leash, at the end of her belt.

Neither Élise nor I appreciate being pulled that way. But alarm overcomes damaged pride. We finally arrive in the hall of the train station. The heat under the glass roof is unbearable.

Can we buy tickets? Is any train leaving anyway? Looking through the crowd, maman seeks anyone likely to give us information.

The rare police officers around are perplexed when clusters of inquiring and sometimes aggressive travelers approach them. In any case, they have no information to provide. As for the SNCF railway employees, they are nowhere to be seen.

- Everything is so disorganized! Sighs maman.

A moment later, she hides me behind her raincoat while I urinate against a column. Élise is exasperated. She is hungry, thirsty, and she wants to go home. People around us thrash about, behaving as fish caught in a net. Rumors reach us from all sides:

There will be no train today.

The train tracks were bombed.

The railway men are on strike.

Airplanes are about to bomb the train stations.

The roads are even worse!

In the end, maman gives up.

- We go back home, she finally says, exhausted.

We manage with some difficulty to get back to the Boulevard Diderot. The idea of going back in the subway frightens us. Better to go home on foot.

It is dark when we get back to rue des Écouffes, and it is with relief that we push open the door of our apartment.

*

Paul Reynaud, the prime minister, resigns a few days later. He transfers his duties to Marshal Pétain, an eighty-three year old army man and a hero of the last war who immediately declares:

- The battle must stop.

The Armistice is signed on June 22. A few days later, while I stand at the corner of the rue *Pavée*, I see German soldiers marching pompously down the rue Saint Antoine towards the Bastille. It is the first time I see Germans on parade. I think about my history books, about the newspaper headlines, and about my collection of buttons that not so long ago, my child's imagination transformed into a proud and victorious army led by a stylishly dressed officer.

The atmosphere is heavy on rue des Rosiers. The remaining Jews expect the recurrence of pogroms at any moment.

Some of the people wonder whether they made the right decision to come to France or whether they would not have been better off choosing a different destination.

CHAPTER 4

June 1940

The Germans have divided France into two zones, one in the north, and one in the south. Pétain governs the so-called *free zone* in the south; the *occupied zone* in the north and west of the country, including Paris, is under German administration. The line separating the two territories cuts across the country from the Swiss border in the east to the Touraine region in the west and from there, south to the Spanish border. The Italians occupy a zone along their border from Switzerland to the Mediterranean.

After fleeing to the countryside, many Parisians have returned to the capital. The Jews who left, however, are not allowed to return to the occupied zone.

The British continue the war alone. They bomb French factories and military sites that are likely to fall into the Germans hands. The German sympathizers are appalled and view this as hostility. An editorial broadcast on Radio-Paris reports a British raid over the city of Dieppe where stray bombs kill dozens of housewives shopping on the market place.

- The British didn't have enough fighter airplanes to defend us, but they suddenly found enough to kill French citizens and more than 2,000 sailors when they scuttled the French fleet in North Africa… Says someone.

The German forces seize supplies of all kinds throughout France and send them to Germany. Consumer prices rise from one day to the next. Long lines form in front of stores. Parisians with relatives in the country ask them for food packages to make up for all that is lacking in the city.

The government institutes food rationing and it becomes impossible to eat without ration cards. The population is divided into various categories. As a J2 – children from 6 to 12 years old- I am entitled, among other foods, to three chocolate bars per month. Élise who is fourteen is a J3. Adults from 19 to 60 years are classified A.

Food distribution is unreliable. It is one thing to have coupons for 500 grams of sugar, and another to know where to get it. You must be a good customer to receive flour or coffee from one's grocer, even if you have tickets for these staples. The prefecture of police dictates what restaurants are to serve: only one main course each day, a meat dish with vegetables, and only one desert. Soon, authorities will institute days without meat. Saccharine has replaced sugar in cafés. What people call *ersatz* replaces all kinds of goods, for example, roasted barley mixed with chicory replaces coffee. Tobacco contains foreign matters that no one can identify. Bread is black and costs 3.10 franc per kilogram. Bananas are only available dried. Those who can, grow vegetables on balconies and roofs.

A curfew is instituted in Paris and there are daily alerts. No one is allowed to walk in the streets between 8 PM and 6 AM. At night when the sirens sound, people dress hurriedly and rush to the basement where they and sleepy neighbors mix with the odd passerby taken by surprise on the street while playing cat and mouse with the police patrols. Everyone carries a small suitcase with important papers and valuables. The basement walls are damp and covered with coal dust. Children in pajamas huddle near their parents, one hand clutching a doll or teddy bear. After a while, the sound of bombs is heard in the distance.

- Must be the Renault factory in *Billancourt*, someone says in the dark.

*

According to rumors in the neighborhood, the Germans have taken more than two million French prisoners. Every French family has at least one member imprisoned in Germany and no one knows when they will be released. We hear that during the invasion, the Germans had more prisoners than they could handle.

After Élise and I go to bed, maman listens to the war news on the radio. She listens to Radio-Paris as well as Radio-Stuttgart, which broadcasts propaganda in French praising Germany and its power. One day though, she hears a feeble voice breaking through the German jamming. It announces, "This is London. Frenchmen speak to Frenchmen!"

Another day, someone knocks on our door. Two women are selling photographs of Marshal Pétain. Not wishing to standout, maman buys a photograph and hangs it on the wall in the vestibule so that strangers coming to the door think she is a *Petainist*. The others, the Jews, will understand it is only a ruse.

After a German soldier is killed in Paris, the Germans arrest a dozen Frenchmen in reprisal and shoot them at the *Mont Valérien*.

There are long debates about letting prisoners of war come home, but discussions drag on.

*

Simon Crespi's diary

October 3, 1940

Maman sends me to buy bread every day and it's so boring! I have to stand in line for hours. I bring along some magazines, but still... Then I have to watch out so the baker's wife does not cut out more tickets than she should. It happened once and I didn't dare speak up. Maman wasn't pleased, but I was too embarrassed to complain.

People keep talking about the black market.

- Maman says we can't afford it. I know we can't, but I don't understand why the market has to be black. It must be held in the dark so shoppers are not recognized. I wonder where this market is located. One thing I know, it's not in our neighborhood.

Radio and newspapers feed a virulent anti-Jewish campaign. The Lissac's, an old French family who manage a chain of optician shops, launches a newspaper campaign:

Do not confuse Lissac with Isaac.

Later, we hear that all those who had become French citizens since 1927 have suddenly and automatically lost their French citizenship. There is a great number of Jews among them.

Talks of demobilization go on forever but at last, papa returns home. He arrives on a beautiful September day and maman is filled with joy to see her husband home again. But as always, we need money. There is no question for the moment of reopening the workshop. The situation has to settle down first, and papa starts looking for work. Here and there, he finds occasional jobs to complete at home on his sewing machine. Although it is better than no work at all, it is not enough to satisfy the needs of our family. Some French shop owners in the garment district of the *Sentier* make veiled remarks when they see my father:

- So, you're back! Rats are the first to leave a sinking ship, but they return as soon as they see it remains afloat.

Papa overlooks the comments.

In October, the government decrees the *Statute of Jews*, establishing who, from now on, is to be considered as a Jew:

Shall be considered Jewish, any person born of three grand parents of the Jewish race, or born of two grand parents of that race, if his or her spouse is Jewish.

The law details further:

Jews are forbidden to hold the following forms of employment:

- *Any position in education.*

- *That of officer in the army, navy, or air force.*
- *Managerial and secretarial positions in companies that receive subsidies from a state authority.*
- *Any position in enterprises of public interest that are the result of appointments by the government.*

The ruling ends as follows:

This decree is to appear in the official government publication, and carried out as a law of the state.

Established at Vichy, this October 3, 1940.

[Signed]   Ph. Pétain, French Marshal, and chief of state:

The cabinet vice-president, Pierre Laval.

The law effectively prevents Jews from working in education or as civil servants; from holding any position in a public office, in the law, the press, or the arts. In the days that follow, the Germans mandates that all Jews register at their local police station. My mother is hesitant to submit to this procedure but my father insists.

- We have lived in this neighborhood for years; everyone knows us, and everyone knows we are Jewish. What's more, we must not do anything illegal.

- We have to do it, says my father. If we refused to register, we would have to move to another neighborhood, maybe even leave Paris. We would have to change our identity papers and we cannot afford any of that.

In the end, my parents go to the police station on rue de Rivoli with their ID papers on which an officer stamps **JEWISH** in bold, red letters. Later still, an order from the prefect of police requires owners of Jewish stores to post a sign in their window in black letters over a yellow background that reads:

Judisches Geschäft*. Jewish enterprise*

The authorities name administrators to manage the businesses of those Jewish owners who left Paris.

Anxiety mounts. My parents' main concern is to find work, but at the same time, finding food is all consuming. Meat, butter, soap have become extremely rare and expensive. Potatoes, when they are available, have gone from 1.90 to 2.50 francs per kilo. Milk is now more than 2 francs per liter.

Papa says that, on the other hand, luxury items are selling well, since the Germans buy everything they can get their hands on and enjoy going out to good restaurants.

German soldiers parade regularly on the Champs-Élysées. The buildings along the avenue are dressed with huge red standards bearing black swastikas. Road signs in German are mounted at the *Place de l'Opéra* and at all major intersections in the capital.

The legal name of the free zone administered by the French is the non-occupied zone, but people nickname it the *zone nono*. Open communication with the free zone is cut. No telephone, no regular mail. Only *interzone* cards are allowed. They look like postcards and facilitate the job of censorship. These letter-cards are pre-stamped with the effigy of Hitler. One must tick off boxes to communicate. Maman writes to her sister at the last address known:

INTERZONE CARD

This card is strictly reserved for family matters. Complete this card and cross out any unnecessary remarks – Do not write between the lines

ATTENTION – Any card whose information does not solely concern family matters will not be forwarded and will probably be destroyed.

October   3   1940

The 4 of us are: in good health; ~~tired; lightly, gravely, ill; wounded; killed; prisoner; dead;~~

And so on...

French people around us are indifferent to our plight. They act as if discrimination and the attacks on Jews do not concern them. Only two matters worry the French: their prisoners of war, and food supply.

The beginning of the school year is postponed until the beginning of October. A great number of teacher positions are vacant either because they were held by Jews who are no longer allowed to teach, or else by teachers who did not return to Paris after the exodus.

Élise, who is a good student, is admitted to a lycée with an excellent reputation. I am registered at the public school on rue des *Quatre Fils* where, in addition to French students, there are

Jewish, Armenian, and Greek boys. Teachers in class make us sing the new hymn of the French state:

Marshal, here we are

Standing in front of you!

The savior of France!

At recess, fights break out between Petainists and Gaullists. I watch and listen but keep my distance. The Petainists bring newspaper clippings and cartoons to school that caricature Jews with grotesque noses, thick lips, and large ears. Revoltingly, they are described as people who would do anything for money, and are held responsible for the misfortunes of the fatherland. They are called traitors to France.

Simon Crespi's diary

Tuesday November 12 1940

My friend Papazian and I just had a bizarre experience. I would be in trouble if my parents knew about it! Yesterday, November 11 was a holiday, no school. The two of us took the subway to the Tuileries gardens. As we came out of the station, we saw a huge crowd on Place de la Concorde, just at the corner of the Champs Elysées.

Some marchers were walking on the road others on the sidewalks, which are very wide at that spot. We followed out of curiosity. Some in the crowd sang the Marseillaise, others shouted in rhythm: Deux Gaules, Deux Gaules, [I did not understand why two. I think they meant the occupied zone and the free one, but I am not sure]. We were curious to know where the crowd was heading, so we followed along until the Rond Point des Champs Elysées.

There, all of a sudden, we noticed trucks full of German soldiers parked along the sidewalks. The Germans suddenly rushed down from their vehicles, rifles in hand, and started running towards the crowd. We got scared and tried to escape by the Avenue Montaigne, but we could see a mass of French police officers running towards us from the other end of the avenue. Papazian pulled me under a carriage door and we hid in a broom closet in the courtyard. It stank in there! We heard the voices of other people outside, which like us were trying to hide in the courtyard. Then the voices became louder. We could hear cops shouting and people screaming. After a while, everything returned to calm, except for the single voice of a woman crying. We didn't dare come out, fearing more havoc in the street. Complete silence finally surrounded us. I could no longer wait and I relieved myself in the closet. We stayed a long time without moving but finally came out to evaluate the situation. No one was around, so we ran all the way to Place de l'Alma and dashed into the Métro to get home. We agreed not to say anything to avoid being punished, but I wanted to write about it, because it's important.

By coincidence, yesterday, Élise told maman that, she too was on the Champs Elysées with her good friend Martine. It was at the same time Papazian and I were in the closet. They too saw trucks full of krauts along the avenue. Élise said a man was demonstrating loudly in front of the German trucks. The soldiers got down, Élise said, and beat up the poor guy who fell on the ground. They kept kicking him in the stomach and then took him away on the truck. Élise saw a group of people in a café. The police would not let them out claiming they were all under arrest as demonstrators. Élise said she and Martine saw everything from a front row seat.

*

Grocers become arrogant despots. They decide how much margarine or chicory a customer can purchase. They are the ones who cut out coupons on the food card. Maman says she notices some customers are invited into the back of the store where she suspects illegal transactions take place. The same thing happens at the bakery, at the butcher, and at the produce store.

My father spends whole days without work. He shuttles from one clothing workshop to another until they offer him some work. And then, it's always a rush job. He works at the sewing machine until late at night. In the morning while he sleeps, maman sews in the linings and does the hems and pressing, before leaving for her shopping. When she returns, my father has already left to bring back the finished work and to look for a new order.

Élise and I are not allowed outside the neighborhood. We go to school and return straight home to do homework. On Thursdays and Sundays, I have permission to go and play with friends in the building or a few houses away on the street. When people visit each other, the discussion is all about news and rumors. Parents usually bring the children along rather than leave them alone at home.

One Saturday, my mother invites a few neighbors to our house. She serves Turkish coffee. It is not the good coffee people enjoyed before the war, and it is sweetened with saccharine, but it is warm. And you have to offer company something, after all! Maman also serves *soldier's biscuits*, the kind that crumble into dust as you bite into them, then dry up your mouth and make you thirsty.

Madame Perahia, the third-floor neighbor is there. She is a widow who lives alone. Also present is Mademoiselle Faraggi, an unmarried woman who lives across the street on rue des

Écouffes. They are two smart and interesting women that my mother invites frequently. Then, there is Madame Modiano and her husband. They live on rue Saint Paul, on the other side of rue Saint Antoine. Maurice Modiano was a teacher at the Lycée Charlemagne nearby. Petain's *statute of Jews* forbids him from returning to his profession.

- I was two years away from retirement; say's he, as he takes a biscuit and shakes his head in disbelief.

- I don't even know whether I will be able to collect my pension.

His wife's name is Cecile Godard. She is neither Jewish nor his wife, but even those who know they are not married call her Madame Modiano, or just Cecile. At first, the conversation revolves around the children and the difficulty of finding food. Very quickly, however, the exchange turns to the *situation* and the discussion heats up.

- Many Jews have recently left Paris, observes Madame Perahia.

- To go where? Asks Madame Modiano.

- They pay guides who smuggle them across farmland fields into the free zone.

- What about you? Why aren't you leaving?

- I certainly would if I could! But you need a lot of money to leave.

- We are the only ones left in the neighborhood, adds Mademoiselle Faraggi. We, is to be understood here as: we-who-have-no-money.

- Where could we go anyway? And how would we find work?

- Quite a few Jews have taken refuge on the Riviera that is run by Italians.

- In Nice, my father steps in. Fortunée Carasso, Fanny's sister, is on the Riviera.

- With her husband Salvatore, adds maman.

- They can afford it.

. Well, his business did very well, you know, he made a lot of money! He closed his watch business at the beginning of the war. It was on rue La Fayette, you remember? Just at the corner of the Place La Fayette.

It had become a big business, three stories of offices above the store! When he was mobilized into the army and Fortunée was left to run the business alone, the government tried to force an economic administrator upon her. They called that the *aryanization* of enterprises. But my sister- in-law is a smart woman, you know! She had the clever idea to lease a railroad car at the Gare de Lyon, fill it up with furniture, carpets from Turkey, and whatever else she had of value. She sent the whole thing to the free zone. And all this while she was pregnant!

When the administrator arrived, she was gone and the store was empty. I believe they are now somewhere on the coast. They move around a lot. You see, with money one can manage, that's for sure.

- What about your mother? Asks Mademoiselle Faraggi.

- She is with them.

- You could join them too, insists Madame Modiano.

- Yes, they suggested we do that, but I cannot leave Paris. They change locations so frequently, and there is no work for me on the Riviera. We don't know anyone there...

Monsieur Modiano lights my father's cigarette, then his own.

- Let's be patient, my father says, but let's also be ready to defend ourselves. We should be proud of our Jewish origin.

The discussion goes on. Smoking in a corner, my father and Mr. Modiano discuss what steps they could take but don't come to any conclusion. They no longer know what to do.

*

For Rosh Hashanah, many do not dare attend services in synagogues, and most Jews celebrate the Jewish New Year in homes, with everyone bringing what they could. Mattresses on the floor are set up for those who cannot get home before the curfew. For Yom Kippur a week later, the fast is observed at home, without ceremony.

We hear by word of mouth that the London radio broadcasts a program in French. My mother knew this already but had not mentioned it to anyone. The static produced by the Germans makes it difficult to listen, but with concentration, one can follow. One night Churchill addresses the French people:

- We already have command of the seas, and soon we will control the air space. One day we will have control of the land. The German swastika will never wave over London!

My father finally finds a stable job. He is a master fitter for a manufacturer of men suits that currently produces police and military uniforms. The rumor mill suggests the firm might even get a contract to produce German uniforms. The work is steady and my father's work is appreciated.

The shop is in *Pontoise*, outside of Paris. My father gets up early to take the subway to the *Gare St Lazare* where he catches a train, then a bus to the factory. At night, exhausted, he reverses the journey. We try to wait for him for dinner. He enjoys so much spending time with his family, listening to what happened in school, and discussing the events of the day in the neighborhood, what we heard on the radio… But some days he comes home so late he has to eat alone. He does not complain, however, having a regular job compensates for the difficulties.

*

One Thursday evening, the doorbell rings as papa is finishing dinner and maman is still doing dishes. Papa opens the door to Maurice Modiano standing on the landing. He looks nervous and distressed. Without even a hello, he brandishes a newspaper under my father's face as he enters our home.

- Here, look at this trash, read this! He says with controlled anger.

- Come in Monsieur Modiano. You should not be out in the street at this late hour. You risk being arrested! Come and sit down in the living room.

Monsieur Modiano sits on the edge of his armchair; my father takes the newspaper and starts reading. The article is from *Au Pilori,* a particularly inflammatory newspaper of the extreme right. Papa reads the tirade of hatred.

- Death to the Jews, death to the vile double-dealing, and cunning of the Jews! Death to Jewish usury! Death to Jewish demagoguery! Death to all that is false, ugly, dirty, repulsive, nigger, half-breed, Jewish! This is the last resort of white people hunted down, robbed, and murdered by Semites and who somehow find the strength to free themselves from their abject grasp...Death! D E A T H T O T H E J E W S!

Papa folds the newspaper, puts his hands on his knees, and reflects.

- So? Monsieur Modiano asks impatiently.

- Yes it is violent, virulent, and full of hatred all right. I can see that. This is evidently the work of demented minds, Monsieur Modiano. These people are hooligans, you know. They cannot accept we lost the war. Since there is nothing they can do about it, they vent their anger on the Jews, on foreigners, on communists, and on freemasons. They even take it out on our secular school system they would like to replace with one that would be Catholic. You know very well that these are not normal people or ordinary times. He hands back the paper.

- Then we are back in the middle ages! This is not acceptable! They are playing into the hand of the Germans!

- It had to be expected after the repeal of the *Marchandeau law* last August, which protected us by prohibiting excesses and abuses in the press. The repeal relieved journalists of all responsibility for restraint. And now, the hatred of the extreme right is uncontained.

- But what are we going to do, Monsieur Crespi, What are we going to do?

- Nothing! These are nothing but words. We keep going to work in the morning and coming home to our families at night.

- But words can hurt; you know very well that words lead to action.

- Yes I know, but we must make as little notice of this as possible. These people would only be too happy if we reacted and gave them reasons to justify their hatred.

- But that is cowardly, Modiano counters. We must protest and fight.

With a shudder, I remember the demonstration on the Champs Elysées a few days ago, the trucks, the police, and the desperate cries. Maman comes out of the kitchen and takes Maurice Modiano by the arm.

- Just go home, she says gently. Once your justifiable outrage has calmed down, you will see that it is wiser to say nothing and not stir matters further.

Shocked by his own anger, Maurice Modiano moves forward.

- We will talk again, papa says, walking him to the door. Come Sunday morning, we will discuss it. Be careful walking home! Give our regards to Madame Modiano, and good night…

*

Simon Crespi's diary

Tuesday March 18, 1941

I've had enough of these alarms! Again last night, I was sleeping so deeply I didn't hear the warning siren and maman had to shake me before I woke up. I dressed quickly; I took along my bag already loaded with my favorite books: Alexandre Dumas The Three Musketeers, Twenty years later; my favorite comics: the last Bibi Fricotin, and Vaillant; I took also Twenty Thousand Leagues Under the Sea, and finally: In the Wake of the Pourquoi-Pas? The "Pourquoi-Pas?" is the name of the boat that Charcot took to the North Pole.

Of course, I took my diary along. I have not told anyone about my diary. No one knows about it. I would not want anyone to read it. It's personal. Writing comforts me.

Maman makes fun of me when she sees me with my bag. She says we are not going on an expedition, but just down to the cellar. Still, I like to have everything with me. This way I can choose.

I nearly forgot: There's the gas mask! Well, not really gas masks like those of the neighbors. We are not allowed one because we are not French citizens. They instead give foreigners a horrible powder that we're supposed to spread on a wet handkerchief. In case of poisoned gas, you stick the handkerchief under your nose and breathe. I can't do it!

I once tried on a real gas mask. It stinks of rubber in there and you can't see through it. You hear yourself breath and when you talk your voice bounces around like at the Neptuna swimming pool.

Maman carefully stuffs our ID papers, our food cards, money and anything valuable in her handbag. You never know. The house could be blown up to pieces by a bomb, in which case we would not be able to return to our apartment…

Going down the stairs, we met the neighbors. Everyone complained. Suddenly someone shouted:

- And the Bonnards? Where are the Bonnards?

Madame Jacob went back upstairs to see what happened. She came back two minutes later. She said the Bonnards didn't want to come down, they were fed up and preferred to stay in their bed.

Papa heard that Pétain triggers these alarms on purpose so the French people end up resenting the British. Personally, I think the British are right to bomb. The Krauts are cruel bastards. In the meantime, we sit in the cellar. It stinks and it's impossible to see anything. People tell boring stories and the next morning I can't wake up. I yawn all day at school.

*

- Radio rue des Rosier announces...

This is how people sarcastically start their sentences now when they exchange news - or the latest derisive joke. And no one knows whether what they hear is one or the other.

Sometimes the rumor is true and this is exactly what happens with the constant report of police rounding-up foreign Jewish men to send them to work camps. This time maman is very worried.

- You must leave and hide in the free zone, she tells my father.

- And leave you all three in Paris? No way... Particularly now that I have a steady job!

_ I can work too!

- There would not be enough part-time work for you. You would not be able to feed the whole family.

- If you keep taking the subway every day, you will end up in a round up! Your ID card is stamped Jewish! And you are a foreigner! So...

- So I am careful, what do you think? I don't have particularly recognizable features, and in the subway I hide behind my newspaper.

She wishes that at least he would sleep in the maid's room, the one we use as a junk room on the sixth floor. But papa won't hear of it.

- No way, he says.

Radio rue des Rosier announces...

A friend, a civil servant who works at the prefecture of police, warns the café owner.

- A round up, he whispers. Tomorrow or the day after, they plan to arrest Jewish men and send them to Germany.

Many take the news seriously. Some hide in an office or in a workshop. Others take advantage of the hospitality of non-Jewish friends. Still others decide to immediately leave Paris. In the end, papa agrees to hide on the sixth floor. Maman will bring him food, his newspapers, and his books. But it's cold and uncomfortable. After three days, papa decides it was a false alarm, and he comes down to the apartment. Maman is beside herself.

*

The memories of the pogroms of Central Europe and of the recent persecutions of Jews in Germany are on everyone's mind. Still, many like my father go about their regular business. Threats have become banal. Occurring daily, they little by little become familiar and mix with the day-to-day worries of getting food and making money. Logically, each new government ruling against the Jews should be perceived as one more sign of danger. But the necessity to concentrate on the difficulties of daily living numbs the minds. People send children to school and attend to urgent business. What's more, each new policy announced by Vichy is presented as a way to protect Jews from even more drastic measures the occupying forces would take. Finally, many Jews remain attached to the very idea that brought them to France: The country is the cradle of Human Rights.

- France, they say, is a decent nation. It will never renounce the noble ideas born of the French revolution.

*

In Mai of 1941, my father receives a green card from the neighborhood police. It is a summons *"for the purpose of verifying your civil situation"*, it says. Papa makes inquiries. Many Jewish men have received the same card. He must show up at the *Japy* Gymnasium, in the 11th arrondissement, accompanied by a relative or a friend. Is added: *Those who do not obey expose themselves to the "most severe consequences."*

Maman panics.

- Don't go!

This time papa hesitates.

- I won't go, he finally decides.

That day, he goes back to the maid's room on the sixth floor where he will spend his nights from now on. However, he continues to go to work in *Pontoise* every morning.

A period of greater anxiety begins for my mother – and for us. Even a small delay in papa's return brings fear to the household. Radio Rue des Rosiers soon broadcasts news of the unlucky ones who answered the summons: All were transferred to a camp near Paris. Nobody knows for how long…

- They probably want to send them to work in Germany, concludes my father.

At night, alone in his room under the roof rafters, he agonizes. Did he expose his family to serious danger by ignoring the summons? But those who obeyed were arrested at once. The trap is closing. The only solution is to flee. Yes, they must leave Paris and cross into the free zone.

He wakes up early, that morning, and goes down to the apartment to wake his wife up:

- Friday is the end of the month. I get my monthly pay. We will leave Saturday morning. Start packing, and warn the kids. Maman is relieved. She kisses papa through tears of happiness.

Alas, papa did receive his pay, but got caught in the subway station before he could bring it home…

CHAPTER 5

July 1941

Camp of Beaune-la-Rolande

Friday July 4, 1941

My dear Fanny,

I just received your card and it reassured me. I get anxious when I don't hear from you. I worry something might have happened.

I am glad you found work but please do not exhaust yourself more than necessary. If all goes well I should not remain here too long. People say we might go home before winter.

I met Maurice Bronstein, here in camp; he is Jacques' brother, the Bronsteins of the rue de Bretagne. He asks you to go by his sister, Louise Apelbaum's concierge. It is not far; it is at 12 rue de Birague. He wonders whether his sister is still is in Paris; in which case, tell her he needs food packages.

Did you finally receive my pay for the after hours from Pontoise? I already wrote twice to the owner.

I hope the children are well.

I should receive another package voucher next Tuesday. I will immediately send it to you. I would like you to send me soap, my blue bag - the one I keep my tools in; one of my belts, and a tin can or some container to eat soup in.

Here is a kiss for you, my dear wife; be patient and courageous. Do not worry too much about me

Victor

*

My professor at the school on rue des *Quatre Fils* is Monsieur Loiseau. Every year, he organizes two or three field trips for the class. Last year we went to the *Musée de l'Homme*, the Louvre, and the Jardin des Plantes. He announces that the next outing will be at the Palais Berlitz on Boulevard des Italiens where there is an exhibition entitled: "The Jew and France."

I do not mention it at home but I decide not to go. Until the morning of the outing, that is; when I cannot resist telling maman. She replies:

- If the whole class is going, you must go too.

The rule at home is that I must not distinguish myself from the rest of the class. None of us must act as if we were different or intimidated and certainly not as if we are afraid.

- There is no need to say anything, continues maman. You don't have to give any explanation. Some people are from Brittany or Savoie, and we are Jewish. That's how it is, says maman as she passes her hand through my hair.

- It's time to go, Simon. You will tell me all about it tonight.

I sit next to Papazian in the Métro. He knows, of course, I am Jewish, as I know he is Armenian. But we never discuss these things and today is not the day we are going to start. the members of my class around us are happily looking forward to the field trip. I notice that two classmates did not show up today: Kahn and Goldblum.

*

Once we get to the Palais Berlitz, the interest of the students wanes; they are disappointed in spite of Monsieur Loiseau's efforts. The exhibition includes numerous statistics on boards as well as horrible caricatures that pretend to represent physical peculiarities. These are accompanied by long explanations dripping with hate in which the word *race* keeps coming back. *"How to recognize a Jew"* proclaims a panel, while another announces *"The misdeeds of Jews through the centuries."*

I feel increasingly ill at ease, and remain in the back of the group, as far as possible from Monsieur Loiseau. I cast glances towards Papazian. He seems as embarrassed as I am and he tries to reassure me with a smile as if to say, "Don't worry". At one moment, he even whispers in my ear:

- This is all nonsense.

One room is dedicated to *"a morphological study of the Jew."* It shows an enormous head with an exaggerated large nose. It is titled: *The classical Jewish stereotype.* A number keyed to a note at the bottom marks each part of the face.

1] *Large ears, massive and protruding*

2] *Fleshy mouth, thick lips, lower lip forward*

3] *Pronounced nasal furrow*

4] *Weak features*

I keep my eyes on the ground. As we reach the exit, at the end of the visit, I notice the professor looking in my direction. Soon he comes over and says:

- Interesting, don't you think?

I say nothing and avoid his stare, but he insists:

- You should tell your parents about it, Crespi; they might be interested in coming for a visit.

In the Métro, Papazian and I keep to ourselves all the way home. We avoid the subject and whisper gloomily.

- Did you follow the boxing match on radio the other night? I say.

- Joe Louis?

- He kept his title for the thirteenth time!

- Good for him.

*

Maman waits for the mailman before going out. She watches for him at the window, and runs down to Madame Chevrolier, the concierge, as soon as he appears.

- I was just about to bring up the mail, Madame Crespi. Here! There is a letter for you...

Beaune-la-Rolande

Monday September 29 1941

My darling wife, my dear children,

I received your package yesterday, Fanny, as well as the letter hidden in the linen. I read it over and over. Every one of your words is precious to me.

De tu pan no me arti, de tus palavras me conforti...

- What does it mean maman?

- More than your bread that nourishes me, your words comfort me.

The sardines were delicious. They said I would be able to send you a package voucher in two weeks.

There are departures from the camp. Marcel Goldstein, the husband of the pharmacist on rue Saint Antoine had been transferred to the hospital in Pithiviers with angina. He was released, and returned to the camp Tuesday afternoon. Wednesday morning he was among those who left for the Drancy camp ...

We sleep on straw mats swarming with insects. Please send me a skin lotion because these beasts attack us all night. In the morning, we are terribly bitten. I am asking you now, knowing that this product will probably be hard to find, in order that you have time to find it before you send the next parcel. I am in good health and I do what I can to keep my spirits up. I prefer to work outside the camp. Being idle as I am lately is not good for me and I think too much. My mind circles around.

Write as much as you can, my darling Fanny. Your letters are my only rays of sunshine.

Do not worry too much on my account, my darling children. This separation will end one day. In the meantime, help your mother and study hard in school.

Your loving father who thinks of you all the time.

Victor

*

One day in October we hear that an extreme right organization has bombed Paris synagogues during the night.

Life is harder still, now that papa is not with us. He won't be home for months and therefore not able of helping us find food.

I am always hungry.

Diary of Simon Crespi

Thursday, October 23 1941

Last Sunday, maman and I went to get potatoes in the country. Maman thought they would be cheaper on a farm. We hardly find any in Paris, and when they are available, they cost 2.80fr for a kilo. They used to sell for 1.90fr just last year. We took the train, just the two of us. I was alone with maman for once! Élise stayed with her friend Rosa.

As usual, the train was packed. Once again, we traveled standing up in the carriage corridor. It was worse than in the Métro! When we got off we still had to walk for kilometers among a crowd of people, all going to the same place. Finally, we reached the village. A real dump that village! The farmer was waiting in the courtyard in front of a mountain of potatoes. He greeted us with a sarcastic remark:

- Well, hello Parisians, then addressing maman:

- He's kind of skinny, your kid! He could use fattening up and some good country air.

The farmer had an enormous red nose, and the pile of manure in the yard was as high as the roof of the shed where his cows mooed.

We left with a three-week supply of potatoes.

The bags were quite heavy to carry all the way back to the train station! They cut my fingers and I had to keep changing hands. Once on the train, I sat on the bags. The return trip was as painful as going, but mumun comforted me by promising to make French fries That would be a change from the rutabaga they serve at the school canteen. They are really horrible. Somehow, tapioca isn't as bad. I was exhausted by the time we got home, and since I had a geography test the next day, I had to study until 10 PM.

*

Maman returned from her last visit at Beaune-la-Rolande in a panic. Papa was not there and the camp was practically empty. They told her all internees had been transferred to Drancy, another camp established in the Paris suburbs. The next day, Madame Chevrolier handed her a letter:

Drancy December 5 1941

My darling wife, my dear children,

I have been transferred to the camp in Drancy. We arrived last Tuesday and the conditions here are miserable. They put us up in an unfinished apartment block. Come and see me alone, as soon as you are allowed to do so. In the meantime, you can write me at the following address:

Camp of Drancy, block 3, staircase 1, chamber 7.

They say visits will soon be authorized; however, no one seems to know if it will be in a week or in a month.

Write if you can, and more than anything, send food because they give us practically nothing to eat, except for a revolting watery soup which does not fill the stomach.

There are even more rumors here than in Beaune-la-Rolande. It seems some men are to be sent to work camps deep inside Germany, at the border with Silesia. I am told I do not have to worry since I just arrived. Some internees have been here for months.

I also hear they let those with a serious illness go home. Please go and see Doctor Nahmias and ask for a medical certificate of some kind. You must try everything to get me out of here, darling.

My dear children, I think of you often and hope to see the end of this ugly time soon. Then I will be with you again.

I kiss all three of you.

Victor

*

The camp of Drancy is located in a compound called *La Cité de la Muette,* where barracks for gendarmes, and two 15-story towers to house officers are in construction. Another block of low- level apartments is also in construction in the compound.

It is a four-story U shaped complex around a strip of grass. The unfinished apartment block, with a dozen stairways, had until now held prisoners of war. It has just been transformed into a camp for Jews. Doors and windows have yet to be installed. There are only 20 working water faucets in the complex. Internees sleep on boards, two on each plank in overcrowded rooms.

Food is insufficient and internees are only allowed one food parcel a week and one clothes package every other week.

The camp is administered by the Germans but policed by French gendarmes who delegate some responsibilities to internees. Thus, positions of chief-of-chamber, stairway leader and other duties are entrusted to the prisoners.

As before, maman sends letters and parcels. She does everything possible to obtain permission to visit her husband, but to no avail. Visits are banned for the time being. No one knows why.

- You must be patient, she is repeatedly told.

Her efforts to obtain a medical certificate to get Victor out are just as ineffective.

*

The cold season starts early that year. There is a shortage of coal. Even indoors, I need to wear three sweaters, one on top of the other. Each night, maman listens to the London radio broadcasts. The reception is always poor, but improves somewhat at night.

Good news at last: The Americans enter the war against Germany. Everyone is overjoyed; 1941 goes out on a hopeful note.

Diary of Simon Crespi

December 15, 1941

The Americans are with us! Japan bombed one of their islands in the Pacific, so they declared war on the Japanese and the Germans. Now the Krauts are going to get it from both sides.

I wanted to keep my coat on, when I got home from school, but maman insisted I had to take it off. She said I could catch cold when I would go out again. But if I am already cold inside the house, it does not make much difference when I go out. Maman has un-knitted an old sweater of papa's, and made big wool balls. With it, she knits a new sweater my size. Same with my coat: It is an old coat of papa's, which she takes apart and remakes for me. She does the same with clothes for Élise.

People remember with delight, how the entry of the Americans into the fight in 1918 precipitated the end of the war. Rumors of landings burst out everywhere. Another encouraging piece of news: The German army is stopped before Moscow. The optimists remember Napoleon's Russian campaign.

But everyone knows that despite these facts, it will take months before it produces any positive effect. In the meantime, we have to eat, keep warm, and stay out of sight as much as possible.

Towards the end of December, a new German rule forbids Jews to change domicile. It resolves a problem we have had for a while:

Whether to leave Paris or not. It was my father's wish, but maman was never able to do anything about it.

- Why this new rule? Sighs maman. There is not a man left in the whole neighborhood. Either they have been already rounded up or else they are in hiding, she adds, overwhelmed with despair:

- I wonder how long the Germans will keep them…

Strange and upsetting news reaches us. People say that the *Militarbefihishaber in Frankreich* - the German military command in France – has decided to fine the Jewish community one thousand million francs. It is to be deducted from Jewish property, whose assessment will be established by the *Union Générale des Israélites de France*. Maman reads in the *Petit Parisien* newspaper that, in reprisal for attacks against Germans, 743 Jewish intellectuals of French citizenship have been arrested in the occupied zone, with the help of the French police. They are interned in a camp in Compiegne. Thus, concludes maman, the threat is no longer exclusively against foreign Jews…

Drancy December 28, 1941

Mi Fanny querida,

I still have not received the parcel you mentioned in your last letter. With nothing left to eat, I am reduced to the horrible camp soup. I have a friend who works in the kitchen. He gets more food than we do. He said he will try to help me a little, but he warned me it will not be much.

Yesterday, the rain came into our room. At night, I have to protect my things from mice!

I cannot wait to get out of here.

In spite of all, I thank God for all the good things in my life: My dear wife and my two beautiful children.

I kiss you all,

Victor

*

The cold weather persists. It snows in Paris. Without sufficient coal, people put anything that burns in their stove in order to keep warm.

Maman works every day now, and until late in the evening. She does not complain. On the contrary, she appreciates being able to provide for the needs of her family. However, we still have to tighten our belt. There are the parcels to papa to take care of, and maman insists on saving money.

The news differs depending on whether we listen to French or English radio. Moreover, the difference is so striking that maman is at her wits end. She hears one day, of the big progress in the Soviet defense. The Russians report having destroyed 17 German divisions, no less!

- If only it were true, sighs maman.

Another time, Goebbels himself is reported to have advised the German people to donate warm clothing for the soldiers fighting on the Russian front.

- It's a good sign!

In other news, General De Gaulle has named the prefect Jean Moulin the Résistance delegate for the southern zone. Then, this troubling information: The German writer Thomas Mann, in exile in America, denounces "the massacre of Jews by the Germans". What is he talking about? Is it an exaggeration or is it some misplaced propaganda? Where did this man get his information, and what exactly does he mean by *massacre*?

My mother says she refuses to trust such information, but in fact, she does not know what to believe.

Curfew is reestablished in February. Except this time, it is only for Jews! We are no longer allowed to go outside between 8 PM and 6 AM.

Everyone welcomes the arrival of spring with relief, although the daily search for food intensifies. As for me, I am constantly famished. The portions at the school canteen are small. It is the same at home, and maman does not know what to do to satisfy me. In spite of her deprivations, she is under the impression that nothing is ever enough to satisfy her children's adolescent stomachs.

*

Maman has not received permission to visit her husband in Drancy. News confirms the internees are confined in rooms without water or adequate toilets.

Stopping for news at the café, maman meets a nurse who says she works for a charitable organization within the Drancy campsite. Her name is Gilberte. She claims she can arrange a visit, and she will see what she can do for maman. Of course, it will cost a lot of money. Maman, does not hesitate for one minute. Gilberte, in fact promises to let her get into the camp and visit with papa for nearly a whole hour.

- When? Asks maman with a pressing tone.

- As soon as conditions permit it. Be patient.

Gilberte will leave word at the café on rue des Rosiers. When the time comes, she will provide maman with a nurse's uniform. Weeks go by, however, and there is no news from Gilberte. It is April when maman hears from the café owner:

- Madame Crespi, someone called for you, her name is Gilberte.

- She asks that you meet her tomorrow at 6 PM at the café Henri IV, Place de la Bastille.

Maman arrives on time. Gilberte gives her instructions.

- It will be tomorrow at 6 AM. That is when I start my shift at Drancy. We will meet near the camp's entrance. There is a small café across from the Cité de la Muette. You will see…

Take this bag. It contains a nurse's dress, an apron, and a nurse's headscarf for your hair. Above all, don't show you are afraid. Look confident and sure of yourself. They don't check papers. They rely on our uniforms…

- Can I bring a package?

- No, bring nothing that may attract attention…

- But…

- Once inside the camp, I will take you to a shed in the yard. They will send me to fetch your husband and you will be able to spend some time together... Ah! One last thing: The money. Did I tell you how much?

- Maman shakes her head in acquiescence.

- Don't forget to bring it with you.

*

Dressed as a nurse, my mother sits at the café across from the Drancy compound. She got up very early to take the Métro to *Gare de l'Est*, then a commuter train to Drancy. She was frightened during the whole trip. If an accident happened on the way, they would see her uniform and ask her to help. They would then find out she is not a nurse at all! She watches as a group of women in white uniform lingers by the camp gate, speaking to one another under the dim streetlights. The sky is grey and a light rain is falling. The site fits the dismal description of the camp maman has heard about: The ugly building, the barbed wire fences, the gendarmes at the gate... Gilberte notices maman in the café and crosses the street, a smile on her face.

- Come quick, they are about to open the gate.

- My train was late. Can you imagine? Says Gilberte. I thought I would never get here on time.

She lowers her voice and adds in a whisper.

- You have the money?

Fanny takes an envelope out of her handbag and hands it to Gilberte who pockets it.

- Smile, Fanny, do as I do, keep talking and smiling. Maman makes an effort to look cheerful. She smiles as if Gilberte had made a funny remark. She sees the gendarmes open the gate half way. Fanny and Gilberte are in the middle of the group of nurses who gather closer to the entrance. Gilberte keeps on talking, as if everything is normal. She even has a friendly gesture for the gendarme holding the gate.

A little farther away, unexpectedly a gendarme is checking ID's. The man stands with a tough and haughty manner. Maman stiffens. Gilberte holds her arm firmly.

- Above all, don't move. Do you want to be arrested? Don't worry and let me handle this.

When their turn arrives, Gilberte addresses the gendarme with a falsely detached look and a wide smile.

- Just imagine: The silly girl here forgot her ID at home! Be nice, captain. Let her come in so she will not have gotten up early for nothing. She will show you her card tomorrow. You know us all since you see us every morning… You even smile at me. You think I don't notice?

Her eyes never leave those of the gendarme who throws a glance at Fanny and mumbles:

- Go ahead.

*

Maman has the feeling she has always known the wide horseshoe building in front of her. She hears voices, calls burst out from the windows facing the yard. Men drag heavy garbage cans full of a smoking liquid from one end of the camp to the other.

Some look at the nurses with a sad and faraway stare. The yard, however, is mostly deserted at this early hour.

- It's here, says Gilberte pointing discreetly at a wooden shack on the grounds. Come!

The two women enter the cabin. An old man is sitting behind a table. Other tables are piled up with registers.

- She is looking for her husband, Gilberte says.

The man looks up with an enigmatic stare.

- Victor Crespi, maman says. Block 3, stairway 1, room 7.

The clerk slides a piece of paper and pencil towards the edge of the table.

- Write it down, he says. And turning towards Gilberte:

- You will get him?

- Of course, says Gilberte.

Maman has finished writing her husband's name on the paper. The man stands up and looking away opens a register on a table.

- They told you the rate? He asks without turning around.

- Yes…

Maman puts a roll of bank notes held by a rubber band in his hand. The money disappears immediately into the pocket of the clerk who continues looking at the register.

- When did he arrive?

- Last November. He was transferred from Beaune-la-Rolande.

The old man looks a long time at the register before closing it and opening another, slowly turning the pages, wetting his thumb at every page. He finally sits down. He moves the register into the light. He then leans again over the lists of typewritten names.

Maman throws a worried glance towards Gilberte who reassures her with a hand sign.

The old man's finger stops a few seconds on a line. He looks again at the paper maman scribbled earlier. He then pushes back the register; he turns towards the two women and says:

- He left on last Friday's transport.

The tone of his voice is unconcerned, as if discussing a train schedule.

- I don't understand what you mean, says maman with a strangled voice.

- He is no longer here.

- I know he is here! Maman says raising her voice.

Gilberte takes quickly hold of maman's arm and says, almost in a whisper:

- Calm down, Fanny.

- How can you ask me to calm down? I came here to see my husband! I want to see him!

- You will be arrested, if you don't get hold of yourself, they will keep you in camp.

Maman throws panic-stricken looks around the cabin. The man pulls the register away from himself and presents it to maman.

- See for yourself...

My mother takes the register between her hands.

Transport List of March 27th 1942

COHEN, MICHEL, 5.7.96, ODESSA

COHN, CLARA, 10.5.70, VARSOVIA

COHN, FANNY, 30.6.26, LYON

CONRAD, HAIM, 5.8.25, DWINSK

COPFERMAN, SYLVIA, 24.9.75, BUCAREST

COPFERMAN, ELLA, 23.7.79, SMYRNA

COSMARU, HERMANN, 26.4.30, CHAMPIGNY

CRASNOPOLSKI, 18.2.93, TUNIS

CRAZOVER, SMYLI, 5.7.12, VARSOVIE

CRAZOVER, ESTERA, 12.3.11, ODESSA

CREIMER, GEORGES, 1.2.30, MULHOUSE

CRESPI, VICTOR, 5.7.05, SALONIQUE

CROITOR, RIWA, 17.8.28, TOMASZOW

Maman took the train back, then the Métro to Saint Paul. She came home and announced the news with a voice she could hardly control before bursting in sobs. She spent the following days sitting by the window, with swollen eyes and disheveled hair, resisting all efforts to comfort her. At night, she could not sleep. Élise took care of the shopping and cooking for the two of us for maman had, so to speak, stopped eating. This condition lasted three weeks. Then one day, while we are both at school,

Madame Chevrolier climbs the stairs. It is about 11 AM. There is a strange look on the face of the concierge as she hands maman a thick envelop with our address and the words *To the attention of Fanny Crespi*. No sender's address is written on the envelope.

Maman thanks the concierge and closes the door. Her heart beating, she tears the envelope open and three sheets fall on the floor. She picks up the first two. She does not see the third one, which remains on the floor. The first sheet it is a page torn from a school notebook:

I am a railway man at the SNCF. I found these two letters on the tracks between Dormans and Ville-en-Tardenois, in the Champagne region. I am sending them to the address on one of the letters. The second letter has no address. I hope that you will be able to forward it to its addressee.

The first letter is written on a piece of torn out packing paper. The writing is so twisted it is almost illegible. It is signed Victor:

Forward urgently to:

Fanny Crespi, 20 rue des Écouffes, Paris 4e.

My dear Fanny,

We are being sent to an unknown destination. We are moving in the direction of Metz. After that, we do not know, although we all think it is probably, to one of these working camps in Germany we heard about. I do not know the conditions we will find on arrival, but one thing is sure you must be strong and hold on, whatever happens.

Whenever I return - si quiere l'Dio - I will find you.

You must leave right now with the children, and hide. I want you to know that if I do not find you right away upon my return, I will stand in front of our building every first Sunday of the month at 10 in the morning. I will wait for you to return from wherever you are then.

I will write you again, as soon as I can. I will address my letters to the café on rue des Rosiers since - as I hope - you will be going away.

I kiss you tenderly, my darling Fanny. Kiss Élise and Simon for me. I think of you. I will always think of you...

Victor

With a heart-wrenching moan, maman collapses on the living room sofa.

*

Élise, who comes home from school first, finds maman slumped on the sofa, crying uncontrollably. She is unable to speak. Élise makes her drink some water and helps her to her room where she lies silently on the bed, staring at a corner of the ceiling.

Coming back to the living room, Élise tries to collect her thoughts and decide what to do. Should she call a doctor? She picks up the envelope and the two letters on the couch. She then notices the third one near the door and goes to pick it up. She starts reading the note from the railway man's, then the letter from papa. Finally, she reads the third letter written by an unknown hand.

My dear Léon,

You cannot imagine what is happening to me. They removed us from Drancy where conditions were already distressing. But we are not any better now. On the contrary! I am writing you from a train that takes us either to Germany, Poland or Russia. We do not know. We do not know anything.

We are traveling in cattle cars. Mine says, "8 horses, 40 men" on the outside. Eight horses would be more comfortable than we are, for sure, since there are 70 of us, all men including some elderly. Everyone is in a panic. The Germans behaved like brutes. They made us run along the platform to embark. When someone stopped running, they hit him with clubs. I saw people fall and not rise again. They piled us up in the boxcars. We are all standing up, for lack of space. Each time the train stops, the vitiated air becomes dense, and we stop for hours at a time in the deserted countryside. There are sick people among us. We have had nothing to eat. They put two buckets in the car. One for drinking water (none is left) the other to relieve ourselves (it overflows). You can imagine the stink. When people faint and fall to the floor, other people step on them. Some men get into fights and some hit each other.

Each time the train stops, Gendarmes, and German soldiers come out screaming at us from three passenger cars attached to the train. Our car doors are sealed from the outside. Whenever people shout or bang on the door to get out, the gendarmes and the Germans answer by pounding with clubs from the other side. It makes a terrifying sound. The fear is becoming unbearable.

May god protect us.

Shema Israël, Adonaï Élohénou, Adonaï Éhad.

Haïm

Élise has just finished reading that letter when I come home from school.

- Maman is sleeping, she announces.

- What is this?

She hands me the three letters. I read them and look at my sister, terrified.

- Haïm? Who is Haïm? Why is this letter coming to us?

Élise takes back the letter

- I don't know but maman must not see it, she says.

- She has not read it?

- No. Just the other two. This one had fallen on the floor. She did not see it…

I jump up to go to maman's room. Élise holds me back by the arm:

- You must not mention the third letter, Simon. She is resting… Swear you will say nothing of Haïm's letter.

I answer with a nod. I understand. I wish I had never read it myself.

I escape from Élise and pushing the bedroom door I look in.

Maman is asleep, to escape her pain, no doubt.

*

Maman's nervous breakdown lasts for days. Élise stays home to take care of her. As far as I am concerned, I prefer going to school and leaving behind the unbearable atmosphere at home. I feel sad and anxious, unable to rid my mind of frightful thoughts. Our father is gone, and in a sense, our mother too.

But, one day Fanny begins to eat again. That day Élise makes meatballs. Maman hardly touches them, but it's a start. The next day she helps Élise with the housekeeping and cooking. The day after, she tidies herself up. Soon, she insists that Élise must go back to the lycée. It is such a relief, a few days later when coming home from school, I see her behind her sewing machine. She went out and brought back some work.

She has not forgotten Victor's admonition: "Leave!" But with what, how? Runners ask for a lot of money to pass you into the free zone. Then there are all the unexpected expenses. Once in the free zone we would need money until maman can find work, in an unknown city. Maman would of course plan to join her sister on the Riviera, but she only has a vague notion of where she might be now. Each time, Fortunée writes from a different city – *Foix, Toulouse, Cagnes-sur-Mer, Nice*. And communications between the two zones are so difficult. Her last letter dates from a few weeks ago, and it took quite a while for the letter to reach us. Who knows where Fortunée and Salvatore Carasso are today?

*

I am waiting in line in front of the grocery store on rue Saint Antoine. According to rumors, there will be a distribution of sugar. Sometimes you can stand for hours in the rain, and when your turn arrives, there is nothing left. The famous black market never did better. Out of boredom, I listen to others in line.

- Le Havre was bombed?

- Absolutely, and Goering who was visiting was wounded. Two of his generals were killed.

- That just sounds like rumors.

- No no, it was announced over Radio-Londres.

- So you listen to Radio-Londres, now?

- No, but I know someone who does.

- If Le Havre was bombed, we would have heard about it.

- The German navy is finished, that's sure. I have a cousin in Normandy. He says the Krauts tried to land in England, and the British threw them back into the drink.

- All these stories are just propaganda. As far as I'm concerned, the Germans conduct themselves correctly. We were heading for disaster before they came, that's for sure. They can go to hell with their Front Populaire and paid vacations!

- It's lucky De Gaulle went to England.

- Your De Gaulle is nothing but an opportunist. A good Frenchman stays in France; he does not go hide in London while his fellow citizens suffer.

- Move on, damn it! It's your turn!

*

I have just turned eleven. Maman gave me a second-hand Bayard fountain pen for my birthday. She exchanged it for a custom-made dress she tailored with fabric a client supplied. The client had received the material in exchange for a watch. Maman often barters her work for food, like anyone else who can. She came home one day with a small sack of rice from Indochina. Another time, the butcher's wife gave her a roast beef in exchange for a summer dress. Maman says children must eat red meat to stay healthy.

She works on her sewing machine day and night. She works for money during the day and at night to barter.

Sometimes, maman rages against Gilberte, the nurse who she suspects, invented the whole visit to Drancy to take our money. My mother weeps in anger, sniffles, and wipes her eyes with a handkerchief.

- When I think of all the money she stole from me.

- And think of the risks you took, adds Élise. You could have been arrested!

The sewing machine pedal resumes its familiar hum.

*

At the end of May, there is a new rumor in the neighborhood: Jews will have to wear a yellow star sewn on their clothes, to distinguish themselves from others. Maman buys a newspaper to read about it.

EIGHTH ORDINANCE REGARDING REGULATIONS AGAINST THE JEWS

The following measures are taken against Jews in accordance with the ordinance of Mai 29 1942: Jews are required to wear a distinctive sign. They are to present themselves at the police station or the sub-prefecture of their residence to receive the star shaped signs specified in the first paragraph of the ordinance. Each Jew will receive three signs in exchange for one point of the textile-ration card.

Signed: DER MILITÀRBEFEHLSHABER IN FRANKREICH.

The next day maman goes to the police station on rue de Rivoli, where a poster states details of the edict:

1   *Jews older than six are forbidden to appear in public without wearing a Jewish star.*
2.   *The Jewish star is a six-point star outlined in black and of a size equal to the palm of the hand. It is made of a yellow fabric and bears the inscription "**JUIF**" in black letters. It is to be firmly sewed on the garment and clearly worn on the left side of the chest.*
3.   *Criminal provision: All infringement to this ordinance will be subject to imprisonment and fines. Internment in a Jewish camp may be added or substituted to these penalties.*
4.   *The ordinance will become effective on June 7 1942.*

The poster is signed:

Senior chief of police and of SS subordinate of the Militaerbefehlshaber in France

Maman exchanges her textile points for the stars and sews them on our clothes. I look at myself in the mirror. This is quite a conflict for someone afraid to distinguish himself from others. A groan escapes from in my throat.

- We are going out together, says maman. You will see, it is not so terrible...

The outing will remain memorable. I have never been so embarrassed. Maman pretends not to be upset and Élise tries to be indifferent.

We walk along rue Saint Antoine, all the way to Bastille. It feels as though everyone is looking at us, although no one says anything. To toughen us up, maman decides to take the Métro. We board the last car, the only one allowed to Jews. We remain standing, but soon, a woman with a grieved expression gets up to offer her seat to maman. Maman is embarrassed, but she accepts. As for me, I wish I could disappear into a hole. What will happen tomorrow when I have to go to school wearing this star?

We get off at the Chatelet station and walk home through the narrow streets of the Marais.

*

The following morning, I hang around before leaving the apartment. I wait a long time under the door to the street before gathering up the courage to step onto the sidewalk. I pass a few people wearing the yellow star as well. By chance, I meet Papazian and another classmate, also Jewish, and it gives me courage.

A few of us in the class are wearing the star. Other kids look at us with curiosity, but make no remarks. The teacher does not mention it either, although I feel him staring at us. During breaks, I don't leave Papazian for a second. He understands how I feel, and on the way home, he walks me to the door.

- Thanks, I say, it is nice of you.

I get used to wearing the star over the next few days.

Once, a woman on the street crosses herself as she stares at me with surprise. I often walk pretending to scratch my face in order to hide the star with my elbow. I have the impression that others in school avoid me, while in fact I am the one who remains distant. One older kid talks to me from time to time during recess. He is very nice; maybe he guesses my embarrassment. His name is David Berlinsky and he too wears the star.

After a few days, no one seems to pay attention to us anymore. The yellow star has become commonplace and no one is interested. Around that time, I read in the paper:

Wearing the Jewish star.

There have been cases when Jews have violated the ordinance of the star. Either they do not wear one, or else they added some writing over it. These Jews were sent to a camp for Jews.

Then, this information in a column entitled: "Briefly":

The Jewish journalist Marcel Hutin, former editor of Échos de Paris was arrested for refusing to wear the Jewish badge.

In early July, new ordinances prohibit Jews from attending movie houses, parks, theaters, museums, and restaurants. A sign on the gate of the park at Place des Vosges reads:

Entry forbidden to Dogs and Jews.

Around that time, radios belonging to Jews are confiscated – maman hides ours in a wardrobe and forbids us to use it when she is out. Finally, Jews are restricted to shop within specified hours of the day. This harassment is in addition to the curfew. Although non-Jewish neighbors offer to help with food shopping, the conditions are becoming unbearable.

*

Radio rue des Rosiers warns one day that a round up is planned in the next two days.

- What do they want now? There are no Jewish men left in Paris! Complains maman.

Still, she avoids going out on the day the round up was predicted. As for children, we still go to school, since regulations do not apply to us, and in the evening, we do our homework as usual before going to sleep.

CHAPTER 6

July 1942

A sharp ring snatches me sharply out of my dream and deep sleep. I recognize the doorbell and open my eyes. The first light of dawn is barely visible through the window. The doorbell rings again, shrill and demanding, and I get out of bed.

I meet maman in her nightshirt, half asleep in the hallway, her face worried. I stand behind her as she cracks the door open. The door is pushed wide open, and we see two men enter our apartment. One wears a police uniform; the other is in civilian clothes. They push my mother aside and enter our home. They step wide and then stop.

- Get dressed Madame, you are coming with us.

- What have we done?

- Pack a suitcase. You have five minutes. Where is your husband?

- My husband was sent to Germany…

She glances quickly at the kitchen clock. It is 5:45 Am. Maman shouts now:

- What have we done wrong?

Élise appears. She is also in her nightshirt. She rubs her eyes and screams when she sees the police.

- I told you to get dressed, repeats the man in civilian clothes.

He walks down the corridor and opens the bedroom doors while his partner guards the entrance.

- Who lives here?

- Only my two children and me, says my mother.

- They come too.

The police officer then turns towards Élise and me:

- Go get your things. Hurry up!

- What things? Ask maman. Things for how long?

- For three days. What are you waiting for?

Maman stands still.

- I will go with you, she says. But, can I leave the children? They have to go to school and…

- The children come too. Stop wasting my time.

He grabs her by the arm and pushes her towards the bedroom. She starts piling clothes in a suitcase she opens on the bed.

The plain-clothes officer turns towards Élise and me:

- Come on you two. Didn't you understand?

- Sir...

Maman comes back to the doorway of the room.

- I have a little money, she says flustered. If it can help... I would like my children to stay here...

- Nobody stays here. Hurry up!

Mother looks at us.

- Get dressed, she says. Simon, put on two sweaters. You will take them off later... You too Élise, put on two blouses, one on top of the other....

- In this heat? Complains Élise.

In spite of the early hour, it is already hot. Overwhelmed by dread I cast a last glance at our house.

We get ready quickly. Even though we don't know what for.

Maman reopens the suitcase, and at the last moment puts in some food. On the landing, she insists we go to the toilet before we leave. Élise goes first.

The officers don't hide their annoyance. I exchange uneasy glances with the man in plain clothes. I am too nervous to relieve myself in the toilet when my turn comes, but I pull the flush anyway. Maman locks the door and picks up her suitcase. I lift my bundle and we follow the uniformed officer down the stairs. The man in plain clothes brings up the rear. He tells maman:

- Leave the key with the concierge

When we reach the courtyard the concierge, in fact, stands in front of her door.

- Would you mind watering the plants? Asks maman as she holds out the key.

A group outside is standing on the sidewalk. They are Jews of all ages from other buildings on the street, and they too carry suitcases. They look bewildered, resigned, or frightened.

Despite the season, one woman wears a fur coat. Officers in uniform guard the group. A neighbor across the street approaches maman and hands her a can of food. Maman is startled by the gift, and wants to put it in the suitcase, but officers order us to start walking. Mother quickly gives the can back to the neighbor.

- It's very nice, she mutters, but…I'm sorry.

Disoriented and distraught, our little troop starts walking towards the rue de Rivoli.

As we cross the rue du Roi-de-Sicile, I see Rachel Gutman ahead of us on the sidewalk. She is walking towards us. Rachel, who is the same age as Élise, lives on the third floor of our building. Rachel's parents are in our group. Rachel passes a neighbor on the street who knows her and pushes her through a doorway. We hear smothered cries, and when we pass the doorway where

Rachel is hiding a few moments later, she exchanges silent glances with her mother who stares back without a gesture, tightens her jaw, then quickly averts her eyes.

All of us pass in front of Rachel, who stands suddenly transformed like a statue on the sidewalk of the rue du Roi-de-Sicile. We don't know whether to envy her for not being part of our group or to pity her for watching the departure of her parents. I can still picture her white knuckles clutching the strap of her handbag over her shoulder, her terror-stricken face, and her silent pale lips. She was in the habit of spending the night at her girlfriend's apartment in nearby Saint-Gervais, returning home early in the morning. She probably feared a scolding for being late this morning. Instead, she found a more terrifying turn of fate.

*

The sun has not risen above the roofs of the place de la Bastille as our closely watched little group of about thirty men women and children, walks along the rue Saint Antoine. On the opposite side of the street, shop owners stare at us while setting up their morning display of meager goods and produce.

What could they be thinking as we pass? Are they thinking at all? Although their faces are familiar, I can't read their thoughts, just as I cannot comprehend what is happening to us. At the Place de la Bastille, waiters in white aprons sweep the sidewalk in front of their cafés. We walk towards the rue de la Roquette and the Boulevard Voltaire. Bicycle riders turn around to glance at us. Like a robot, I follow my mother. Where are we going? What will happen to us? The questions bounce around my head. My mind is a blank and I keep thinking of my mother's repeated question: "What have we done wrong?"

*

Our destination is the Japy gymnasium. I was here once with Papazian and other kids to watch a wrestling competition. The place is already filled with people like us; people taken from their homes, people dressed in hastily chosen clothes, people carrying a bag full of their belongings.

Their nervous eyes search around, expecting disastrous news. Some find the courage to laugh at the situation, but it is a laughter tainted with anguish. Others complain quietly.

- They could at least tell us what is going on, whispers one.

Behind a long table, officers check the new arrivals ID's on a list. Afterwards we wait, seated on our suitcases or against the wall. No one gives us information, or anything to eat or drink.

In the afternoon, old city buses arrive. Maman, Élise, and I file with the others between two rows of uniformed officers who push us towards one of the buses. I watch the mound of luggage tossed haphazardly on the rear deck of the bus trying to keep track of maman's suitcase. The officers are the last ones on the deck. One of them puts his head in the compartment and yells:

- This door stays shut! Anyone trying to escape, I shoot!

People exchange stunned looks. Have we become criminals that they threaten to shoot at us?

*

Crossing Paris, I stand up in the aisle, risking a tumble each time the bus brakes. I look through the window and think how strange it is that life outside continues as if nothing had changed. I have always felt I was different from others, a difference that lay heavy on my heart. Today's events evidently have something to do with it. Parisians on sidewalks are going about their business, a living tableau from which Jews have just been forcibly extracted. Torn out of their daily lives, they are cast into obscurity.

Our bus stops on rue Nélaton, in front of the *Vélodrome d'Hiver*, an indoor track for bicycle competitions and commonly known as *"le Vél d'Hiv"*. Buses are lined up bumper-to-bumper on the street, and the police are out in force. There are no Germans in sight.

Each bus advances slowly to the stadium gate where it discharges its contingent of Jews. People struggle getting off the bus with their bulky gear. They recover suitcases from the tangle of luggage on the rear deck; they then take a place in the long line. The three of us are horrified at the sight that greets us inside. The center elliptical track, sloping in the turns for bicycle races is swarming with people. From four stories of bleachers surrounding the track, habitually echoing with the shouts of fans encouraging their favorite, surges a terrifying bedlam of yells and cries. The smell under the huge glass roof is awful. We are like fish caught in a net. A few daring souls might try to escape but a line of parisian police officers and gendarmes closes off all exits.

Near the entrance, lies a heap of torn half-open smashed suitcases, bags and cardboard boxes tied with a string, blankets hastily tied to form bundles. Whose belongings are these? Carrying her suitcase, maman clears a path for us through the panic-stricken crowd. Children cry, arguments gush right and left, loudspeakers spew out unintelligible orders. I try to listen to the announcements with a vague and confused hope. Looking up at the loudspeakers

I see instead the spectacle of thousands of Jews huddled together on the bleachers above.

A massive lament suddenly rises from the crowd, resonates under the glass roof, increases like a wave then ebbs before I can catch its cause.

The few Red Cross staff here are overwhelmed. Among those assembled are sick people who need medication, pregnant women, children who are thirsty. Their inability to satisfy the demands made on them exasperates the police. They become impatient, brutal, and inhumane.

*

We pass by the toilets whose conditions are repugnant. People have been relieving themselves wherever they can; in a corner, against a wall, behind a door. It is of course impossible to wash. The revolting stench that emanates from this place mixes with the overall suffocating smell we encountered when we first entered the Vélodrome. Why is there such chaos and confusion in this place? People don't know why they are here, what offenses they have committed, how long they will be detained, and when they will have a chance to defend themselves. Each thinks he is victim of a misunderstanding, and rumors of all kinds circulate.

Maman, Élise and I look for a space up on the bleachers. There we meet the Barzilai family, Turkish Jews who live near us on rue des Archives. They are all here except for the father. Anticipating that the Germans would only arrest Jewish men, Alexandre Barzilai slept at a friend's house, and so he had not yet returned home the morning the police knocked on the door. The officers took away his wife, his children, and his mother-in-law. Madame

Barzilai complains about the heat and fans herself with a piece of cardboard. She moves aside to make room for maman, and asks:

- Have you heard anything? What are they going to do with us?

- Nothing, maman answers, placing her suitcase on her lap, and squeezing closer to make room for Élise.

I walk down the few steps to the railing and watch the scene below. Nurses with their Red Cross scarves on their heads mill around a tent set up in the center of the elliptical track. I tell maman I'm going down to see if I can get any information.

- Be careful...

Down below, it is impossible to walk. The underpass that leads to the center of the track is full of people lying on their belongings. Some are talking; others cry, out of despair, some are asleep.

I am about to go back up when I hear a commotion near the gate. Inching closer to the entrance, I see a truck backing into the entryway in reverse. It is loaded with breads that two officers throw haphazardly to the crowd.

The detainees rush forward reaching for the loaves. But, the breads break and crumble in the hands of the few who manage to grab them.

- I am beginning to understand, I say to myself, it's every man for himself, here.....

I manage to squeeze towards the front of the truck and find myself near the entrance gate. Suddenly I realize that in the chaos surrounding me, I could easily slip out. For a minute, I imagine myself walking in the fresh air through the streets of Paris, returning to rue des Écouffes... But how could I abandon maman and Élise waiting for me on the bleachers, worrying about me? I am torn apart. What to do? Seize my chance? I imagine my mother's anguish not knowing what happened to me, and I decide to stay. What would a boy of eleven do alone in Paris, anyway? Perhaps there will be another chance later for the three of us to escape. I return to the great hall trying to believe in that hope, knowing deep inside it is only a dream.

*

The buses near the entrance keep disgorging more waves of Jews swept up throughout Paris. A despondent crowd disembarks in a daze, cries out in shock at the scene before them. People entering are swept up in the horror of it all, knowing there is no chance to go back.

Among the buses, an occasional ambulance stops to unload its cargo of wounded and sick people on stretchers or in wheelchairs. The officers don't make a move to help, they remain on guard, but they summon volunteers. I find myself helping by pushing a wheelchair towards an area just cleared, where the pile of luggage was a while ago. Then, I return to the bleachers where my mother has been worrying.

- So? She asks.

I don't mention that for an instant, I saw a chance to escape. I tell her instead about the old people who arrived by ambulance. Maman is distraught.

- They came from the Rothschild hospital, I say.

As I offer this bit of news, walking across the bleachers on the level above ours, I recognize a friend from the lycée, David Berlinsky. I remember he comforted me in the schoolyard when I was upset about wearing a yellow star. He made light of the star on his left side in order to reassure me. Now he is among those herded into the stadium with his family. He sees me coming towards him.

- Hey Simon!

He trips on the steps that are crowded with people, trying to make a path towards me.

- Let's meet downstairs!

I go down below. Two minutes later, David appears. His presence is comforting and takes a weight off my chest. In our lycée days, he reminded me of Napoleon--short but sure of himself and full of confidence. I was flattered by his attention and his friendship.

- We've got to find a way out of here, he says in a low voice. This place is unbearable...

- How do you manage to keep your spirits up in here?

- I tell myself there's always a way.

- Even in this hell?

- Even in this hell!

I tell him I could have managed to sneak out, when the bread truck came in, but could not bear leaving my family.

David nods in agreement.

- In my family, he says, we even have Grandma.

A woman suddenly dizzy stumbles in front of us. David barely catches her before she hits the ground.

- Get her other side! He says. We'll carry her to the infirmary.

We head for the passage carrying the woman. Some people press to the side to let us through while others are too dazed to move. No one notices us when we finally reach the tent.

- Hey! Shouts David to a passing nurse. This woman has fainted.

- Lay her on the ground, the nurse replies the exasperated nurse.

- Where?

- Right here.

- Aren't you going to take care of her? He asks.

- We do the best we can! We only have two doctors!

We set the woman on the ground as best we can. I take off my sweater and slip it under her head. Her face is unbelievably white. Dark circles ring her eyes. She suddenly look at us, and her mouth twists in a frightening grin. Then she starts to cry.

- Stay with her a moment, says David.

He enters the tent with determination and comes out a few minutes later with a half-glass of water.

- It's horrible in there, he whispers in my ear.

We help the sick woman drink. She closes her eyes again. Did she faint again? Maybe it's for the best. We stay with her close to an hour.

*

By the time I rejoin my mother on the bleachers, she is so anguished and distressed that I hardly dare look at her. Maman, usually so strong, so determined, so good at resolving problems, utters not a single word. I am afraid she will fall into depression as she did when we received the letters from papa, written on the train that took him and Haïm to Germany.

I feel lost. I realize suddenly that I have only my own resources to count on and I am overwhelmed! Do I have the courage to survive this nightmare? I look around for my friend David. Where did he and his family go? I am gripped with anguish and I feel the sudden urge to throw up. I stand up and trip over bodies attempting to reach the wall where I lean, with my hands on the cold cement. How can I throw up with an empty stomach? Painful spasms grip my guts and I vomit on the ground, on the wall, over my shoes, and on the bottom of my pants. Maman is suddenly behind me with her cool hand on my forehead. She wipes my mouth and holds me.

- Come, she says, come and sit down, now.

*

My efforts to adjust to the confusion and chaos are futile. We have no choice but to endure the pain and the senseless misery as best we can. Some cry, others scream, and none of these primitive reactions has a chance of improving the hellish situation. The hardest for me is to see my mother lose control. The Jews are doomed, I think to myself. I am a Jew therefore, I am doomed.

My father could not escape his tormentors despite his precautions. They caught him in the subway, sent him to Beaune-la-Rolande, then Drancy, and from there to an unknown destination. Where is he now? Does he have any idea of what is happening to us? Does he suspect that his persecutors have now captured his wife and children?

I am overcome with bitterness. Why do I belong to a family whose origins condemn me? Why must I bear a name if that names sentences me? Why must I belong to a family altogether? Had I been alone a while ago, near the truck loaded with bread, I would have run off and escaped my fate as a Jew. I would have run down into the subway where no one could recognize me. Why can't I be like the other boys without this curse that has followed us forever!

People around me are talking. They still think they will return home, once the police have verified their identity. They will prove their innocence. There might even be an apology, and they will be free to go home… I know they delude themselves. I no longer share these illusions and I know maman does not either. But I don't say a word, and maman avoids discussing the point with me. We are both trapped by our own anguish, not able to share our pain for fear of raising the other's. Silence is our only protection.

With my head on maman's shoulder, I fall asleep despite the uproar all around. When I wake up the glass roof is dark and blackness envelops the Vel D'Hiv.

I get up carefully to avoid waking up maman, and climb down the bleachers in the vague hope of finding something to eat. I return empty-handed but find maman and Élise awake. We share the last bar of chocolate that maman had in her suitcase

*

A while later I find David who tells me he can't sleep. We walk around the crowded hallways, where people sleep leaning against the wall. We step over the bodies of others lying on the ground.

- If we were here just to check ID's it would be over already, I say.

- They might be planning to send us to a work camp…

- Children in a work camp? People on crutches, old people?

- Then what?

- Then I don't know. Maybe they will send us to join the men who left earlier for work camps.

- Hey! What's going on?

A roar rises from the bleachers. A shadow goes quickly by over the railing. We watch in horror as a body bounces with a dull sound on the ground below. People rush over.

- A suicide, I say with a choking voice.

*

The faint light of dawn brightens the blue of the glass roof above our heads. Maman, Élise, and I go down looking for food. After a long wait, a truck enters the Vélodrome in reverse just like yesterday. It is loaded with large containers of a blackish liquid and baskets of breads. People push and shove, anxious to have some food. Some get into fights. They are hungry, exhausted, and fed up. I manage to get a hunk of bread and a bowl of tepid liquid that I carefully hand over to maman amid the jostling crowd. The miserable breakfast doesn't last long, and Élise pecks the last crumbs from her blouse. We return to the bleachers, but new arrivals have taken our seats while we were downstairs. Luckily, no one has touched our suitcase.

- Come, I say, we'll look for another place. We must stay together.

I am now determined to avoid being separated.

*

People ask repeatedly: What day is it? What time is it? Little by little, we have lost all sense of time. Even at night, when the glass roof is dark, the heat is stifling. The stench, like the anxiety, gets stronger all the time.

On the fourth day, loud speakers announce that the "internees" will be transferred to a "gathering camp". The news is foreboding since no one knows what to expect, but we greet the information with some relief. Anything seems better than this inferno. We eventually get more details: Families will proceed to the entrance at the call of their name. I am so anxious not to miss our turn that I stand below a loud speaker and listen carefully as each name is called out. At last, in the afternoon, I hear our name

- Crespi family...

Élise who, has also heard, claps her hands.

Mother stands up painfully from the corner where she had crouched. I hurry to help her with the suitcase. A long line, moving slowly towards the exit awaits us downstairs. Everyone holds a suitcase. Faces are tired, bodies smell, words are few.

At last, we breathe fresh air and I try to cheer maman with a hopeful smile. We keep moving forward where a bus awaits us. We are told *the gathering camp* is located in the south of Paris.

Once again, I watch the unreal spectacle of everyday life from the bus window. Delivery boys pedal bicycles or pull a cart on the streets; housewives return from the market, nurses push baby carriages. I watch people sitting on café terraces leading a normal life, while Jews cross Paris in requisitioned buses. Which is reality? Here in this bus or there, just a few meters away, on a sidewalk bathed in sunlight?

The line of buses passes in front of the Jardin des Plantes and turns around at the *Gare d'Austerlitz* before stopping, along a railroad track out of sight, where a long train of freight cars is stationary. There, for the first time, we see German soldiers. They are in uniform, among the French gendarmes, lined up along the tracks. They carry guns on their shoulders and hold dogs on leashes that begin barking as soon as the buses arrive.

I am taken aback by the reflection of a woman near me:

- As long as we stay in France, nothing bad will happen to us.

My eyes are riveted on the wide-open freight cars each fitted with a ramp; the floor of each one is covered with straw. On the outside of the cars a sign is stenciled. It reads: *8 horses, 40 men.* Are we going to travel in these? Anxiety grips me once more. I don't dare look at maman.

Dogs barks, commands fly, faces around me are stunned. We are ordered to exit the buses with our luggage, and to line up along the tracks. With painful legs, and stooped shoulders, people obey. Fretful children ask nervous questions that no one has the heart or the knowledge to answer.

The Germans conduct a roll call, which takes a long time in the July sun beating on dirty stiff necks. After the roll call comes the count, and after the count, a recount. Each group is given the order to board at the blow of a whistle.

I trade a glance with Élise whose lips call a name in silence: Haïm. Tears roll down her cheeks, and I frown to remind her to watch herself in front of maman. The doors slide shut with an ominous bang, plunging the car into darkness.

*

Squeezed against one another, everyone inside the car remains standing. The Germans run along the tracks and shout orders, sliding open the door of a car to push someone inside, or ordering someone out, without regard for broken families. The heat is suffocating because the train has been left in full sun for hours.

Slowly, my eyes adjust to the darkness. The sanitary facilities consist of a single bucket in the corner. A little sunlight falls from a rectangular slit window just under the roof on one side. It is hopeless trying to get near it. Gashes between the planks under our feet reveal the stones on the roadbed below.

After an endless wait, the train finally pulls out, but it stops just outside the station after only a few minutes. Again, we wait before it starts again. There will be many other such stops. Pushed beyond their limits, a few men try to force open the door of the car. Some cheer them on, while others want to hold them back.

- Have you lost your mind?

But, the doors had been sealed before we left.

Once the train gathers a little speed, the tiny skylight, and the spaces between the planks let in a little air that everyone is eager to breath. It barely refreshes the putrid air inside the car. Pressed against each other, most of us remain standing. A few take turn sitting down.

After much shoving, I make my way below the slit window. From the shadows on the floor I figure out we are traveling southwest. I report this to Élise who shrugs her shoulders not seeing the value of this information, and neither do I.

The sun is getting low on the horizon when the train stops. Shrill whistles, shouts, footsteps, and cries resonate. A huge commotion is taking place outside our car, but we can't tell what it is. The door of our car remains shut. Once more, we wait with no explanation. From the report of a man looking out the slit window and from the disturbance outside we figure out the Germans have emptied a number of cars, but ours remains closed.

The train rolls out again, slowly. We stop again an hour later. I manage to peek through the space between two boards and to read a town name: Beaune-la-Rolande. I inform maman who shakes her head, stupefied. Suddenly the door slides open to the relief of everyone. French gendarmes stand on the station platform ordering us to jump down from the freight car, but children and old people hesitate. I help maman down onto the platform, and Élise holds the hand of an old man who barely escapes falling to the ground. We are ordered to form a single large group, and we start marching, surrounded by gendarmes.

Local residents await us outside the train station. They offer to rent wheelbarrows to carry people. Families among us with older relatives agree to pay.

- They were waiting for us, I remark to Élise. They knew we were coming.

We move on, each carrying a suitcase. I recognize the road; we walked here when we came to visit papa. The gendarmes keep telling us it is not far, but I remember that the distance is three long kilometers and everyone is already very tired. I worry about maman and hope she will hold out. I tell her she can lean on me but she refuses. Shadows on the road draw longer, but the heat persists.

- Here you are! A gendarme, points towards the silo at the entrance of the camp.

We are exhausted.

I recognize the corrugated metal roofs of the watchtowers where stand armed gendarmes.

We are searched as soon as we arrive. Men line up in front of one barracks, while women and children stand in front of another. The operation takes hours while we wait in the dust, thirsty, hungry and tired. We are however permitted, a few at a time, to use the latrines in an outside hut before returning to our place in the line.

The mothers have lost the energy to comfort their crying children. Some of the youngest are falling asleep on the ground.

Inside the barracks, the search is entrusted to no nonsense women from a nearby village. Cold and unconcerned, they take everything of value: money, jewelry; but also cigarette lighters, matches, key holders and pocket knives. These so called *volunteers* are often cruel and without compassion. I watch, horrified, as one of them pulls on the earring of a woman who hesitates to take it off. Blood gushes out of the poor woman's ear and stains her blouse.

The plunderers don't find the bank notes maman hid on her body, but they take her jewelry and her few gold coins.

After the search, the men go one way, women and children the other. I am secretly pleased to be too young to be sent to the men's barracks and to remain with maman and Élise. Our new prison contains two rows of triple level bunks covered with straw. The three of us settle in a middle bunk. There is no prospect for dinner, but we are too exhausted to dare ask. Most of the internees go to sleep immediately. The gendarmes lock the barracks door. Compared to the experience of the Vél D'Hiv, our conditions have improved. We toss on the hard bed looking for a position that lets us sleep, despite the straw that slips under our clothes and pricks our skin.

*

In the morning, a long line forms in front of the few faucets in the camp. We all need to wash after three days in the stench of the Vél D'Hiv. When I am done, and it takes hours of wait, I look around the camp. Nothing has changed since my father was imprisoned in this place. There is nothing here but barracks surrounded by barbed wire.

Twice a day, volunteers come back from the kitchen carrying heavy tubs full of a clear liquid, a kind of soup in which float beans and unidentifiable vegetables. You have to be starving to eat such food.

I am itching. Along with others, I have caught fleas from the straw in the bunks. Maman insists I join the column of men waiting to have their head shaved. I find David Berlinsky waiting in line.

At first, we don't recognize each other, but eventually we get used to our bare heads. He tells me he managed to pass as younger than his age because of his small size. He is in a barracks with his mother, grandmother, and sister.

Gendarmes occupy the watchtowers around the clock. Others patrol the camp with menacing dogs on leashes. We know, from their threats, not to get near the barbed wire fence or they will release the dogs.

*

We are hungry all the time. David and I stare resentfully at the fields of wheat and sugar beet surrounding the camp. We walk aimlessly along the barbed wires, under the watchtowers, and by the sentries with their dogs. People all around us look worn out and dejected

There are thousands of us here, arrested and held three days in the Vél D'Hiv, transported to this camp, searched, pilfered from and imprisoned. What do they want from us? What will become of us?

The same questions haunt us repeatedly: Would the Germans have taken women, children, the elderly and sick if they intended to send us to work camps? The most popular theory around is that they plan to send us back to our countries of origin.

David read a message carved on a wood partition in his barracks. He knows it by heart: *My name is Hermann Fisher. I live in Paris at 31 rue des Petites Écuries. I arrived here in April 1941. We are leaving tomorrow but we don't know our destination. Please warn my wife. It has been eleven weeks since she's had news of my whereabouts.*

- I heard his wife is here now, David adds.

At night, everyone must be in the barracks by 8 PM, the time of curfew. Many children are sick; others cry in their sleep and have nightmares.

*

Days and weeks go by. Maman discovered her hair started turning grey soon after our arrival. Now, she is losing large clumps each time she combs her hair. Élise suffers continuously from a stubborn cold, and coughs day and night. There is only one doctor in the camp, and a severe shortage of medicine. We hear reports of cases of scarlet fever.

*

A rumor one day reaches us: The internees are to be transferred, but no one knows where. Some say Germany, others Poland or even to a camp on the outskirts of Paris.

- That must be Drancy, I tell David.

In an atmosphere of fearful uncertainty, we all prepare to leave. On the day before the announced departure, a new rumor: Parents will leave first; children under 16 will stay in the camp and join them later. We can't believe this news. Who would take care of the little ones without their mothers?

The cynics among us say:

-. Was the Vél D'Hiv unbelievable? And what about the early morning roundups were they credible?

A fever of anxiety spreads through the camp and mothers are panic-stricken.

Nervously, maman tells us:

- Listen to me. Whatever happens, we must stay together. Did you understand Élise? You both must state you are over sixteen…

- But they put me in the women barracks with the young children! I reply with a tone of exasperation.

- Do as I say.

Fear gives my mother renewed courage and resolve. She divides among up what little hidden money she had. If ever we're separated, we'll meet again at home. OK? Her tone does not invite disagreement.

- And wherever they send us, the goal is the same: we meet at home when we return...

- It is our rendezvous point, I say.

- Right. Élise?

- I understand, maman.

- For now we'll do our best to stay together.

Élise is fifteen and won't have a problem passing for older than her age. Still, maman takes no chances, she stuffs her bra with paper. In my case it's more difficult. Maman somehow finds a cap and a pipe. She insists that I keep the pipe in my mouth at all times to make me look older. It belonged to someone else, it is chewed up and disgusting. I find the idea absurd but maman insists and I give in.

Our last night in Beaune-la-Rolande is tormented. Doubt and fear plague us. I am sure maman's idea is doomed; I will never pass as a 16-year old, being short for my age. Even if I manage to pass the gendarmes with my ridiculous getup, I'm sure to be eventually discovered, and then I'll be separated from my mother and sister...

I cuddle all night against my mother in the darkness of the barracks. The children's cries are more desperate than usual, as though they anticipate the coming tragedy.

*

I stick close behind my mother during the morning roll call. The loud speakers suddenly confirm that mothers will leave without their children in order to prepare for the little ones' arrival. Children will remain in the camp. The announcement creates a huge uproar. The gendarmes order the mothers to enter a small barb-wired courtyard. Mothers scream and refuse to obey. A gendarme tries to grab a small boy, and like a wild animal, the mother throws herself on the gendarme who is forced to retreat. The mothers tighten into a threatening crowd. The gendarmes move back to deliberate. They return with clubs. Side by side, they advance in a straight line towards the mothers who shield their little ones with their bodies. In a rain of blows, bodies fall to the ground and are hit again; blood spurts and splashes. The air fills with cries of despair punctuated by the dull thud of clubs against flesh and bone. Women stagger and collapse. The gendarmes haul children squirming and screaming in fear, towards one barracks. The struggle goes on and on.

I lose my cap and my pipe in the crush that follows the assault of the gendarmes, and I find myself separated among a cluster of men. I see maman and Élise in a group of women that are pushed by the gendarmes towards the small courtyard where those mothers already separated from their children are assembled under guard. A string of gendarmes blocks me from joining them. From the main courtyard where I am still standing, I see at a distance maman looking for me, and I can read the cry on her lips:

- Simon!

- Maman…

I am seized with panic.

My sister looks as well and finally finds me but I can only wave at them. I have the idea to slip unnoticed to the side and lose myself in the last group of rebellious mothers, but a hand grips my shoulder.

- Better to come over here, says David.

He leads me towards one of the barracks occupied by the already separated children; they are crying and calling for their mothers. Their faces are disfigured by fear of abandonment and bewilderment. A group of sweaty and wounded gendarmes guards them. I choke on a sob. I also want my mother. As once before, David tries to comfort me, but I can't hear him now. I want to go back outside.

A truck then enters the courtyard and stops to let out a company of armed German soldiers who take up positions around the yard. Soldiers point their guns at our crowd and install machine guns on tripods. Not a shot is fired, but the turmoil is suddenly replaced by a hushed feeling of horror. The exhausted women lie in the dust. Children cry in the barracks. Gendarmes bloody with wounds and slashes on their faces keep their clubs raised, ready to strike again. I return inside and watch from a distance. The central courtyard is now almost empty, occupied only by Germans behind machine-guns, a few gendarmes with clubs, and the inert bodies of several mothers on the ground. One of them, driven by madness, repeatedly hits her head against the ground.

- Maman, I utter softly.

David is next to me again.

- They are in the other barracks, he says, behind the small courtyard.

I suddenly leap and start running in that direction, but a gendarme outside blocks me with a raised club. He pushes me back with a blow across my chest. I stagger and fall back a few steps and glare at the gendarme above me. He is ready to hit me again, his face contorted with anger...

- Get back inside! He yells.

Defeated, I turn back. I ignore David coming towards me and instead I return to my barracks where I throw myself on our bunk, sobbing and grasping the straws with my hands. It is then that I find maman's tortoise shell comb, the same she always wears in her hair. It must have fallen off during the night. I hear the sound of engines in the courtyard, of trucks going away. I run outside, just in time to see the last truck carrying the women disappear on the road.

*

In a dream during the night, I see myself on the platform of the Saint Paul subway station. Maman stands on the opposite platform. I call out to her, but she doesn't hear me. I jump over the rail to join her, but I stumble and fall on the electrified rail. I wake up with a start. Everything around me is dark and for an instant I wonder: Am I alive or dead? Slowly, I regain consciousness and reality hits me. I hear groans and cries throughout the barracks. I jump from one nightmare to another. Nausea suddenly overtakes me, as it did in the Vél d'Hiv. I make my way to a corner of the barracks and I vomit on the ground in painful spasms. I can't sleep when I return to my bunk. The first light of day comes as a relief.

In the morning the spectacle outside is horrible. Young children come out of their barracks calling for their mothers. Toddlers who have just learned to walk stumble around. They are dirty, their diapers overflowing with urine and feces. They cry even louder when they fall on the dusty ground. They are hungry, thirsty, and terrified.

I wander alone aimlessly in the camp until late in the afternoon, passing near the children's barracks I see David coming towards me.

- Help us take care of the little ones, will you?

- What do you want to do?

- They need to be washed and comforted. We can't leave them like this.

I follow him. The oldest ones have already started helping out and, overcoming our repulsion at the filth and smells, we join them. It takes a huge effort to reassure the children, because we too are afraid, we too are hungry and thirsty, and we too were separated from our mothers.

Later, we go into another barracks permeated by a terrible stench. More children are here. I learn that the doctor is still in the camp, in the gendarmes' barrack. Three Red Cross nurses help him, but they can't do much without equipment or medicine. By the end of the day I am cutting makeshift diapers from clothes the mothers left behind. The business distracts me from my own distress.

Gradually, the lives of the older children take shape around the care of the younger ones, some of whom are still babies. We quickly learn how to carry them, rock them, change their diapers and speak to them. Many of them withdraw, sucking their thumb for hours, staring at some invisible spot where they hope to see their mothers return; the weakest have fallen in a stupor. But weak or strong, they all are sick with diarrhea, infections, and sores. The doctor does what he can. He is the last remaining Jewish adult in Beaune-la-Rolande.

Even older children begin to act strangely. One group plays an endless soccer game with a ball made out of rags. The most depressed ones wander around the camp oblivious of others. A few become aggressive, even violent.

Little by little, I begin to listen to David. While he is no less skeptical or bitter than I am, he seems more determined to do something. He hasn't lost confidence in his own resources, and is convinced we can still affect what happens to us. He believes we must fight back.

- We have to defend ourselves, he advises me.

CHAPTER 7

August 1942

I exasperate David. He thinks I am weak, easily discouraged, and ill prepared for life's hardships. He thinks I am the type of kid who never lets go of his mother's apron strings. On the other hand, I can tell that he likes me. He feels responsible for me, as he did in the schoolyard, on rue des Quatre-Fils, the day I was so embarrassed to wear the yellow star. He confides in me:

- I have decided to escape, he says in a low voice.

I don't know what to say. I feel a lump in my throat. If David leaves, I will be left alone, on my own. I know our friendship means something to him. He is clever and resourceful, and through all the disasters that we've encountered he has been like a big brother to me.

Not knowing what else to say I whisper:

- It's dangerous.

He gives me an ironic smile. He must think I am a coward. I try a different argument:

- They said we will be reunited to our families. Won't it be better to wait? They can't keep us here forever.

- You still trust these sons of bitches? Not me. I am going back to Paris, and from there, I will go to Drancy, see what I can do...

His eyes fixed on the camp's gate, he repeats

- I am getting out of here. I am going to escape. Impulsively I say:

- Then take me along.

David is quiet. He avoids looking at me but after a while, he says:

- You think I need to be weighed down by a chicken like you? It's not going to be easy, you know...

- I am not a chicken and I will do whatever you tell me to.

-Without arguing?

- Without arguing.

- You're sure?

- I swear I won't argue.

David says nothing.

- I'll have to think about it, he finally adds and walks away, his hands deep in his pockets.

*

- It's here, have a look.

David leads me to the fence. We approach it slowly as if out on a stroll. We pretend we are talking but we keep glancing towards the barbed wires strung from pole to pole.

- Make sure you get a good look, Simon. You see the soil dipping under the lowest wire near the stake?

- You don't expect to get under there?

- I do.

- But the hole is so small.

- Are you already forgetting your promise? You are not so big and neither am I. We should be able to wiggle under the wire...

- They will see us from the watchtower....

- They won't see us. Come here...

We take a few steps, before David resumes:

- You see this barrack? It blocks the view of the fence. It creates a blind spot for the sentries in the tower...

-Are you sure? David sighs with exasperation.

- I studied it very carefully... You can still change your mind, you know. If you don't think you have the guts...

- I do, I say suppressing my fear.

- That's what you promised...

- You can count on me.

- Let's not hang around here; we don't want these brutes to notice what we are up to.

As we walk back to our barrack, David continues:

- Anyway, what do we risk if we get caught? They'll bring us back to camp, that's all.

- They'll beat us.

- So? We can take it. They won't kill us…

- I'm worried about how we will reach the wires without being seen.

David thinks a moment, and then says:

- There's an opportunity at noon, during the change of guards. I'll choose the time carefully.

- You've studied their movements, I suppose.

- I have counted up to 300 between the moment when the first team comes down from the watchtower and the time when the second team climbs up to the platform. That gives us… about four minutes. That's plenty of time to get to the wires. The important thing is not to make any noise.

I can't help but be impressed by my friend.

- Any other question?

- When are we leaving?

- Day after tomorrow

My legs already feel weak.

- OK, the day after tomorrow, I say trying not to let my voice quiver.

*

The discussion resumes as we lie side by side on the barracks beds. David whispers:

- One problem is that once we are outside the camp people will spot us right away with our shaved heads.

- We could say there were lice in boarding school.

- You forget this is summer vacation.

- Then we can say we caught lice in summer camp.

- That's a good idea, Simon. Good for you!

A feeling of pride swells my chest.

- There is another problem to deal with, David adds. We will need money to eat, once we get to Paris.

- I have 200 francs my mother gave me.

- Good, but it's not enough.

I lean on one elbow, scrutinizing his face in the dark; afraid to hear the idea he has in mind.

- How do you plan to get the money? I ask cautiously.

- Not just money. Jewelry too.

- How? Where?

- Where people threw belongings away, rather than hand them over during the search when we first arrived.

- You mean…

- Exactly!

*

The sun beats hard on us the following day. Everyone in the camp stays inside the barracks. Even the gendarmes keep away rather than sweat in their uniforms. David takes me to the shack that serves as latrines. On our way over, he picks up a rake that is leaning against the outside wall of a barracks.

- I warn you, it's going to stink.

The smell, as we enter, is worse than I had imagined. We hold our breath. We don't intend to stay here any longer than we have to.

- Do as I do, says David, and he throws me a dirty cotton scarf and covers his own mouth and nose with a filthy handkerchief from his pocket.

- You look like a real cowboy, he tells me.

I guess his smile under his mask. His eyes, however, show no fulness.

- Let's get to work, he says sternly.

David grabs the rake. To cheer himself up, he adds:

- You never know, we might get rich…

- The septic pit is under a flimsy roof made of lumber and tarred paper. Over the pit itself are benches of coarse boards with holes at regular intervals. Feces and pieces of torn paper float in a muddy brownish pool under the benches. Our makeshift masks are useless. Nausea takes hold of us. I suddenly feel sick.

- Go stand watch outside, says David. Knock on the wall if you see anyone coming…

- OK.

I go outside, relieved to breathe clean air. I look around casting occasional glances towards the latrines where David starts his work. Kneeling on one of the boards, he slowly rakes the cesspool; stopping each time his tool hits a hard object. He then carefully raises to the surface the salvaged object between the teeth of the rake and drops it on the ground. With twigs he brought for that purpose, he scraps off its coating of filth. For a while, he only picks up stones and pieces of wood. But after a few tries he finds something with shiny reflection in the sludge. It turns out to be a gold bracelet.

- It's a start, says David in a whisper.

The heat under the roof of the cesspool makes our work even more difficult.

David straightens up and joins me outside.

- It's your turn, he says putting the rake in my hands. I'll go on watch...

The effort is such an ordeal that tears come to my eyes. I work taking small breaths of stinking air. My knees pressed against the dirty boards ache. Stirring the liquid makes the foul smell even more nauseating. Here and there the rake hits a hard object. I try to catch it and, no matter how repugnant, bring it up to inspect so that I can decide if my catch is worth salvaging. I get discouraged after a while. The rake is hard to maneuver and I feel faint. I am afraid of falling in the pool...

- Simon...

David whispers questioningly.

- It's useless, I reply. We are wasting our time. I have had enough of this.

- Keep going... I will relieve you as soon as you bring up something worthwhile.

I am angry and irritated with David for insisting that I do such disgusting work. Curiously, my anger stokes my energy. My nose adjusts to the vile stench, which clings to every pore of my skin. Having exhausted one area of the pool, I move to another and continue scraping the bottom of the filthy pond with my rake until I hit a hard object. I move the handle around to determine its contours. It has the shape of a brick. Probably another stone, but it feels lighter than rock. I carefully raise the thing. A brown liquid drips from the dense object between the teeth of the garden tool. It looks like a small package wrapped in a rag. I drop it on the ground between my feet, and lay the rake behind me. Then I begin to slowly clean the rag with twigs. Separating one side that opens more easily. David comes over to see my catch.

- You won the lottery! He says.

What I fished out is nothing less than a wad of banknotes, which one of the detainees has thrown in the latrines upon arriving in camp, rather than give it to one of our greedy wardens. David unfolds a large rag he had rolled around his waist and spreads it on the ground. He puts the wad and the gold bracelet in its center.

- That's enough, he says.

Careful not to be noticed, we head for a washbasin carrying our precious treasure. The bracelet is easily washed, but the banknotes are another matter. We must be careful not to damage them and we wipe them one at a time. It takes forever. We have to stop and hide everything under the sink each time someone comes by, and resume the work when they leave. However, we smell so bad, we get disgusted glances and people leave quickly. We are so excited that we forget the stink and the stains on our worn out clothes. After we are done, we wash under the faucet without soap, and return to the barracks. But first, we take a long detour through the camp to let the stench that clings to us dissipate, and we change into clothes we find in a barracks.

*

After a fitful night, I watch anxiously as light of day filters through the windows. We exchange a quick glance as we get up.

- See you later, at the place agreed upon.

- Have you got our treasure?

David answers with a tap on his belly: The bracelet and the banknotes are hidden under his shirt. In a reflex gesture, I shove a hand in my pocket where my fingers squeeze my mother's tortoise shell comb. From now on, my good luck charm…

Fear and impatience about our escape project haunt me. Although the younger children need attention all morning, I find it hard to concentrate on them. They passively let me wash and change them. For them I am an adult. David and I meet behind the barrack at the agreed time. We keep watching the critical watchtower. Nothing moves for what seems like a very long time. At last, two gendarmes start down the wooden ladder.

- Now! Whispers David

According to our plan, we undress behind a barrack wall. We keep our underwear and shoes on, and stuff the rest of our clothes in our sweater that we carry as a bag. The idea to undress has of course come from David who thinks it will be easier to slip under the fence if we are almost naked, with no clothes to grab hold of the wires.

- We are going to get scratched all over, I say while wrapping up my bundle.

- Too late to change plan, answers David.

Ready before me, he stands at the corner of the barrack and spies the watchtower. The gendarmes have reached the ground.

- Let's go! Says David.

With no sentry in sight, we reach the barbed wire in about twenty strides; David leads the way. My heart is pounding hard. I don't have the nerve to turn around. I follow David and slide my bundle under the fence. David lifts the bottom wire and holds it up with a stick he brought for the purpose. He takes one last look towards the camp, and signals me to go first. I crawl on my stomach. Even with the wire raised, the space is very small!

- Shit, hurry up! Whispers David.

Just at that moment, we hear shouts coming from the direction of the barracks and a dog barks. I wiggle as fast as I can.

- Quick! Says David slapping me on the thigh.

Frantic now, I dart under the fence. My back scrapes against the wire. The pain is sharp, but I keep going. I am sweating profusely. My shoulders have gone through. I keep crawling, with my head down. My buttocks now go through, then my legs. I crouch on the ground, my hands over my head. My back is on fire. The screams and barking started again. I hear David:

- Move over! I need to get through. Keep going! Don't stop!

- What are these shouts?

- It's not for us.

I look back to hold up the bottom wire. David has a hard time going under the fence. But he twists and turns and finally makes it through.

We are crawling behind one another in the fragrant grass, our bundles beside us. I am still in front. I stop in about twenty meters, exhausted. It feels as if my heart is about to burst. The air is hot, the shouts and the barks inside the camp have now subsided although the relieving sentry crew must have reached the watchtower's platform. Will they see us? Has David considered that possibility?

- The wheat field, he instructs, catching his breath. Straight ahead!

He is now next to me. His head resting on his clothes bundle.

- How? Do we run for it?

- No, keep crawling.

- They'll see us. They'll shoot at us…

David is not listening to me. I watch him scrambling ahead of me; his naked body makes me think of a snake slipping through high grass. I lift my head. The wheat field seems so far away!

- Wait for me, I say between my teeth. Don't leave me behind.

By the time I reach the edge of the field, David has disappeared deep among the green wheat stalks. Overwhelmed by fear, I expect to hear the shouts of sentries and the bark of dogs at any moment. I picture the gendarmes dashing out of camp in pursuit, catching us, and taking us back to the camp's courtyard. I imagine them clubbing us as they clubbed the mothers the other day. Fear and pain bring tears to my eyes. And where is David? I keep crawling between the wheat stalks. This is a very big field. The soil is damp; a faint and greenish glow colors the air around me. When, for a moment, I try to turn on my back and rest, I feel a sudden sharp pain as my injured shoulders rub against the soil and pebbles on the ground.

- Simon…

I see David's white face through tears of pain. He whispers:

- Keep crawling. You go first.

My underpants catch on the grass and thorns. My elbows hurt. The ground is full of sharp stones. My fear recedes somewhat when I realize that at last, the sentries can no longer see us. Only physical pain, and apprehension for the future, remains. How will we cope after we escape the attention of the gendarmes? Freedom is nice, but it requires so much resourcefulness...

- Keep going, whispers David behind me. You're nearly there.

- In fact, I can see the edge of the field through the thick growth. What if we find ourselves at the feet of a farmer eager to call the Germans? They would come to fetch us and bring us back to camp.

The field ends along an embankment, leading to a paved road above. The bank is full of stones, undergrowth, and pieces of rusty broken-down fences

- We can rest here a while, says David.

- You don't think they can see us? I ask.

- If you can't see them, they can't see you either. He too is worn out and out of breath.

- We're not yet out of trouble.

- What d'you mean?

- We said we would rest.

He closes his eyes. His face looks stiff; his lean and naked chest hardly rises with each intake of air. He resembles one of these statues on top of tombs I have seen in history books. I wonder if he is still breathing. Images keep going through my mind: the school, the Marais district, the café on rue des Rosiers, our apartment, papa sitting at the sewing machine. In my head, I see maman sewing the lining of a jacket under the lamp; her black hair is rolled in a bun and held by the shell comb she customarily uses to retain her hair. Coming back to reality, I lower my eyes on the bundle of my clothes...

- Look at your back, whispers David.

- It's OK.

Seated at the bottom of the embankment, we dress in silence. Our legs, chests and arms are covered with painful scratches. What hurts me most however, are those on my back. The pain returns each time my shirt rubs against the wounds. We climb the embankment, clinging to roots and bushes, and hoist ourselves onto the paved road.

- Bend down to cross, says David.

Beyond the wheat field, stand the watchtowers of the camp.

- No more crawling, do as I do.

He runs across the road, body bent in two and tumbles down the embankment on the other side. I am right behind him. We are now in a field of beets, and the road above us hides the watchtowers. We run as fast as we can.

*

Beyond the beet field and after walking for a couple of hours along a country lane bordered with fences demarking fields, we reach the village of Montbarrois. The little community is deserted, as if all its inhabitants were taking a nap. We walk down the main street. The café with its sheet-metal sign above the door is open. We dare not enter, even though no one is visible inside. Our heads are shaved; we are dirty and probably still smell of the latrines. Indeed, we look like two escaped convicts. It does not take long to cross the village. We keep going, walking along a paved road lined with electrical poles. The sun is strong; we are tired; we are hungry and thirsty.

- You were right, I say, we are not yet at the end of our troubles.

- We are free, and that's a lot.

- Yes, but for how long?

I am annoyed with myself for feeling depressed and lacking confidence. I would so much prefer to be a good partner and live up to David's expectations. After all, were it not for his resourcefulness and courage, I would still be in that horrible camp guarded by French gendarmes in the pay of the Germans.

- I am sorry, I say.

- Don't worry Simon; we'll get out of this. Here is another village.

A church steeple shows up on the horizon. This one is called Saint-Loup-des-Vignes. A few farmers wearing overalls and berets are talking in a group in front of the church. A wheelbarrow full of tools stands nearby. The men keep silent as they see us walking towards the café across the street. The terrace of the café consists of a couple of metal tables and some chairs under a plane tree.

- How about a drink? Suggests David with a mocked laid-back attitude.

His joke would make me laugh, if I were not so tired. We sit down, pretending we came out to quietly chew the fat around a drink. A woman appears in front of the door. She stares at us as if she just saw a couple of Martians. David orders two lemonades and the woman moves back inside without a word.

- Aren't you afraid she might call the gendarmes, I say in a low voice, leaning on the table.

- Don't worry.

David gets out the banknotes and sorts through them to pick one that is not as dirty as the others, and does not smell like shit. The woman comes back holding a glass of lemonade in each hand. David has slipped a five Franc note under the Fernet Branca ashtray. He then asks:

- Can you make us sandwiches, Madame? A smile lightens his dirty face with dark rings under his eyes. We don't have any ration coupons with us, our parents kept them in Paris. We are on vacation in a kid's camp. We were touring for the day around the countryside and we got lost. So now, we have to go back, but in the meantime, we are hungry…

- Cheese sandwiches. Will that do?

- That will be perfect.

David and I agree on one point: These are the best sandwiches we have had to eat in the course of our short life. In the meantime, the farmers in front of the church have disappeared. Women crossing the square replace them. One of them carries a chicken by its legs; head down.

- They have enough to eat around here, observes David. They don't worry about the rationing as we do in Paris.

The woman gives us change. David, who notices a newspaper stand inside decides to buy a local paper called *L'Écho de Pithiviers*. Now satiated, we leave after politely saying good-bye and leaving a tip on the metal table.

*

Later in the afternoon, as we try to put as many kilometers as we can between us and the camp, we notice a stream some 100 meters away from the road; sheltered under a weeping willow. We decide to take a break to bathe and clean ourselves. We are in the water just a few minutes when we hear the sound of a car on the road. We are relieved when we notice it is not a the van of the gendarmerie. For an instant, up to our chest in water, we just shared a moment of fear, imagining once more the Germans' machine-guns, the dogs, the latrines, the children forcibly torn from their mothers and abandoned...

Just as quickly however, the camp seems far away; suddenly we become conscious we made it, we succeeded, we escaped! We explode with laughter that we don't even try to control.

After bathing, we take a little nap under the willows to soothe our wounds. Then we continue on our route. Night comes upon us as we are stuffing ourselves with beets in a middle of a field that will be our bedroom for the evening.

*

At dawn we are awakened by singing birds. We are hungry, but we have had enough of beets, and we get back on the road. Soon we are in sight of a farm. A dog barks in the yard as we approach. A middle-aged woman comes to the threshold of her kitchen door and stares at us, surprised and speechless. She waits for us to speak.

- Hello, starts David.

- What do you want?

David tells one of his typical stories. We are on vacation, we are camping here and there, and we are looking to buy something to eat. He has taken the precaution of choosing a few more among the cleanest banknotes. We leave a few minutes later with some bread, eggs and milk in a bottle with a cap. We find a place and stop for a picnic. David shows me how to make a pinhole in the shell of an egg and gulp it down with a straw.

- Where did you learn this? I ask, surprised.

- In a book, answers David, while spreading the newspaper bought the day before in Saint-Loup des Vignes in front of him. It is subtitled *News from the Beauce and Gatinais farming region*.

I watch him as he chews on a piece of bread and interrupts himself to toss down some milk. For the first time since the police barged into our house on rue des Écouffes, I feel safe, and I know I owe the feeling to David.

Listen to this, he says. The inhabitants are delighted to know that Jews and freemasons are held behind barbed wires rather than at the head of big organizations as in the time of Leon Blum... Shall I continue...?

- This is worse than reading the *Crapouillot*, that anti-Semitic piece of shit ...

- You haven't heard anything yet: All-powerful yesterday, the filthy Semites today are no more than concentration-camp-jailbirds. You want some more...

- One can't get enough of it.

- Look at this ad... I lean over the newspaper:

LOOKING TO RECRUIT GUARDS FOR THE CAMP OF PITHIVIERS

1050 francs per month, plus meals and lodging.

- Pithiviers is the twin camp of Beaune-la-Rolande, David says gloomily.

He carefully folds up the paper and puts it in his pocket.

- We'll use it to wipe our ass, he says. Now, how about getting back on the road?

*

We walk until late. As night falls, we hear the sound of music as we reach the village of Nesploy. The town square is decorated with garlands strung between trees. The owner of the local café has installed his tables on the square and arranged a dance floor on top of which people, dressed in their Sunday best, are moving about. A man on a platform plays the accordion. As we come closer, David locates an empty table. He gestures to the owner while we sit.

- Can we eat?

The man gives us a suspicious look. This time, I give him our camping story managing to include that we have money. Soon a young woman in a white apron brings us an omelet and French fries.

The first stars come out in the clear summer sky above the village, as if inviting us to a dream; our worries, however, are not far away. Where are our mothers and our sisters right now? Where is my father? No need for David to guess my thoughts. Similar ones cross his mind. How can villages be so undisturbed while whole families are torn out of their homes and driven to camps where they are left to fester without an explanation; while gendarmes beat mothers with clubs to separate them from their young children…?

Still eating my tasty French fries, I watch the villagers spinning on the dance floor, raising dust with their shoes. At the end of each dance, men wipe their foreheads and women return to sit down with their women friends. People around us talk as if the world was at peace. Young women in low neckline dresses let out sudden bursts of laughter. A group of standing teenage girls has formed on one side. They are waiting to be invited to dance. They throw glances our way and laugh. I sit, dumbfounded, as David suddenly gets up and walks towards the group. He bows with class in front of the nicest looking young woman. I can't hear his words but I can guess he is inviting her to dance. The young woman motions her rejection with her head then looks away.

Somewhat sheepish, David comes back and sits next to me. I am so relieved. I have an instant of panic just at the thought he could have abandoned me to pursue a flirtation.

- You have some nerve! I say with sincere admiration.

- We had better look for a place to sleep.

*

We spend the night in a road maintenance shack on the way, not far from a crossroad where a sign indicates the road to Paris, without specifying the distance. The next morning we walk all the way to Bellegarde where we spend a few banknotes on food. As we leave a bakery shop, I see my reflection in a window.

- Did you notice? Our hair is beginning to grow back.

There is a movie house in the village, and the poster advertises: *La Route Enchantée*, The Enchanted Road, with Charles Trenet and Marguerite Moreno, two well known stars of the French cinema.

- This is quite fitting, says David. How would you like to see a movie tonight?

The theatre is filled with farmers from the village and surrounding area. They look like nice people. Do they even know that Jews are no longer allowed to take their children to the movies? The lights dim and we hear the familiar rattle of the old projector as the screen lights up. The show starts with a documentary on horses, then, the emblematic cock of the Pathé Movie Company appears, announcing the news.

- What horrors are they going to show us now, whispers David in my ear.

The lights of the theater are suddenly turned on again. David turns towards the projection room while unease suddenly grips my guts. Whistles and catcalls rise from the audience. What is going on? German officers have appeared on the screen while the whistles redouble.

- I get it! David explains; they put the lights on to prevent disturbances and the audience making fun of the Germans during the news...

Indeed, the audience calms down as soon as the Germans leave the screen and the lights are dimed again. David and I exchange a glance of understanding in the dark,.

*

The next day, hot sunny weather ends with rain. We look for protection from steady showers along the way. Our lack of progress - just two kilometers in one day! - affects our moral. By evening, the rain increases in intensity. We look for a farm where we can ask for shelter. We stop at a large farmhouse surrounded by wheat fields. Inside, two men and a woman, seated at a table, are having dinner.

Soaking wet, famish and depressed, we mumble our explanations, which we know, don't hold water.

- We are looking for something to eat and a place to spend the night.

- You got money? Interrupts one of the men.

A puddle is forming under our feet, right on the flagstones of this kitchen-dining room. Smells of soup, of wine and good bread reach our nostrils. The other man, probably his brother, looks a little older and acts as the head of the family. After staring at us for a while, as if to decipher the enigma of our presence in his house, he stands up, comes near us and says:

- Follow me.

He throws a raincoat hanging down from a peg on his shoulders, lights a portable lamp he swings from its handle and goes out of the house. We follow him, zigzagging between the puddles in the yard. A dog barks.

- Hush, Milou!

With a shove of his shoulder, the man opens the door to a barn. It's nice and dry inside. The man casts the light of his lamp over bales of straw stacked against one of the walls.

- Your bedroom, he says, adding:

- That will be forty francs with dinner.

- It's quite expensive.

- It's the war...

He lets us think a moment then concludes:

- If you prefer the water outside...

- We prefer sleeping where it's dry, says David quickly.

- You got to pay first.

Forlornly, David gives the money, and the man leaves.

A short while later, the woman brings in a basket laden with bread, wine, cheese and a few plums. She has even taken care to include glasses and napkins.

We eat in the dark, without a word. We get to quench our thirst with wine, and it is a little drunk that we fall asleep, in our dirty clothes on our bed of straw.

*

It is still dark and raining when we are awakened by the sound of an engine outside. A light through the barn's window makes me blink. A van has stopped in the yard. We hear voices, the door to the barn opens abruptly, and the portable lamp of the farmer is shined in our faces.

- Stand up gentlemen. I don't recognize the voice.

We lift ourselves up from the bales of straw. Three men face us: The farmer and two gendarmes. One of the gendarmes is a brigadier. He speaks first, while in the yard the engine keeps idling.

- Wouldn't you be from the camp of Pithiviers, by any chance?

- No, replies David.

- Have you got your papers with you?

- No sir, I answer.

- And your parents. Where are your parents?

- In Bellegarde.

What is the address?

- In fact, muddles David, we are from Paris... We are on a trip, and...

- A trip, you say? Follow us. We are taking you with us...

- We have not done anything! Complains David.

- That is what we will verify. Come on.

*

The constabulary van jolts us about in the night. Its headlights illuminate each white pole as we pass alongside the road. The brigadier dozes off, his head leaning on the window. His colleague at the wheel says after a while:

- We are in front of your house, chief. I'll drop you here. Go get some rest while I take care of the youngsters. The brigadier hesitates a moment, then turns towards us. He looks grim and tired.

- Ya! It's been a long day, he says.

He seems ready to go home. He opens the door and puts one foot on the ground.

- Make sure you keep them cool, he says, glancing at us from the corner of his eyes. I'll call Pithiviers in the morning. And watch out, these are no choirboys, in my opinion.

- Have a good night, chief.

- See you tomorrow, the brigadier says again before slamming the car door.

The van continues on its way. The ride is monotonous. I despair at the thought of finding myself again in the camp, although I am hoping David is right now thinking of a way of sneaking away. A few kilometers further on, the gendarme turns towards us:

- Where in fact are you from?

David and I exchange glances. I signal for him to answer.

- From Paris, as I told you.

- At what address?

- He lives near Bastille and me, at République

The gendarme weighs David's answer. A long silence follows, the gendarme resumes, without taking his eyes off the road.

- I'll leave you on the outskirt of Montargis. You'll have to wait until morning without anyone seeing you. OK?

We can't believe our ears.

- There is a bus in the center of town, continues the gendarme. You'll find it easily; it's on the market square… Then he adds:

- I don't want to see you dawdling around after daylight. Is that understood?

- Understood, but…

- We'll say you ran away when we got to the police station. Take the bus tomorrow morning and disappear, that's my advice to you.

The gendarme slows down as we pass the sign announcing the city of Montargis. The gendarme stops the van, opens the door, and tells us to get out. As he bends down to close the door, David holds it back for an instant:

- Thanks...

The gendarme nods his head and takes off. The sound of the engine rises as it goes through each gear then diminishes and dissipates at the end of the road.

*

The bus is on time at the market square – Many of the passengers on the old Citroen bus are farmwomen laden with baskets. We sit behind the driver and the bus leaves in the rain, to the accompaniment of the regular rhythm of the windshield wipers. David makes suggestions for what to do when we arrive in Paris.

- You will have problems managing without ID papers, ration card or much money, he explains.

The thought that we will each have to go our own way alarms me. How will I make decisions on my own?

- What are you going to do? I ask.

- Like you. Try to find my family.

- In Drancy?

- I heard they don't keep people very long in Drancy. They send them somewhere else. To *Pitchipoï*, as I heard some people say euphemistically.

He looks my way and sighs:

- But we have to try anyway. After a while, he adds:

- Didn't you tell me you have family on the Mediterranean Coast?

- Yes, my grandmother. She's with my aunt and uncle. But I don't know exactly where they are staying. Anyway, what I really want to do is find my mother and sister.

I am terrified at the thought of our expedition ending. David may feel the same way but if he does, he knows how not to show it. In my case, just to control my voice is an effort. Paris, the city where I grew up is suddenly a foreign land; it has become a maze in which I will endlessly stumble over malicious obstacles. I am depressed. My head against the window and rocked by the bumps of the road, I withdraw into myself, my thoughts take me away and become dreams inhabited by familiar yet far away faces…

- We're nearly there.

David shakes my shoulder gently.

I recognize Paris. We pass by Place d'Alésia, then Denfert. The bus stops at the terminal at the end of Boulevard Saint-Michel.

Listen, starts David, perhaps aware of my anxiety, I have to go to my house and see what happened. Try to manage as best you can for a few days.

I nod my head, swallowing my tears. David continues:

Let's meet again next Monday at Bastille.

- At the Métro?

- At the Métro at 10 a.m. At the subway exit on the corner of rue St Antoine. OK?

- OK David.

We walk to Place du Chatelet and continue towards Hotel de Ville. German patrols are everywhere. People walk fast on the sidewalk avoiding the stares of other pedestrians. Once at Saint Paul, I follow David in the café *La Pointe-Rivoli*. No one pays attention to us at the counter where we drink a soda. We then go to the toilets where we hide like thieves to share the leftover banknotes, most of which still smell bad. I see for an instant in my mind's eye the cesspool of the latrines and all we have achieved since then. The camp seems so far away now.

- See you Monday, Simon.

One instant we shake hands like two men, and the next I see David go down rue Saint-Antoine. I follow him with my eyes until he turns the corner on rue de Turenne.

CHAPTER 8

August 1942

How am I going to eat?

It was simple enough to say our parents kept our ration cards during our escape through the Beauce region. We paid black market prices and that was that. But here in Paris, things are not so simple.

Won't it be dangerous to return to the apartment on rue des Écouffes? What will I say to Madame Chevrolier the concierge, when she asks me for an explanation? I raise my shirt collar as I approach and walk through the building entrance. No one is around, and I cross the courtyard unnoticed. Maman used to hide a spare key near the garbage cans under the stairway. The key is there.

Listening for the slightest sound, I climb the stairs cautiously, on tiptoe. At our landing, I find the door to the apartment ajar. I wait a moment holding my breath. Nothing moves, no sound comes from inside. I finally push the door open and immediately the mix of smells that identifies our home greets me. However, everything is in shambles. The drawers in my parents' bedroom are open, the bed is turned over, and the clothes are thrown on the floor. My father's ties are on the floor. I know we didn't leave the place in such a mess when the police dragged us out! The apartment was burglarized! In my bedroom, all my books are on the ground, same thing in Élise's room. The sewing machine is missing in my father's workshop. Returning to my parent's room, I throw myself on the bed and burst into sobs. After I recover a little, I go to the kitchen and open the cupboard. I guess the burglars were not interested in food because all of maman's canisters are untouched, including the sugar box where she hid her savings. I quickly count the remaining few banknotes and stuff them into my pocket. After eating some canned food, I return to my parent's bed and I fall into an agitated and troubled sleep.

*

On the day maman left for Drancy dressed as a nurse, she told my sister and me how she would get there by Métro and commuter train from the Gare du Nord. Once in Drancy, I get strange looks when I ask my way. It isn't hard to find the notorious place; barbed wire fences enclose the compound. Numerous police vans are parked along the side. Clustered near the gate, gendarmes form a somber and hostile gathering.

I enter a café across the street with the uncertain hope of collecting information. This is no doubt the place where my mother met Gilberte. The café is crowded. I'm not, it seems, the only Jew searching for news. I sit at a table and order mineral water. Most people are keeping their eyes on the camp entrance, as if trying to decipher an enigma or guess how to obtain what meager information they can. Bits of conversations reach me:

- A sizeable transport three days ago...

- For sure, they intend to empty the camp...

A woman is staring at me from a distance. I avoid her gaze as I finish my glass, and wonder whether I should go and inquire directly of the gendarmes near the entrance. I've just about made up my mind to do so when the woman studying me comes towards me.

- You shouldn't stay here, she whispers. It's dangerous...

I look at her dumbfounded – but I understand very well.

- Do you at least have ID papers? She continues.

I shake my head negatively.

- They searched the café yesterday and checked everyone's identity. They took away a man because he wasn't wearing his star.

I know I'm not wearing a star either. I lower my eyes to my chest, and then look up again. I am not sure how to interpret the woman's gaze. She keeps staring at me, combining fear and sternness in a desire to protect me from danger.

- I'm looking for my mother, I finally confess.

- And you think she's there?

- Yes, my sister too. My father was also interned in this camp before they sent him to Germany or Poland, I don't know for sure…

- They don't let anyone in, you know. It is no good hanging around. What is your name?

- Simon.

- Where do you live?

- At Nation.

I am embarrassed to lie to this nice woman. It is clear she does not wish me any harm, but instinct tells me to be suspicious of everything and everyone. A part of me has learned harsh lessons from the Vél d'Hiv, Beaune-la-Rolande, and the burglarized apartment. Why isn't David here to help and protect me? Although the woman understands my suspicion, she persists:

- Try not to go outside until your hair has grown back, or else wear a cap. Everyone knows they shave men's hair in camp. And don't come back to Drancy, it's not safe…

- Go home; this is not a place for you, she continues, these are harsh times!

I nod and get up without a word. I feel close to panic. I control myself so as not to start running.

*

Once back on rue des Écouffes, I walk around in circles in the apartment trying to decide what to do. I stay away from windows to avoid being seen by neighbors. I wanted, after Drancy, to go food shopping but didn't dare enter a store. Without ration cards, my hair too short, and without a star, I see merchants as enemies. Were I to be stopped, denounced, or just caught in a raid on the street, I would lose my independence. So I stay in. I exhaust maman's last food reserves, and sleep in my parent's bed. When boredom becomes unbearable, I open a book and read until there is no more daylight.

I am angry with myself for being incapable of making any decision. What will I say to David when he asks what progress I made? Embarrassed, I finally change my mind and decide to go out and walk around the neighborhood. I have money, after all. I can at least buy what I need. If asked, I'll say I lost my tickets.

I close the door behind me and shove the key in my pocket. As I am about to go down the stairs, I hear steps below. I quietly reenter the apartment. After judging it's safe to go out, I try again. I make it to the courtyard. The concierge's room is empty. The building seems deserted. No one on rue des Ecouffes either. I walk towards Saint Paul, hoping to find a store to enter. I stop in front of the grocer on rue St Antoine and watch the sullen-faced merchant in grey overalls clip the coupons of one of his customers. I have known this man forever; yet now he seems a stranger, maybe my worst enemy...

- Simon...

Someone grazes my shoulder. It is Madame Modiano, a friend of my mother who used to visit with us. She recognizes me. As I turn toward her, she is taken aback. How I must have changed looking half-starved and disheveled. She is searching words. Everything has become so complicated...

- How is your mother?

I can't hold back and burst into tears. People turn around on the street. Madame Modiano doesn't know what to do.

- Come, Simon.

She directs me towards the church, empty at this hour. She holds out a handkerchief she takes out of her handbag. I wipe my eyes. I want to return the handkerchief but it is now as dirty as my face.

- Keep it, she says.

Once a properly dressed and well-behaved young boy, I am now a lost soul, and the feeling of disgrace touches us both. When I stop and regain control of myself, she continues:

- We must not stay in the street.

She glances quickly around, and then offers to go to her house. I remember she lives, on rue Saint Paul.

*

- Hurry, come inside.

Closely watching the stairways, Cécile Modiano pushes me inside her apartment and hastily closes and locks the door. After she drops her shopping bag in the kitchen, we enter the living room. I don't dare sit down for fear of soiling the seat.

- Don't worry, she says, guessing my thoughts.

She knows papa was arrested last year, but she does not know what happened to my mother, my sister, and me. She had noticed she no longer met Madame Crespi in the street as she used to, but so many familiar faces had disappeared lately anyway. Shy and uncertain at first, then gathering my courage, I tell her everything. I tell her about the round up at dawn, the revolting conditions in the Vél d'Hiv, the journey in sealed cattle cars to Beaune-la-Rolande, the separation of mothers from their children, the bludgeon blows of the gendarmes, my escape with David Berlinsky, the good fortune to meet a compassionate gendarme in Montargis.

- How did you manage to survive? Asks Cécile Modiano.

She doesn't doubt my word; she is just amazed. How could two kids have escaped from a camp, fed themselves without any help, and reached Paris on their own? I don't dare mention the cesspool episode, so I answer, diverting my eyes:

- We managed.

We both remain silent for a while. I look around at the warm and comfortable living room, before Cécile Modiano continues:

- You know, my husband too was taken in a round up. She throws up her arms in a sign of helplessness. Tears run down her cheeks. She gets up to find a handkerchief.

- I have family in the country, but I prefer to stay in Paris. I take care of my mother who lives on Boulevard Bourdon. What's more, I want to be here when Monsieur Modiano returns.

She adds with a breaking voice:

- I can't understand what is happening, but it can't last forever. It will have to stop one day.

She looks at me, then goes on:

- As for you Simon, you can't stay in Paris, or else you're likely to be caught like the others….

- I don't have anywhere to go…

- You have family on the Riviera. You must try to get in touch with them…

- But how?

- We'll think about it, and then you'll go and join them. Cécile Modiano adds:

- In the meantime, you'll stay here with me.

I am not entirely happy with the idea. I would feel awkward sharing the quarters of this woman, certainly caring but elderly and not a relative.

- I prefer to stay at my house, I say.

If she's disappointed by my answer, she doesn't show it. She surely understands I went through difficult times – as she herself and most people in the neighborhood have. She tells me neighbors in her building are watching out for her. There is not a day one of them doesn't come knocking at her door with some dish she cooked and to make sure she is OK. None however, is Jewish. The Jews have all disappeared.

- At least you are safe, I say.

- You can't be sure of any one, these days. Even of your neighbors, especially the concierge. So maybe you're right, after all. It's not such a good idea for you to stay here.

We agree I will stay in hiding in my apartment until my relatives are contacted.

- Our apartment was burglarized, I say.

- I am not surprised! Many have been. Wait a minute...

She disappears into the kitchen and comes back with some bread, some cheese and a bottle of milk.

I'm coming with you, she says.

*

Diary of Simon Crespi

August 27, 1942

Gosh, how my life has changed in a short time! Here I am alone, no family, and unable to find my mother. I was so proud to have escaped from that rotten camp. Thanks to David! But my rewards are terrible loneliness, and fear.

Madame Modiano is convinced that the only way for me to be safe is to get to the free zone. True, my uncle, my aunt, my cousins, and my grandmother are there. But I cringe at the idea of going even farther away from maman. Who knows? What if they were to set her free from Drancy? What if papa where to come back home? Then you need an ausweis form issued by the krauts upon presentation of an ID card, to cross the line of demarcation. I don't even have an ID card... I heard say there are smugglers who guide those who want to cross secretly into the free zone.

Madame Modiano said she would make inquiries for me…I am lucky, despite my difficulties, to have met this woman who is willing to help me.

The days are long and depressing, alone in the apartment. I sleep a lot. When I wake up, I walk around in my socks; I eat something before returning to lie on my parent's bed with a book. I read "The Viscount of Bragelonne", I reread "The Three Musketeers", and I read for the third time "Twenty Years After". I will soon know them all by heart. The burglars who visited our apartment didn't care for literature. They were not very shrewd either, since I found our radio set at the back of the wardrobe, behind old clothes! I remembered maman had hidden it there. She refused to bring it to the police station when the authorities decided to seize radios owned by Jews. I place the radio on the bed, next to maman's tortoise shell comb, I adjust the sound to a minimum and I listen with my eyes closed to songs, commercials, and news coming from a world so far away it hardly seems real.

*

When I hear a scratch on the door early in the morning, I know it's Cécile Modiano bringing me food, books and clean clothes. I chat with her about David. I worry about him and feel guilty not to have gone to our planned rendezvous. After all, it's thanks to him that I'm free.

- How was your husband arrested, Madame Modiano?

It was two months ago. A Saturday…

The Modianos were finishing lunch. Someone knocked on the door. It was the police, two men in uniform. The concierge gave them the names of all Jews living in the building. They asked the Modianos to show their IDs. They noticed that Cecile's last name was Godard and her husband Maurice shrugged his shoulders without answering when they asked him why his papers were not stamped: "JUIF". The officers then asked them to pack a small suitcase.

- Mine is ready answered Maurice, but leave my wife alone. She is not Jewish.

- We're taking you both in...

- But Godard is not a Jewish name, Godard! Can't you read!

The remark earned the Modianos a trip without empathy to the police station on rue de Rivoli where they were made to wait for hours in a room where other Jews, some with children, kept arriving. Finally, a van stopped in front of the police station. A police officer came out and addressed Madame Modiano. He gave her back her ID card and told her:

- You can go but he stays. He is Jewish.

Maurice Modiano immediately opened the suitcase to give his wife her clothes back. Eyes blurred by tears, his arms shaking, he hugged his wife. She too was crying. Cécile Modiano went back home by way of the rue de Rivoli. She hasn't heard from her husband since that day.

*

Adjusting the radio's knobs, I hear a recurring refrain that reminds me of a music box maman had bought for me a long time ago at the market. I distinguish voices in the background. I realize the refrain is the German jamming of the broadcast to thwart us listening to the British radio. At night, when radio reception is best, I pick up bits of information. News about combat, defense, resistance.

It is the first time I hear about resistance... Is it about resisting the Germans? Sometimes the words I hear make no sense: "The ant found herself quite unprepared; three times", or: "In April don't remove even a single thread; one time"; or again: "Hindered by her skirt, she fell to the ground"...

After I am done listening to such poetic but undecipherable messages, I talk to myself-- following my wandering thoughts and telling the story of my life to an invisible buddy who keeps me company and sometimes has the face of David Berlinsky.

One day follows another, dull, and colorless. I can no longer tell what time it is, what day it is. I eat when I'm hungry; I re-read the same book a hundred times. I am bored. Often drowsy, I fall asleep in my clothes. I have become completely lethargic.

- Don't let yourself down that way! Admonishes Madame Modiano.

- I'm fed up.

This type of remark discourages her. Why should I upset such a kind woman? As soon as she leaves, I regret my behavior and I am angry with myself--all the more because she has struggled for weeks to find the trace of my family in the South, all while taking care of me and her mother.

Cécile Modiano doesn't inform me about the recurrent roundups in Paris and elsewhere in France. Jews everywhere are continually picked up and sent to Drancy. She doesn't repeat the conversations heard waiting in line on rue Saint Antoine., when people say those interned in Drancy are sent to an unknown destination.

Some people waiting in line are compassionate:

- Just think of these poor souls sent to work in Germany.

Others are glad:

- Good riddance!

She doesn't tell me that a big raid to round up Jews took place just last week in the nearby 11th arrondissement.

*

- Read this, she tells me with a satisfied smile, as she shows me a letter she just received.

Nice, September 20, 1942

Dear Cécile,

My God! What misery has befallen us! How grateful I am to you for taking such care of my nephew, in spite of your own affliction.

Right now, we are making the necessary arrangements so that you and Simon can join us as soon as possible. You'll be safer in the free zone than in Paris. We think we'll be able to give you concrete details in a few days.

Have you any way to find out about or receive information regarding Fanny and Élise? They must be in the camp of Drancy. We wrote but never received any answer. Tell us, if you know, to whom we should apply. Have you received any news from Monsieur Modiano?

God bless you Cécile.

Fortunée Carasso

- There's another letter, says Madame Modiano handing me an envelope.

My dear little Simon,

I'm so happy to hear about you. Your uncle Salvatore and I want you to come and join us here, very soon. You'll stay with us until the return of your parents and your sister. We're trying to get information about them, but it's very difficult now.

Madame Modiano will soon tell you what to do so you both can join us. Listen carefully to what she says.

Your uncle Salvatore, your cousin Sarah, your other cousin Sophie whom you have not yet met, your grandmother and I send you a big kiss.

Aunt Fortunée

I read the letter one more time. I am speechless, unable to react.

- You don't seem happy, says Madame Modiano surprised and a little annoyed.

Uncomfortable, I finally venture:

- I'd rather stay in Paris…

- Don't say that, Simon! I know you're depressed, but Paris is getting more dangerous for you every day...

I keep returning to the same deeply felt argument: When maman returns, she'll need me. Who will take care of her if I am basking on the Riviera? What I do not tell Cécile is that I also harbor somewhat less dignified feelings: I have adjusted to an empty life in which nothing ever happens. I got used to a life without responsibility, made up of endless waiting and allowing events take their course, whatever they are. Had I reconnected with David, everything would have been different. We would have made plans together, taken initiative, pursued our search. We would have fought... But I didn't go to our rendezvous. I lost all will to fight.

Exasperated, Cécile Modiano no longer hides her annoyance.

- Don't you want to see your aunt, your cousins?

Again, I remain silent. Of course, I like my aunt, but I can't stand my uncle. Salvatore is harsh and arrogant. He always behaves as if he is better than my father. Madame Modiano insists:

- It's your family.

- I want to be left alone! I suddenly say, leaving the room and taking refuge in my disorderly bedroom.

*

I remain apathetic for a few more days, until Cécile Modiano comes scratching our agreed-upon code at my door. Her face is drawn and tense. She reminds me that what she's doing is well intended, out of friendship for my parents and for me, and because she is outraged by what they are doing to the Jews... I suddenly feel terribly guilty to have behaved so unfairly.

- Another letter has arrived...

She takes an envelope out of her pocket. In a letter addressed to her, Fortunée explains how to get to the free zone. Madame Modiano will accompany me by train to a small village in the countryside near Dijon; there she will find a man called Monsieur Robert waiting for me. He is a friend of Salvatore's who will help me cross the line of demarcation. On the other side, a second man will take me to Nice. The departure date is set. All the details are in place.

- And what about you? I ask.

Cécile shakes her head. Her eyes become watery.

- I told Fortunée I didn't want to get to the southern zone...

- But why?

- It looks like the roles are reversed, she tells me hesitantly. Then she adds.

- I have my mother here; then, she adds forcing herself to smile in order to hide her tears: I am not Jewish.

*

- Walk faster!

Cécile Modiano drags me towards the Hotel de Ville, to a *Photomaton* photo booth in the Métro station. Cécile helps me set the stool height. She's used to it. She was here not so long ago, with her husband who needed photos for his ID papers. A flash burst fills the booth, then after what seems like a very long time, the ID photos drop in the slot.

- Wait a while, says Madame Modiano, let them dry. Then looking at the snapshots: You look more human, now.

I nod.

*

Early one morning, I hear Madame Modiano scratching and her key going through the lock. I jump out of bed.

- Did you sleep well?

I don't have the time to answer before she takes my ID papers out of her handbag and hands them to me:

- Look.

Still tousled and sleepy, I sit on a chair. It's with some apprehension and confusion that I take note of my new identity. From now on, my name is Simon Bouchard.

Cécile sits across from me.

You are going to have to forget your real name, she says in a low voice.

- Forever?

She can't help but smile at this childish reaction

- No, but for as long as necessary.

I remember a phrase my father once said. For Jews, changing address is changing destiny, and changing name is a new life.

- How did you do it? I ask.

- I managed...

I am mindful Cécile Modiano is one of these generous women, who feel compelled to help those in need. Unable to help her husband, she left no stone unturned to obtain the papers that might well be the key to my freedom.

*

This will be my last evening in the apartment. I slowly pack my things in a small suitcase: My books, toiletries; clothes that have been washed and pressed by Madame Modiano. The tortoise shell comb goes into my pants pocket. Later, lying on the bed, my suitcase still open, I won't easily fall asleep.

Cécile Modiano arrives to pick me up early the next morning. She is dressed up wearing suit, a hat and glossy shoes. She holds a small valise in her hand.

- Good morning, Madame Modiano.

- You look terrific.

I am wearing a suit my father no longer wore and which she tailored to fit me. Madame Modiano smells good when I kiss her cheek. Her face is smooth and powdery. We walk together along deserted streets to the Métro Saint Paul.

At the Gare de Lyon, the train is already on the platform, under the big glass roof. We settle into a compartment. Cécile Modiano keeps checking the tickets anxiously.

- You have your ID Simon?

- Of course, I say tapping the pocket of my suit jacket.

She is worried. Vichy militiamen or Germans soldiers often check papers on trains. If a man looks suspicious, they may even ask him to lower his pants to check if he is circumcised. If the traveler is a child or a teenager, it is even easier to intimidate him. If such misfortune were to happen to us, my brand new ID card would only contribute to our guilt... The compartment is soon filled.

*

The start of the trip is very unpleasant. After leaving on time and gaining some speed, the train stops in the middle of the countryside, evoking painful memories of the departure for the camp. When someone in the corridor asks a conductor why we are stopped, he answers:

- We are waiting for a green light.

It's hot in here. The sun bakes the roof of the car. The air around the tracks is still. Travelers wipe their worried faces in silence. What if the train doesn't start again? No one forgets this is wartime; the country is occupied, and the unforeseen is always to be expected, even in the most ordinary circumstances. At last, the axles grind again and the train proceeds. Relief is on everyone's face.

We are three hours late when we reach Dijon. Madame Modiano is pleasantly surprised that no one has checked our tickets or IDs during the first leg of our trip. She kept them in her hand all the time. We have to transfer to a local train. The flurry of activity around the station takes me by surprise. Engines noisily spew jets of steam and smoke on the platforms; loudspeakers emit garbled announcements we can't decipher.

- Dijon is an important railroad hub, says Cécile, to reassure me or perhaps to reassure herself. She has some trouble finding our train on the board.

- We should ask someone, I suggest.

I observe she is watching something. There is a checkpoint at the platform exit conducted by men in civilian clothes. Behind them, German soldiers look on. Travelers are lining up to pass through.

We take place in the line. I grit my teeth. I don't have the courage to look at Madame Modiano still holding our papers in hand. What if these people were suspicious of my brand new ID card? I have the odd feeling that when they read "Bouchard," the Germans will immediately think "Jewish". They will pull me out of line and take me to an office. They will discover my real identity and send me to a camp... A hand in my pants pocket, I squeeze my mother' tortoise shell comb.

- Papers?

One of the civilians looks at my card as if it concealed an enigma. He stares at me and looks at my photo. My heart beats hard under my jacket. While with one leg up I hold my opened suitcase on my thigh, the man carefully checks its contents He then turns towards Madame Modiano:

- Are you a relative?

- A friend of the family.

- Shouldn't it be in school?

- His grandmother just died...

- His grandmother was from Dijon?

- No, from Vergèze.

- And what is this?

He opens my notebook, the diary of Simon Crespi...

- I am writing a novel.

The inspector looks doubtful. He closes the notebook and puts it back in my suitcase. I close the suitcase, and the civilian gives me back my ID card. I seem to have crossed the hurdle and avoiding eye contact, I walk passed the expressionless Germans.

- Young man!

The voice in my back is that of one of the Germans. The man must suspect something. I feel the body of Madame Modiano suddenly stiffen next to me. We stop in our tracks and turn around. The German is staring at me while the following traveler has trouble opening his suitcase. I feel dizzy.

- What is your grandmother's name?

- Mamie Huguette, I say.

Heart beating, I hold the stare of the man until he looks away to continue his work. Madame Modiano had taken the precaution to tell me what to say, in case we were asked: We were going to the funeral of Mamie Huguette.

*

The transfer to Vergèze is delayed. The train will now leave late in the afternoon. We sit in the waiting room. Cécile Modiano gets the rest of the food she brought on the train out of her bag. After a while, I need to walk around and I wander through the station. Outside, German trucks are parked on the square.

- We're going to be late for the rendezvous with Monsieur Robert, I remark to Cécile Modiano when I come back to sit next to her.

- Yes, particularly since the rendezvous is not in Vergèze but in *Velais en Barois*.

- Is it far from *Vergèze*?

- Just a few kilometers.

I sigh with impatience and try to chase away depressing thoughts and images. Everything so far has worked well, after all. Cécile is the perfect guardian angel. At last, the train for *Vergèze* puffs in. The carriages are equipped with running boards the whole length of the car. Local people in our compartment have such a pronounced accent from Burgundy that Madame Modiano can hardly communicate with them.

We arrive in *Vergèze* before nightfall, but the railcar for *Velais en Barois* left long ago. We'll have to spend the night at the *hôtel du Commerce*. Cécile is relieved to note there are no visible Germans in town. The middle-aged woman standing behind the hotel counter squints under the curls of smoke rising from the cigarette hanging from her lower lip. She takes our IDs and makes detailed notes in her register.

- May I use your telephone? Asks Madame Modiano.

- To call where? Asks the woman rolling her r's.

- Velais. It's a local call. Our train was late and we missed our connection ...

The demarcation line is so close that I wonder whether the woman hasn't guessed the reason for our being in *Vergèze*.

The room has two single beds. Cécile takes the one nearest the door. My sleep is strange and full of labyrinthine dreams. Around midnight, however, Cécile shakes me:

- Get up... We must get out. They're going to search the hotel.

On her way to the toilets on the landing, my guardian angel heard, passing near the stairway, the hotel owner talking to a man in the office downstairs where the lights were still on. The conversation alarmed her. She clearly heard the man inquire if there were Jews registered in the hotel tonight, and then ask to look at the register...

We left furtively through the back door, dragging our suitcases. We advanced cautiously, under the stars, in silence, our steps echoing on the paved streets. Certainly, Madame Modiano had given in to panic, but who could say she didn't make the right decision? We reached the darkened and deserted train station, and spent the rest of the night on the wooden benches of the waiting room.

*

Once in *Velais en Barois*, we enter a café and order coffee and some bread. I can see that Cécile Modiano is exhausted by a sleepless night. Although I know how much affection she has for my parents, I wonder whether she regrets having taken the risk of accompanying me all the way here. After my benefactor has eaten, she recovers somewhat and whispers:

- Mr. Robert promised he would be at the station at noon.

If it were not for the stationmaster wandering along the platform wearing his regulation cap, I would wonder whether this charming little pavilion along the tracks is a train station at all. We sit on a bench. The air is mild; birds flutter through the foliage. Time passes slowly. Once or twice, a red and white local train stops in the station. A few travelers come down and move away, some towards the village, others towards the countryside.

- I hope he comes, I say after a while.

- He'll be here.

Around noon, a graying middle-aged man with the refined manners of a man from the city walks towards us.

- Madame Modiano?

His suit, tie, and hat seem out of place in this pastoral environment. This traveler without luggage is Mr. Robert – although his real name is Daniel Finkelstein.

- I no longer expected you. I couldn't have waited much longer...

- This is Simon, Madame Modiano hastens to say.

We shake hands but it is clear Mr. Robert wants to get right to the purpose of our meeting:

- We're going to be taken to *Saint Marc du Fenouillet*. It's a village right on the line. We'll be part of a group going across tonight ...

On the other side a Mr. Rémi, another relation of my uncle Salvatore, is expected to meet us. Mr. Rémi will bring me to Nice by train.

- As for me, I'm meeting my wife in Limoges. We're looking for a way to leave France... I'll let you say good-bye while I get my luggage at the place where I spent the night. And he walks away briskly.

It's time for farewells.

- Give a kiss to your aunt Fortunée for me, says Madame Modiano

- Thank you for all you've done for me. I wouldn't be here without you... We'll see each other when all this is over.

- Of course...

- Here is Mr. Fink... I mean Mr. Robert with his luggage. He is waiting for you, adds Mrs. Modiano.

The handsomely dressed man waves at us.

As a local-train rolls along the platform and stops, the stationmaster announces the train returning to *Vergèze*.

- I'm not good at good-byes, says Cécile Modiano, climbing on the car's footboard. So, quick, give me a kiss!

- Take good care of yourself, Simon...

We exchange a nervous kiss while Madame Modiano holds on to the door handle. Tears run down her cheeks and down mine too. I watch through the window as she takes a seat and signals me to move on, as if chasing me away. As the train rolls slowly away, I see her curling up to cry.

CHAPTER 9

September 1942

The hooves of a horse clatter on the cobblestones as a cart approaches the station. A gigantic workhorse, blinded by long white hair falling over his eyes, draws the cart. The man seated high on the driver's bench wears black velvet pants and a blouse that drops to mid thighs. He clicks his tongue and the carriage stops in front of us.

- Let's go! Says the man leaning towards Mr. Robert who, without removing the pipe from his mouth, throws his suitcase in the back of the carriage and invites me to do the same. We climb up and sit on the wooden bench next to the farmer. With a heave, the carriage lurches forward. Elbows on his knees, Mr. Robert throws worried glances right and left while still smoking his pipe.

- Do you know my Uncle Carasso well? I ask Mr. Robert.

- I was his manager on rue La Fayette.

Our path cuts through the countryside. The air smells of cut grass and horse manure. Still high in the sky, the sun beats hard on our shoulders. Few words are exchanged for the duration of the journey that takes over two hours and leads us to a small village.

- Here we are, says the driver.

The village consists of a few low buildings along the unpaved trail. There is a fountain next to a small pond where a couple of ducks swim. The air is filled with smells of cut grass and curdled milk. A man wearing overalls and a beret comes out of one of the house and greets us:

- You'll have to wait here.

We jump off the cart and collect our luggage. Mr. Robert takes out his wallet and hands a banknote to our driver who leaves right away, while the man with the beret leaves, heading across fields. The place is quiet. My imagination races: What if someone in *Velais* has denounced us, and the Germans suddenly appeared. … Mr. Robert next to me doesn't seem any more at ease than I am. I drag my suitcase to the fountain where, all at once, I wash away sweat and dark thoughts. I am eager for night to fall when we will be on our way to cross that line, which in my imagination appears as it does in children games: a chalk line on the ground. Beyond the chalk line is freedom. But what is freedom after all, and what has happened to my parents?

We have been sitting by the fountain for a while when another horse-drawn carriage appears. It is much larger than the one that brought us here. It stops a few steps away. It is overloaded with a collection of people that seem out of place in such a bucolic setting. One by one come down: a man in a black suit; a young woman in high heels wearing a hat and veil, she carries a fur coat over her arm; a small and pudgy man in a suit too tight for him, followed by his plump and clumsy wife who insists on leaning on her husband's shoulder to get down from the cart. There is also a young couple with a little girl asleep in their arms. Finally, two men wearing city clothes climb down from the carriage. The driver takes money from everyone before smacking his tongue and leaving in his wobbly carriage.

The plump lady comes directly to the fountain to wash her face. Then she sits on a stone and calls out to her husband:

- *Ven aquí! No me decha sola!* Come here; don't leave me by myself...

In the space of a second, my heart starts beating hard. The sound of the familiar language takes me back to the warmth of my family. How long since I heard Ladino spoken?

I exchange glances with the husband when he comes near his wife, but neither he nor anyone else is in the mood for introductions or conversation. Each of us has a unique preoccupation: cross the demarcation line between occupied and free zone, escape fear, and find security.

The sun is setting when the man with the beret returns accompanied by a heavyset man whose prominent belly is held under a flannel belt. The man instructs us to gather around him. It is soon apparent he is not one given to civilities and he speaks roughly to us.

- We leave as soon as night falls, he begins. You have to follow my orders without argument, OK! The least mistake could put us all in danger...

He then adds sullenly:

- The Krauts patrol every night. We need to go around them. It's very simple: I know how, and you don't. There is still time for you to change your mind.

He looks at the man with the beret and then at us before adding:

- It's five thousand francs per person. Paid in advance.

Hands plunge into pockets without hesitation and start opening wallets. I turn towards Mr. Robert who is already counting bills.

- Young children are also five thousand? Asks the father of the little girl.

- Five thousand per head, answers the runner with a no nonsense look before specifying:

- The little one, she will have to keep quiet. No shouting, no crying.

- I'll give her some cough syrup, says the mother. It will make her sleep.

- You can double the dose, says the man.

The runner counts and recounts the banknotes before shoving them in his pocket. As the discussions continue, the sun is setting.

- Ok. Now for some serious matters, resumes the man. We're going to have to cross muddy fields and even a stream. So, no fancy shoes… Do you have flat shoes you can wear, Madame?

- These are the only ones I have.

- Give them to me.

The woman takes off her high heel shoes and hands them to the runner who starts to leave, then stops after a few steps and turns around.

- I'll be back. My wife will serve you some soup before we leave.

We the refugees sit down around a large table inside the house while a woman serves a hearty soup. The runner returns and hands the shoes back to its owner. The heels have been sawed off.

- And now a most important point: Don't forget to go to the bathroom before we leave. Afterward, it will be too late.

*

Under the cover of complete darkness, our pathetic group heads out over the uneven ground. The suitcases are heavy. The young father walks ahead of me, carrying his sleeping little girl on his shoulders. Wrapped in her fur coat, his wife is at his side. I can't see our guide who is at the head of our single file line. A series of shushes followed by angry muffled protests are heard each time someone lets out a groan. Awakened by a nightmare, the little girl cries out.

- Keep her quiet, damn it! Whispers an irate marcher.

Then nothing more is heard than the sound of our steps on the difficult ground. Little by little, our eyes adjust to the darkness and we are able to distinguish more easily the trees that border the field where we are walking.

My mind wanders. I think of my father, of Turkey, a country I don't even know. I reflect about the destiny that for centuries has forced Jews to run away and to surrender their lives to smugglers. From time to time our little group stops, the guide checks to make sure he has not lost anyone, and then moves on. A dog barks in the distance.

Is it a guard dog on a farm or the police dog of a German patrol? We soundlessly endure branches whipping our faces. The scent of the countryside changes as we progress: dead leaves, then mushrooms; tree sap, then cut grass.

Crossing the stream is the most difficult and its swirling waters are terrifying. The guide retrieves a makeshift bridge made up of planks that has been hidden under a tree. He sets it on flat stones on each side of the flowing water. There are just a few steps to cross, but the boards bend and slide under the weight of the stumbling marchers. The pudgy lady protests in Ladino--her foot deep in water, she demands her husband's arm. The young mother refuses to venture onto the hazardous boards. She says she prefers to fall into the hands of the Germans. Her husband tries to reassure her without waking up their daughter.

- I'll help you says the guide, holding the woman's arm.

Behind me is Mr. Robert, his pipe still between his teeth, although extinguished by order of our guide. After crossing the river we take a muddy footpath through a swamp emanating unpleasant smells. The footpath winds between two rows of reeds, which will eventually, we are told, lead us to the free zone.

- Can't we stop for a minute? Whispers someone.

- It's out of the question.

This is the most dangerous spot, the runner warns in a whisper. Patrols pass close by. But the marchers are all panting. A woman falls, still holding on to her heavy suitcase. The runner looks down the whole line.

- Two minutes then, he sighs, and not a sound.

*

Beyond the swamp, the footpath leads to yet another open field. We are about to enter, when the guide abruptly stops us. We bump into each other along the line. The guide walks ahead alone.

- What did he say?

- He said to wait.

He comes back flapping his arms up and down in the dark, indicating we must lie down on the ground. We squat and make ourselves as small as possible. Everyone does the best he can. Our guide also lies on the ground, but a little away from our terrified group. I glance at the little girl who has just reopened her eyes and is on the verge of tears. Her father puts one hand over her mouth. Three suitcases remain standing tall above the grass.

Approaching footsteps and voices break the silence. A beam of light appears; we hear the dogs panting on their leash. Holding our breaths, we listen to the patrol go by. I peek and count five helmeted German soldiers and the tip of their guns above the high grass. What if the dogs pick up our scent? I know the answer to my question and I am capable of fully assessing the consequences. The runner would disappear, and like helpless frightened animals (and burdened by our luggage and city clothes), we would be arrested. Should someone try to flee, there would be shots, and there would be dead corpses abandoned on the ground. There would be tears and despair. Trucks would arrive at dawn to take away those who survived. We would end up in a camp where the terrified little girl would be torn away from her mother.

I make up my mind: I refuse to return to a camp. Should things take a bad turn, I'm thinking of taking off and running straight ahead without looking back. I'll take the risk of being shot in the back before crossing the line. The patrol disappears in the distance. My hands are shaking as I look in the direction of the runner who now stands up. We resume our march.

Now stimulated by fear, no one feels tired and no one complains. We leave the field behind. The footpath now cuts through a hedge and once behind a row of bushes, the runner stops. We gather around him.

- You are in the free zone, he says with a normal voice. I don't go any further but you keep walking on this path. We look at each other, petrified by the same thought: have we fallen into a trap?

The guide points with his arm extended.

- Straight this way…

- Where does it lead to?

- To Moncereau. You will see houses after a 15-minute walk….

- Is there a train station in Moncereau?

- The station is in Mézaille. People in Moncereau will take you there....

He walks backwards as he talks. In the following instant, his body dissolves in darkness.

*

Don't they have a curfew here? Someone asks. A house ahead of us is lit as though it were peacetime. We walk with our suitcases in careful and suspicious steps towards that house. The father of the little girl hands the child over to her mother. Unable to contain his anxiety any longer, he starts speaking in a low voice, retelling stories of smugglers who delivered the Jews to the Germans pocketing money from both sides. We are now just a few steps from the house. A sign hanging above the door reads *Café Restaurant*. The door opens and a man in a white undershirt and wearing a beret appears.

- Come on in.

We enter the café furnished with tables and chairs and a counter along one of the walls. The man shows us where to stow our luggage. His wife appears, wearing a grey apron and slippers. She looks at us without a word. We all sit down, noisily dragging chairs on the flagstone floor. Mr. Robert takes the pipe out of his mouth and asks:

- This is the free zone, isn't it?

I can read on his face how painful the crossing has been for him. His features are lined with fatigue and fear.

- You don't have to worry anymore, says the restaurant owner, before adding:

- We can give you something to eat and drink, and then you can rest.

- You often have people…like us? Asks the young father.

- It happens now and then.

A woman places glasses and water pitchers on the tables.

- We only have bread, pâté, and hard-boiled eggs.

- We're at war, sighs the husband of the plump lady.

*

Later in the night, a small horse-drawn carriage arrives and the driver offers to take those willing to leave right away to Mézaille. A few in our group stand and pick up their luggage. Throughout the night, farmers appear and offer their services. Each time, a few of us Jews say good-bye, then leave.

- What about us? I ask Mr. Robert.

He looks at his watch and answers:

- We are waiting for Mr. Rémi.

Although we have successfully crossed the line, I feel strangely depressed. I am overwhelmed by loneliness and the weight of being far from anyone close to me. I think of Madame Modiano who by now, must have returned to Paris. She will be suffering the same feelings of injustice that those who have loved ones in camps feel. And what about David, whatever happened to him? Where would I be today, if he hadn't taken me under his wing in the courtyard of the school? It seems so long ago…What is the meaning of this war, and why is there a zone called free?

Mr. Robert touches my elbow. A man just entered the restaurant; his clothes are halfway between city elegance and leisurewear. Mr. Robert stands up, takes the pipe out of his mouth and speaks to the newcomer. It is Mr. Rémi, the envoy of Salvatore Carasso, who has come for me. He looks at me:

- You must be Simon.

He addresses Mr. Robert:

- I have a taxi waiting. We must hurry… Are you taking a train in Mézaille, Mr. Finkelstein?

- Yes.

- Then, come with us.

We pick up our things and wave goodbye to the restaurant owner. The car is a strange vehicle equipped with a series of long containers on the roof.

- I would have come earlier, Mr. Rémi explains while closing the door. I had found an ambulance ready to bring me here, but there was an accident and it could not get to me.

- Strange car, I say.

- This on top is a gas producer. The car runs on charcoal instead of gasoline.

The driver opens a little door on a tank on the side of the car and stirs the burning charcoal.

- We are ready now; the driver sits down and starts the car.

*

In Mézaille, we left Mr. Robert, his pipe, his lost look, and his plans to depart France for another country. Our train brought us to Lyon where we transferred to another line to continue our journey south. I slept most of the time, succumbing to the physical and emotional exhaustion of recent events. I felt the relief of finally experiencing a measure of security. When I reopened my eyes, the whole world around me had changed. The light of the countryside was different. There were pine trees and Provençal style houses I had only seen in magazines.

- We'll be in Nice in half an hour, says Mr. Rémi. I notice a bit of a southern accent in his voice. I look out the window; soon it will be night. Once more, I am arriving in a new place, seeing new faces, talking, explaining, crying and being filled with sadness… I was so comfortable in our Paris apartment.

*

My uncle and aunt are on the station platform. Aunt Fortunée with open arms, hugs and kisses me. Tears run down her cheeks. Emotion renders her speechless. Uncle Salvatore, whom I don't much care for comes to her rescue.

Fortunée recovers and dabs her eyes with an embroidered handkerchief. My uncle Salvatore, whose manners have not changed, leaves me in her care while he has a hushed conversation with Mr. Rémi. Money passes from one hand to the other. Now, Fortunée won't let go of my arm and torments me with questions. She wants me to tell her everything. I answer, reluctant and unwilling to give her the information she seeks. She doesn't realize I need to recover and adjust before I can be coherent.

When we reach the front of the station, Mr. Rémi shakes my hand.

- Quite a little guy, your nephew, he remarks to Salvatore before he goes away.

- Aren't you anxious to meet your cousins? Asks Fortunée.

- Let's go, says Salvatore, walking towards his car parked nearby.

*

The Carassos live in an imposing building on *boulevard Raimbaldi*. Their apartment is spacious, with high-curtained windows. On my arrival I meet Esther Mechulam, my grandmother, who is impatient to see me, but incapable of speaking, now that I am in front of her. She can only cry. She gives us cookies she baked for the occasion. My cousin Sarah hardly lifts her eyes from her book to mutter hello. To her I am just a ghost landed out of nowhere. They bring in Sophie, the baby, just a few months old. Marguerite, the maid, comes in and offers to take my jacket. I refuse because I know I smell of sweat.

In the end, this reunion is quite depressing. Too many people are missing. What has become of my father, my mother, my sister? Why aren't they here with us? The fact that no one dares speak their names upsets me even more.

*

Diary of Simon Crespi

Nice, September 27, 1942

I have been in Nice for the last three weeks. I am staying with my uncle, my aunt and my two cousins. There is also my grandmother Esther, great as always at making Turkish pastries. My little dark room was a junk room until my arrival. This is where the Carassos still keep the crates of watches they brought from Paris. But how can I complain? My life here is so much easier than it was in Paris, and I was terrified crossing the demarcation line! Then there is the sea and a pebbly beach. We live on Boulevard Raimbaldi, a nice street close to the big hotels on the Promenade des Anglais; an avenue with large sidewalks and palm trees. The sea is so blue, so intense, and so mysterious that I could watch it for hours on end.

However, my instinct tells me I won't stay in Nice very long. That's why I keep my life in my suitcase: my clothes, my underwear, my diary, my pen, my books and my mother' tortoise shell comb.

My cousin Sarah is a little older than I am but younger than Élise. I can tell she doesn't like me. She prefers her books. As for Sophie, she is a baby. In other words, I am alone for the most part. Being alone seems to be my destiny...

However, I get along well with Marguerite, the maid. Yesterday she was making gnocchi's on the kitchen table. I helped her cut dough cubes on the table coated with flour. Then she rolled each one over a fork to ripple it. I was sitting at the table and we had a good conversation. She has a funny accent but I can understand her. When she speaks in the patois of Nice, I find it as appealing as her cooking. She sometimes has long discussions around the oven with my grandmother. We ate the gnocchi for dinner. They were really good.

My uncle Salvatore has always been a tough and very proud man. He doesn't think much of my father, and I think he doesn't care to have me here either. Aunt Fortunée must have insisted, and in the end, I must say, he has done a lot. Without him, I might be in a camp right now, and in camp, you don't have the chance to think about the blue of the sea. I like my aunt. I was shocked when I first saw her on the station platform. The two sisters look so much alike, I thought for a second that maman was in front of me. I had to suppress my tears, while my aunt held back hers.

The most embarrassing situation for me is when I am around my grandmother. She lives nearby, but in fact, she is always at our house. She only goes home to sleep. She won't stop repeating the same thing. She tells me that I am the image of my mother, and then she bursts into tears. I am forced to hold back my own sadness. There is not a day when, at one time or another, my grandmother and my aunt don't leave the room hurriedly. They think they are hiding their sadness and tears from me. In the end, when I need to cry, I go to my room. Sarah rolls her eyes whenever someone gives in to emotion and Salvatore never cries.

*

The Italians occupied the Riviera coast of France after they declared war in June 1940, and their soldiers are everywhere in town. Soldiers wearing grey-green uniforms and a feathered cap control traffic at crossroads. Many Jews have taken refuge in the region. Jews fear the Germans and mistrust the French, but they are not afraid of the Italians. The French might well be collaborators, members of the Vichy militia or Pétain sympathizers. Then there are the French police, who persist in pursuing Jews. They operate with the help of denunciations, which are easy money in Nice as elsewhere. All it takes is a discontented neighbor, a jealous concierge, someone holding an old grudge, and an anonymous letter goes out. The letter is followed by the visit from the police. People are taken away without explanation and often, never seen again.

Checking of papers is frequent in the street, and my new ID card in the name of Simon Bouchard is very useful. The Carassos don't have the fateful JUIF stamp on their IDs either. They had the good sense not to declare themselves as Jewish. They are French and speak French without accent. Furthermore, Carasso can easily pass for an Italian name.

After my uncle learns that a catholic priest in nearby Monaco offers to baptize Jews, he decides the whole family should pay him a visit.

- You never know, he says. A baptism certificate can be useful in today's atmosphere.

Always practical, Salvatore adds:

- Saving one's life is well worth a mass.

On the designated day, we get out of the car in front of a chapel adjoining the bishop's residence. We are all here, including Esther Mechulam, and even Marguerite who, although baptized when she was an infant, will hold little Sophie in her arms.

For me, it is the first time I enter a catholic house of worship. Candles burn on each side of a large golden cross. The priest makes us kneel, chants prayers in Latin, sprays us with holy water, and draws a cross on our foreheads with his thumb, then we leave, baptism certificates in hand.

*

Every night before going to bed, Fortunée goes out to check on Grandma Esther. One day she comes back panic-stricken. Grandma is not home!

- We must go to the police! She says fearfully.

Uncle Salvatore hesitates. What will they think at the police station if he goes looking for a Jewish woman? They may decide to take the whole family! Salvatore eventually gives in to Fortunée and goes to see the police commissioner. After checking, the commissioner informs him that, Esther Mechulam was picked up in a round up.

- A round up, asks Salvatore, but where?

- On rue Lamartine.

- And where is she now?

- On a train, the official answers, unruffled.

Her baptism certificate won't have helped her much, thinks Salvatore, getting back in his car.

Fortunée is despondent upon hearing the news, and I feel all my anxieties reawakened.

- What are we going to do? Asks my aunt.

That's the problem, there's nothing to be done, and I ought to know, I reflect, shrugging my shoulders.

Fortunée does not speak anymore; she doesn't do any of the things that usually fill her days. She cries all the time.

Two weeks later a postcard arrives from Drancy. My aunt who has been walking around every day with red and swollen eyes, reads it with disbelief: As soon as she arrived, Esther attempted without success to get some information regarding my family. She says that for a long time already, entire trains have been leaving Drancy for Germany. As far as she is concerned, she writes, she does not have much to complain about. True, the living conditions are horrible, but the authorities decided she would be sent back to Turkey, given that the country is not at war with Germany. She hopes to rejoin her husband in Istanbul. The news is met with relief.

*

The Turkish government in Ankara has all along fought to repatriate Jews in France of Turkish citizenship. They have been forceful enough to resist the stubborn refutation of the Germans and most of all of the French Vichy government who insists Jews are Jews, no matter what their citizenship. The consuls of Turkey throughout France were only able to enforce their regulations when Ankara threatened to retaliate in similar fashion against French citizens living in Turkey.

*

More and more Jews arrive in Nice, and the situation becomes more dangerous every day. They are seen in restaurants, in hotels, on the famous *Promenade des Anglais* and on the *Croisette* in nearby Cannes. The result is a more forceful persecution by the French police who intensify controls and round ups. Small hotels are particularly singled out.

I sometimes visit a friend my age named Henri Moscovitch and we play chess together. Henri lives with his parents in a hotel room on rue de Paris. My aunt and his mother are friends, and while they're out shopping one day, I stay in their room with Henri and his father. We start a game while my friend's father reads a book on the bed.

We suddenly hear the sound of an engine stopping, followed by the commotion of steps down in the street. We look over the balcony's guardrail. A police van has stopped in front of the hotel and a group of police officers, some in uniform, others in civilian clothes, is entering the hotel.

- Come back in, Henri's father tells us.

He goes out on the landing to observe what is happening then returns to the room and calmly locks the door. My friend's father then opens the large wardrobe and the three of us squeeze in between coats and jackets. He then skillfully closes the wardrobe from inside. Standing in the dark, we hear quarrels, orders given, and dreadful yells. We hear steps in the corridor outside, and distressed cries. Soon someone is banging on the door to our room.

- Police, open up!

- Don't make a move, whispers the father.

We remain motionless. I clasp my hands over my knees to prevent them from shaking.

- Open up!

- Shhh, says the father.

The commotion spreads throughout the hotel. There is no longer any way to determine whether they are beating on our door or on the room next door. From the smell, I guess Henri is peeing in his pants. A woman cries out in the corridor. Is it the voice of my aunt, Henri's mother, or another hotel guest who soon will be climbing on a train for Drancy before embarking on another for Germany? We hold our breaths for a long time.

The clamor finally subsides and a measure of calm returns.

- Don't move, insists Henri's father.

The smell of urine in the wardrobe is becoming pungent. I am angry with Henri for his weakness. And yet, didn't I pee in a closet when pursued by French gendarmes near the Champs Elysees, didn't David get angry at my own softness while we walked the country roads of the Beauce after our escape? How many times did I risk messing up everything by my lack of nerve?

A door slams in the corridor. Steps tumble down the stairs, and then silence returns. We stay in the wardrobe a long time. Does the silence mean the police left, or is it a trap to make us come out? At last, Henri's father carefully reopens the wardrobe's door, which squeaks behind him as he walks into the room. I come out next. The father walks cautiously to the balcony, looks down, and returns after closing the window. The van has gone away. The three of us lay down side by side on the bed, silent and without making a move. After a while, the father addresses his son:

- I think you can go and change clothes now.

A while later, my aunt and Henri's mother return. They were coming back to the hotel when they saw the police van in front of the hotel. They had to wait, incapable of doing anything. They saw a dozen people taken into the van, men, and women, Jews, evidently.

- We must immediately change hotel says Henri's mother hugging her son in her arms, still loaded with parcels.

- Certainly not! Says Mr. Moscovitch. Lightning never strikes twice in the same spot.

CHAPTER 10

October 1942

Villefranche-de-Rouergue is a thirteenth century *bastide,* an ancient fortified town whose architecture is a mix of styles of successive periods. It is a dense urban center, distinguished by red tile roofs and situated at the crossroads of ancient routes connecting Albi, Montauban and Toulouse in the Southwest of France. From the old fortified church, known as *La collégiale,* narrow streets run down to the Aveyron River. The *Place Notre-Dame,* the square in front of the imposing church, is paved with pebbles from the *Aveyron* riverbed. Shady arcades supporting three-story houses of medieval character surround the square.

After storing most of their household goods in a warehouse of Nice, Salvatore and Fortunée choose to hide with their family in this small town. They decide to rent an apartment rather than live in hotels that are the object of too much close attention from the authorities. A couple of weeks after our arrival, the five of us crowd into a small apartment on rue *Saint-Jacques,* a narrow side street in front of *La collégiale.*

Because a sick old man occupied the tiny apartment before us, Fortunée has the walls cleaned with lime. Nothing, however, prevents the pungent smell of mildew and mold that emanates from the old spiral staircase and reaches the landing in front of our door.

A flight of stairs leads to the apartment above us occupied by a widow. Higher still is the attic, part of which will be outfitted to become Marguerite's room. She too is depressed and homesick for her native Mediterranean. Marguerite's bedroom is adjacent to a garret space in which we will soon raise chickens.

The contrast with our life style in Nice makes my aunt feel miserable. Standing at the center of the kitchen, she looks distressed as she takes in the large stone sink, the wood burning stove, and a wobbly table pushed against a wall at the back of the room. In the tiny dining room, which also serves as a living room, a slow burning wood stove called a Salamander stands in the fireplace. Light is poor and even more dim in the two adjoining bedrooms.

Sarah goes to the lycée Saint Joseph and I attend the boy's college run by priests. I am registered as Simon Bouchard, my borrowed name, and pass as a Catholic; although as soon as I return home, with Ladino spoken around the house I become Simon Crespi again. I would be so happy to belong to a family that behaves like any other French family! When I walk in town with my uncle and my aunt, and we meet parents of my schoolmates, my biggest fear is that an innocent word in conversation will expose my religion and real name.

We try to make believe that the members of the Carasso-Bouchard family are good Catholics. We attend Mass every Sunday. In church, we dip our fingers in holy water; we make the sign of the cross; we kneel in front of the altar like all Catholics. We move our lips during the service, but we stop at the hurdle that communion represents.

I wonder what the local paper *Le Villefranchois* thinks of the refugees in their town, and whether they understand why they are here. I sometimes think of the Spanish Jews my father used to tell me about. Called Marranos, they remained secretly Jewish and practiced their religion clandestinely, although they were forced to convert to Catholicism.

I cannot escape attending classes in catechism at school and I am required to attend the weekly confessional sessions. I wait my turn seated with other kids on a bench. One at a time, we pass in front of the priest whose shoes extend below the wood partition of the cubicle. When my turn comes, I enter and immediately look down to see if I recognize the shoes of my confessor, or else I peek through the lattice to make out the face of the priest. One of them I recognize immediately by his wine breath. I recite the litany of the sins I have prepared. We each get our dose of repentance: so many Our Father's... so many Hail Mary's... that we recite kneeling in front of the altar. Each priest behaves differently. Some are very inquisitive and ask sharp questions. They suggest in detail situations leading to sin. You must watch out to cleverly escape their ambush. I get out of it by lying, never quite sure whether my deceptions have convinced the adversary.

One day I leave the booth feeling terribly guilty for having forgotten to confess a sin. Then I suddenly remember:

- It doesn't matter since I am Jewish!

For a brief moment I had forgotten my real identity. I try to keep my deception to a reasonable level, and resent that my uncle constantly urges me to become a choirboy and to assist the priest during Mass. The limits of what we can do are plain to me: Esther Mechulam was saved because she had the good fortune of being a Turkish citizen, not because she held a baptism certificate. Similarly, I was saved in Montargis because I had the good luck of meeting a more humane gendarme than others.

We live among a small community of Jewish refugees in Villefranche. Those residing at the Hotel Moderne spend as little time in their rooms as possible. Their goal is to remain unnoticed and avoid potential raids by the police, the gendarmes, the Militia, or even the Germans passing through town. It doesn't take long, however, to exhaust the conceivable activities in such a small town. The Jewish refugees are weary of lingering, day after day, in one café or another.

To help a little, my aunt Fortunée organizes afternoon teas in her house. On these days, our table is laden with cheeses and cold cuts brought back by my uncle who scours the countryside on his bicycle. Our living room resonates with discussions, opinions, and deliberations in Yiddish, French, or Ladino. There is Monsieur David, a diamond merchant from the rue de la Paix who left Paris with Esthelle, his companion. The Segal's used to run a fashion designer boutique in Bordeaux. Mr. Blum manufactured dresses in the *Sentier* garment district in Paris. Both Régine Steiner and her husband Léon were lawyers. Edgar Benbassat was a professor at the Sorbonne. He is here too with his wife. They lost the right to teach their profession when the laws on discrimination were promulgated. There is also Max Bernstein with his wife, his son Jacques, and Max's mother who speaks hesitant French with such a strong Polish accent that they tell everyone she is from Corsica. Endless discussions lay out various scenarios about how all this will end.

*

Fortunée lacks proper tableware but she manages as best she can. One afternoon Monsieur David knocks on her door. He comes in with his hands deep in his pockets.

- Close your eyes, Fortunée.

My aunt complies with a smile. - What is it? She asks impatiently.

- We just had lunch at the Auberge Sénéchal, and…

- Can I open my eyes?

Monsieur David solemnly takes out two glass tumblers out of his pockets that he stole from the restaurant during lunch. It is a gift for my aunt. Fortunées face lights up. They are only mustard jars, but we lack so much that they are greatly valued.

*

Early in November there is a lively discussion during one afternoon tea: The Americans just landed in North Africa! The French citizens in Morocco and Algeria welcomed them warmly although they are called traitors in our local French press. This is seen as good news for the Jews of Villefranche.

- At last!

Our joy is short lived. In response to the landing, the Germans invade the free zone. Now German as well as French discriminatory laws against Jews will apply everywhere in France.

*

The sun has not yet set and we are about to sit down for dinner one day, when we hear the growl of engines at the end of the street. It intensifies and becomes a steady roar. Rushing to the balcony, we see an endless column of armored vehicles rolling by on the boulevard de Haute-Guyenne, the ring road around town, at the end of our street. Even at a distance, we can clearly see guns barrel and the Wehrmacht helmets of soldiers seated on the trucks. We can also make out the Swastikas on the doors of vehicles. Stunned, I recognize Parisian TCRP buses loaded with soldiers. No mistaking them, they are the very buses that took us to the Vél d'Hiv, and to the Gare d'Austerlitz when we were transferred to Beaune-la-Rolande. But this time, they boast that grey-green camouflage color the Germans are so fond of. Fortunée hurries everyone inside and tells Marguerite to serve dinner, although no one can eat. Fortunée, elbows on the table, holds her head in her hands. Anxiety etches her face.

- *Me muera yo! Como vamos escapar de esto?* My god! How will we survive this?

She looks at Salvatore who remains silent.

- Go on, eat! Says Marguerite to the children.

My aunt suddenly stands up, closes the window and turns off the lights. We whisper in the dark. What can we do? We discuss various options but none seems suitable. Fear has overtaken Fortunée. She is convinced the Germans are coming after us.

*

I cannot sleep. The frightened look on my aunt's face has reminded me how much she looks like my mother. I read tonight the same fear in her eyes that I saw on my mother's face while we sat on the bleachers of the Vél d'Hiv, and once more while we were being separated at Beaune-la-Rolande. These and other thoughts of my mother flood my mind. I miss her so much! When will I see her again? When will my life return to normal? I hear Fortunée's sobs on the other side of the wall while Salvatore attempts to calm her. The somber hum of his voice in the dark insinuates disaster. Images of the column of armored cars tumble around in my head.

I wonder what Villefranche was like before the war. Today, two entirely different groups of people live side by side: there are the inhabitants who know each other well, and who speak Occitan among themselves; and then there are the refugees who have come from all over. There are numerous Alsatians among the exiles. They lived on the border with Germany, near the Maginot Line, and were transferred to the Dordogne region by the authorities when the war broke out. In time, some of them came down to Villefranche. There they found other refugees from Belgium and the northern regions of France, and the Parisians who fled during the exodus. Mixed among these groups are Jews who are prohibited from returning to Paris or anywhere in the occupied zone. The status of refugee provides an anonymous cover for the Jews.

*

The next day is Thursday, market day on the Place Notre-Dame. Everyone is talking about the Germans.

- They were just passing through, they did not stop.

- Some soldiers got out of their trucks for a while.

- Just to direct traffic.

They painted white arrows that pointed south on walls.

- They will be part of the welcoming committee in case the Americans decide to land in Provence.

The anxiety level among Jews goes up a notch. They visualize all kind of possible danger, sometime imaginary, sometime reminiscent of events in Central Europe. Should we get out before it is too late? But where exactly can we go?

*

The law requiring Jews to stamp their ID cards now extends to the whole of France. The Jews of Villefranche, however, have learned their lesson. Everyone knows someone rounded up after making the mistake of registering as a Jew; now everyone has false papers and very French names, just as I do. The names are borrowed from civil records destroyed in the bombings at the beginning of the war. The Segals, for instance are now called Duvals. The Blums became Plouviers and the Benbassats, Thevenots. The Carassos however, did not change appellation thinking their name could easily pass as either Spanish or Italian.

Now that they occupy the southern zone, the Germans pressure local authorities to be more suspicious. Combined patrols of gendarmes or militiamen in brown uniforms and black berets check people in the street, with particular attention to refugees. Anyone stopped must supply evidence of his identity. ID cards are no longer sufficient. But many administrations are entitled to issue IDs, and each jurisdiction has a different stamp and photo; for one the portrait on the picture must be facing front, for another it must be three quarter. Fake ID's are common. Consequently, additional evidence must be presented: a military record or paper attesting that its holder was discharged from the army; a marriage certificate, a driver's license, or an official family book in which children are recorded at the time of their birth. Ration cards are also used to show ID, since they are only issued to those who have legal papers.

Gendarmes come up from Rodez to conduct interrogations. The questions they ask make it clear they now search for more than Jews. They are also after members of the *maquis*: people in the Resistance. While people fear the Germans more than others, the militiamen are well known for their extreme cruelty. Many of them are criminals let out of jail in exchange for service in the militia. Police and gendarme authorities now focus on finding those they call terrorists: Young members of the Resistance who drive stolen cars and attack banks, German vehicles, and installations. Whenever one of their soldiers is shot, the Germans retaliate by executing ten hostages, usually including a good number of Jews.

One day, two black front-drive Citroens with little FFI flags enter Villefranche. FFI is the official acronym of the Resistance; it stands for *Forces Françaises de l'Intérieur*. The occupants park in Place Notre-Dame. Someone must have alerted the Germans because at 2 AM we hear shots coming from the café where the group has gathered. Listening tensely under my blanket, I imagine the whole of Villefranche awake. The next morning I walk by the square where I see the burned out shell of one of the cars.

*

A rumor from Nice reports that all foreign Jews are being rounded up and deported, by order of the local prefect.

- Good thing we did not stay in Nice, remarks Salvatore.

We all agree, having realized for quite a while now that the distinction between foreign and French Jews no longer applies.

We welcome the New Year of 1943 without joy. When will all this end?

The good news is that Morocco and Algeria are liberated. The bad news is that Rommel's *Afrika-korp* resists fiercely. Although the Germans are having a hard time in Stalingrad, we have the discouraging impression that they still dominate the conflict.

In mid-January, Sarah's arms are suddenly covered with red spots that Marguerite attempts to cure with old wives' country remedies. Two days later Salvatore finds similar spots on his legs. Father and daughter return from the doctor with a diagnosis: they have scabies, a contagious skin disease. The whole family has to take sulfur baths at the Sisters of Saint-Viateur hospital. We are taken to a small poorly lit basement with a large steaming bathtub whose stench grips my throat.

- It smells like rotten eggs, says Sarah, with a disgusted look.

Flashbacks of the Vél d'Hiv suddenly seize me and I panic. I have the urge to run away.

- I am not getting in there! I tell the assisting nun.

- Just do what you are told! Grumbles my uncle.

I try to escape, but he grabs my arm and hauls me back.

This torment is repeated over the next weeks.

*

My parents often appear to me in dreams and nightmares. Papa, maman, and Élise are walking away on a road. I call out to them: - papa, maman, wait for me!

But they do not hear me and keep walking away. I try to but never can catch up with them. I wake up frightened and screaming. I sit up in bed, panting and covered with sweat.

*

More workers are required in Germany. The collaborating Vichy government institutes the Compulsory Work Service. The *Service de travail Obligatoire*, familiarly called STO. It mandates that young French men will work in German factories. The French authorities spread rumors asserting that cooperation is essential and that for each three new workers, one French prisoner will be allowed to return home. Many young men see through the deceit and escape to join the *maquis*, instead.

In February, the Germans lose the initiative on the Russian front and General Von Paulus capitulates at Stalingrad. In the Libyan desert of Africa, the Nazis are in retreat and Rommel returns home.

Every night, British and American flying fortresses attack German industrial complexes, the industrial North of France, and Belgium as well. Meanwhile, round ups continue across France. Jews in large cities are the most vulnerable. In Marseilles, in Lyon, in Bordeaux, in Toulouse, the trap closes on the unfortunate who are loaded into cattle cars and sent to Drancy. From there, they soon leave again for an unknown destination. There are hearsay reports about camps in Silesia, and atrocities in Central Europe. But how can we believe what we would rather think are just exaggerated horrible stories? The British radio reports a revolt in the Warsaw ghetto leading to its total destruction.

*

One day while walking home from school, I linger on the Promenade du Languedoc, and hear the sound of an engine on the road below. Looking over the balustrade, I see three German trucks and a Parisian bus stopped on the street. A couple of armed soldiers gets off the rear platform of the bus and enter the café at the corner of the Boulevard de Haute-Guyenne. Soon after, I hear shouts and gunshots coming from inside, and the doors to the café, reopen; coming out laughing loudly the soldiers get back on the bus and leave. I am frozen with fright. I never found out what happened that day...

*

- A round up! Announces my aunt, shaking with fear.

- When?

- The day after tomorrow.

According to the rumor, the police secured a list of Jews in hiding in Villefranche. The information comes from the owner of the *Hotel de L'Aveyron*, the mistress of an officer at the gendarmerie in Rodez.

Fortunée rushes to friends' home outside of town to arrange for them to keep the children for the night. Subsequently, they go to nearby Villeneuve and rent a room in a house for a couple of nights. They pay in advance and return home to pick up some clothing. Marguerite will remain in the house. If questioned she will pretend the Carasso-Bouchards went to visit relatives in Montauban.

By evening, Salvatore and Fortunée return to Villeneuve. Without explanation, but perhaps sensing danger, the landlady returns their money saying she no longer can rent the room. She suddenly needs it for her goddaughter who is about to give birth.

- We have nowhere else to go at this late hour, protests Salvatore.

- Let us at least sleep there tonight, begs Fortunée.

The landlady refuses.

Without an alternative at this late hour, my uncle and aunt go back to sleep at the apartment on rue Saint-Jacques, to the amazement of Marguerite. They lie down fully dressed expecting the worst.

- At least the children are safe, says Fortunée.

Two o'clock in the morning: heavy knocks on the door downstairs startle them. Still convinced only men need to hide, Salvatore goes up to Marguerite's room. The poor woman is shaking in her nightshirt. A finger on his lips, Salvatore begs her to remain quiet.

- It's only me, Monsieur. He locks the door behind him and says in a soft voice:

- Whatever happens Marguerite, do not open the door!

- But...

- Just say you are too frightened to open.

He hoists himself out the window and onto the roof, hiding behind a smokestack. Salvatore keeps his ear cocked for the sounds coming from inside the house. Steps under his feet resound in the stairways. Doors are opened; doors are closed then, silence returns. Time passes. Not a sound, not a car down in the street. Villefranche is asleep.

- Salvatore!

It is Fortunée's voice. Leaning around the corner of the chimney my uncle sees his wife leaning in Marguerite's window. She signals him to come back inside.

- What happened? Asks Salvatore, as he jumps back inside the house.

It was just the upstairs neighbor's niece arriving in the middle of the night. Her bus had broken down in the countryside. As for the rumored round up, it never happened. Maybe it was a false rumor, or perhaps rescheduled for a later date, or it possibly took place in another town...

*

During that summer, the Carasso-Bouchards listen regularly to the BBC, ear close to the radio, the volume set low so neighbors will not hear, although the neighbors themselves are probably listening too. The allies land in Sicily, then Italy capitulates. Soon, the Americans cross the Strait of Messina and land in Salerno.

Monsieur David, the diamond merchant from the rue de la Paix, has hung a map of Europe on the inside door of his bedroom wardrobe, marking with push pins the progress of the Allied armies. Estelle complains that when people come for tea, they always end up in heated discussions in her bedroom. The Allies continue their advance through Italy with heavy losses.

In France, after the Germans, replacing the Italians occupy the Savoie and Riviera region, Nice and Grenoble have become treacherous traps where round ups occur on a large scale. In Cannes, men suspected of being Jewish are stopped on the Croisette and ordered to lower their pants, those circumcised are immediately taken away.

However, Cannes and Grenoble are far from Villefranche-de-Rouergue, and Italy is even farther. Still, militiamen goose step on parade in Rode, and Figeac just a few kilometers away. They terrorize the population and provoke young men to reveal which side they are on. It is now common in Villefranche to find clandestine Resistance leaflets posted on walls.

*

We are in August, and the atmosphere in the little apartment is stifling. Fortunée has given up trying to keep me inside. She lets me hang out with Julien Daydou, a classmate whose mother runs the grocery store on the rue Giraudet. We play cards, we meet other kids on the square, and we go down to the river to chase ducks or skip stones. Sometime we go as a group to the Popular

Kitchen, which serves afternoon snacks to children: enriched cookies and a cup of hot chocolate which in fact is nothing but a brown milk drink with saccharin.

Until recently, the occupiers garrisoned in Rodez and Albi were not very visible in Villefranche, but now German officers frequently walk the streets. They arrive one day to inspect school buildings. Mr. Fontange, the mayor of Villefranche accompanies them. He is easily recognizable, having lost his left arm in a car accident before the war.

Activity in and around the college intensifies; townspeople notice whole trucks of cots and other furniture unloaded in the schoolyard. Soon, over fifty German soldiers are quartered in the school and an SS sentry is permanently on guard at the entrance.

Germans in town are courteous and make efforts to stay on good terms with the inhabitants. They seem too busy to chase Jews. Around the same time, French gendarmes suspend their routine checks in hotels. Still, the atmosphere in our house is tense. My uncle avoids going out and only leaves the apartment to go to Mass on Sunday.

*

My aunt heard that, as soon as the Germans took residence in the school, the Jews of the *Hotel Moderne*, left Villefranche to hide in the surrounding countryside. My uncle prefers to remain in town. He thinks we are in relative security since we live in an apartment, not a hotel.

Otherwise, life outside appears to continue normally and I am still allowed to go out as I please. I wander along the promenade du Giraudet with my friend Julien Daydou a local boy not at risk. Here and there we hear unsettling talk.

- People say they are Cossacks.

- You mean barbarians!

Cossacks or barbarians, they parade through town every morning belting out marching songs. They frequent the shops and spend time on café terraces. According to some rumors a German soldier struck a resident; another shot a dog with his handgun. The mayor who speaks German, complained to the military authorities. Another rumor reports they are Croats not Cossacks, and all of them are Muslims. As far as I am concerned, they wear a German uniform so they are German soldiers.

*

On the way back from the Popular Kitchen with Julien, a commotion draws our attention one day, and we cross the bridge to see what's going on near the railroad station. There, a group of so-called Croats is unloading a freight train and a young soldier is carrying a heavy bundle of hay on his shoulders. The soldier slips on the ground, muddy from rain that fell during the night and falls with his load. One of the German officers yells at him angrily. The young soldier picks himself up and stands at attention. The officer shouts an order and everyone around is surprised to see the soldier fall forward in the mud without even breaking his fall with his arms. He then picks himself up and, ordered by the officer, he falls again several times. The cruelty of the scene outrages the town's people watching. Tension mounts as the crowd shouts insults at the Germans.

- Let's get out of here, I tell Julien.

- Wait a minute; it's getting interesting.

I have no desire to watch one more time people beaten with clubs or worse. I grab Julien by the arm.

- What's the matter with you? Are you scared?

*

It is 8 AM. Sarah, who went out to get milk, returns yelling:

- There is gunfire in the street!

A skirmish apparently took place near the Consuls' bridge, and shots were heard from the direction of the Hotel Moderne.

- Did you see soldiers shooting? I ask Sarah.

- No, that's what people said.

We suddenly hear gunshots outside and we hurry to close the shutters. When silence returns, my aunt goes downstairs to try and find out what happened.

- It's over, she says when she returns, looking apprehensive and frightened.

- What exactly happened? Asks Sarah.

- They say a band of communists attacked the Germans.

Everyone looks uneasy. The explanation does not make sense.

An unusual calm gets hold of the street in the hours that follow. Now and then Salvatore opens the curtains to see what he can through the shutters. For a long time nothing happens, but suddenly cries come out of the square followed by bursts of submachine guns. It lasts only a few seconds but my heart stops beating. We exchange worried glances in the semi-darkness of the apartment. Sarah opens a book pretending to read in the dark. My aunt, head in her hands, sits at the table. Marguerite knits, lifting her eyes now and then to follow my uncle who nervously paces back and forth. The image of my mother as I last saw her when we were separated at Beaune-la-Rolande fills my mind. The image trigger others: the terrifying vision of mothers beaten up, little children with dirty diapers running aimlessly around; machine-guns set on tripods; feces covered banknotes and jewelry retrieved from the cesspool ... I twist and turn a piece of wire between my fingers to escape these distressing thoughts.

My uncle turns on the radio, the volume set so low we can hardly hear a thing. In any case, there is nothing to listen to, but regular programming. Frustrated, my uncle turns the set off; wipes his forehead with a handkerchief, and mutters a few words to my aunt. A happy cry comes from the crib in the corner of the dining room where Sophie is waking from her nap. No one has the heart to return her joyful smile.

Around five in the afternoon, we hear the roar of engines and slammed doors. I join my uncle near the window where his finger has already slipped between the curtains. Armed men are running up the narrow lane that amplifies the thud of their boots on the cobblestones. Dark shirts and black berets with a brass gamma letter insignia pinned over their foreheads tell us they are French militiamen. They bang the door just across from ours with the butt of their rifles until the lock gives in. The door flies open and slams against the back wall while the militiamen rush through the narrow corridor. Boots bang against the steps; shouts come out of a second floor, then out of a third floor window. Evidently, a struggle is taking place. The brawl lasts about ten minutes before the militiamen leave, the sound of their engines fading in the distance. What kind of military operation was this?

- What happened? Asks Sarah.

- I don't know.

What could have happened in the house across the narrow street? We imagine the worse.

- Are they communists? Sarah asks again.

- Maybe people who helped the Resistance, I surmise.

- Keep quiet, says Fortunée. We just don't know.

The room gets darker as night falls. Sarah curls up next to her mother. Little Sophie plays quietly in her bed.

No one says a word while we tensely eat dinner without enthusiasm, the silence only broken by Sophie's babble. We eventually go to bed although no one sleeps. Each of us is wondering, waiting, and watching. Late in the night, bursts of machine-gun fire still resonate in the distance.

Early the next morning, my uncle decides to ask our neighbor Mr. Érignac what is happening. He trusts him more than others. From the top of the stairs, I listen to their discussion down in the entryway.

- It is the Croats, says Érignac. Apparently, they revolted against their German officers. I hear they killed many of them!

- What else; and what happened afterward?

- Most of the Croat soldiers fled. It seems they are hiding here and there… They are all Muslims, you know.

- Yes, so?

- So, the Gestapo came from Mende and Rodez.

- The Gestapo, what for?

- To recapture them, of course!

- And did they find them?

- They caught a few of them hiding in town. I have to go, now. It's not good to be seen hanging out on the street…

- Wait a minute Mr. Érignac, insists Salvatore. What did they do with the Croats they found?

- They finished them off, Érignac adds after a pause. Be careful, Mr. Carasso.

- Careful, why?

- They think the population is helping and hiding the Croats. They could start searching houses.

- There is no particular reason for me to watch out, says my uncle defensively with a voice he has trouble controlling. I am not hiding anyone.

- I am just saying… And Mr. Érignac hurries away.

My uncle remains on the doorstep an instant, absorbed in thoughts before returning upstairs.

It is about noon when a little stone hits the windowpane. I look down from the window.

- It's Érignac, I tell my uncle.

I join my uncle downstairs, this time.

- They are confiscating arms held by the population, says Érignac. Even hunting rifles. Do you keep arms at home?

- No…

- Because if you did, you would have to bring them to the school. That's the order given. Got to go.

We watch Érignac walk away and disappear into his house. He did not say whether he himself kept arms at home.

- What are we going to do? I ask in a low voice.

- I just hope they don't start searching houses, replies Salvatore.

We go back up to the apartment. Salvatore recounts Érignac's remarks to Fortunée who concludes:

- There is nothing to do except be patient and wait.

After lunch, Salvatore asks Marguerite to go out to get news. The poor woman is afraid to step out and attract attention by asking questions. You can see that what she really thinks is:

- If Monsieur needs information; Monsieur can go look for himself. My uncle tries to justify his spineless plea:

- I just thought it would be easier for you, Marguerite.

Fortunée tells him in Ladino that he should be ashamed of himself and to leave Marguerite alone.

A scream occasionally pierces the relative quiet of the street and we hear sporadic shooting throughout the afternoon. It comes from every direction. We remain rooted in the small apartment now overtaken by darkness. We feel trapped and cannot even count on the relief of sleep. We twist and turn in our beds, our agitated slumber filled with nightmares.

In the middle of the night, I hear a sound. It seems to come from downstairs, maybe from the hallway near the door. I get up and put my ear against the landing door. Once again, I hear a shuffle. I quietly go to my aunt and wake her up. She sits in bed, her hair in disarray and listens anxiously to my worries. She then wakes her husband up and both of them quietly tiptoe to the landing and listen. The floor squeaks under our bare feet.

- There is someone downstairs, concludes my aunt in a whisper.

We listen for some long minutes. The house is wrapped in a thick silence.

- There is no one, says my uncle. Go back to bed. You too Simon.

- Shush…

The shuffle starts again, followed by a faint groan. There is definitely someone downstairs in the hallway. We hold our breath to listen. Sarah has joined us on the landing. All of us return to the dining room where we sit in the dark. My aunt says, in a low voice:

- Listen Salvat, if it were a thief, he would come up. The same is true if it were the Gestapo or the Militia…

- So, what do we do?

- We have to go and see who it is.

- I will wake Marguerite and ask her to go and see…

- Don't even think about it! Says Fortunée in an irritated whisper.

We sit around the table the rest of the night, too frightened to move, incapable of making a decision, while now and then bewildering sounds come from the stairwell. None of us wants to return to bed. At last a faint morning light pierces through the shutters; birds on the roof start chirping. Gradually, we distinguish shapes in the room. Fortunée shakes my uncle who in spite of his fear had dozed off.

- Marguerite will come down soon. We have to check now.

Armed with a heavy frying pan, Salvatore goes slowly down the steps, almost in slow motion, as if walking on eggs. I follow at a distance.

- Anybody there? He asks.

A moan answers.

We continue down. Half way down the stairs, I recognize the shadow of a man lying under the stairway. His face is covered with grime and he is wearing a dirty German uniform. I stop. My aunt catches up with me.

- Is he armed?

- It's one of the Croats!

- He doesn't look dangerous. Maybe he is hurt. We should see if we can help…

- You want to get us all killed? Mutters Salvatore between his teeth.

- Well then, tell him to go away! Oh, you can be so clumsy, sometimes!

My aunt approaches the soldier. I get close too. He seems very young, just a few years older than I am.

- What do you want? Fortunée asks him.

- Kroatisch! Mutters the soldier with a plaintive voice. Kroatisch! Kroatisch. Kein übel, Deutsche mich zu töten.

We don't understand what the soldier is mumbling. His arm is covered with dry blood.

Now Sarah comes down.

- He can't stay here, says Salvatore.

- Let's get him upstairs, says my aunt.

- It's impossible…

We start arguing about what to do. It is obvious the man does not have the strength to walk on his own and if he did, once outside he would immediately be shot down. After all, he is a deserter. Nevertheless, my uncle wants him to go away. In the end, Fortunée makes a convincing argument: The soldier is sure to collapse as soon as he gets outside and this would attract the Germans to the front of our house.

Salvatore holds out his hand for the wounded man to grab. However, the soldier does not have the strength to stand up. I lean forward and wrap my arm around one shoulder while my uncle does the same on the other side. The soldier stinks. A beard a few days old covers his dark face. His bushy hair is unkempt.

From the landing above, Marguerite who was coming down to make coffee looks at us in shocked silence, her hand covering her mouth.

We climb the steps carrying the wounded man as best we can. Marguerite helps us sit him down on a chair in the dining room. Slowly, he drinks a glass of water she hands him. She removes his jacket, then his shirt. Although superficial, the wound has bled profusely. Marguerite cleans the wound and prepares a makeshift dressing.

- *Danke*, mumbles the young soldier staring at Marguerite.

- What are we going to do with him? Asks Salvatore. We have to ask him to leave as soon as it is dark tonight.

- Not wearing this uniform! Says Marguerite. Find him some clothes and shoes. Then she adds:

- To begin with, give me a towel...

I smile inwardly, noticing how suddenly roles have reversed. Marguerite has taken over and gives orders.

- *Danke, danke,* repeats the deserter, then with a hand on his chest:

- Milos.

- Simon, I answer.

The whole family now introduces itself: Fortunée, Sarah, Salvatore, and then Marguerite.

- The baby is called Sophie, I add.

Milos feels better after he eats some bread and drinks coffee with us. His spirits improve as well but we still don't understand a word of what he is trying to tell us, and we have not yet decided what to do with him. I have an idea: I bring paper and pencil and after I wet the lead on my tongue, I draw a doorway and an arrow as well as a little man leaving the house towards the countryside with cows and trees.

Milos borrows my pencil to draw a car followed by a question mark. No, I motion with my head as I draw a pair of legs. Milos looks disappointed, but he grasps what I meant. I then draw a map of the region. Salvatore, who knows the countryside well from scouring the area looking for food, writes down the names of places where people are likely to help the deserter. When we are done, Milos goes up to rest on Marguerite's bed.

We are still discussing around the table when Érignac as has become his habit, throws a pebble against the window.

- I am coming down, Salvatore tells him.

- Wait, I am coming up replies Érignac.

Usually so evasive, he now wants to come up. We exchange worried looks.

- Let him come up, sighs Fortunée, but he must not stay long.

A minute later Marguerite serves him a cup of coffee. All of us watch closely worried about Milos resting upstairs. We all hope he does not decide to come down to the dining room! Érignac remains unaware of our concern.

- The situation seems to be improving, he says, look! He takes a poster out of his jacket and spreads it on the table while Marguerite hurries to sweep crumbs away with her hand.

TO THE POPULATION OF VILLEFRANCHE

The declaration is printed on two side-by-side columns. One is in French, the other in German.

Following recent events, I have been named commanding officer of Villefranche and consequently I order the following:

Villefranche is placed under martial law.

All civilians are forbidden to circulate in the streets and public places between 9 PM and 6 AM. Anyone violating this order will be arrested and punished. Doctors, midwives, and public service employees will receive a pass provided by the mayor upon presentation of evidence.

Anyone found in possession of arms will be shot.

The text is followed by other practical instructions and the warning ends with the following summons:

I count on everyone not to let those aliens to your country such as Jews and British people influence you. This riff-raff only wants your destruction!

The poster is signed:

Hanke, commanding officer of Villefranche.

According to Érignac, martial law was established 24 hours ago. The mayor's negotiation savvy succeeded in getting the order lifted this morning.

*

Milos feels better and eats dinner with us that evening. I spend part of the day writing notes for him to keep in his pockets:

I am looking for a hiding place, The Germans are after me, or *Please help me!*

After dinner, my aunt gives Milos some money and Marguerite prepares him a substantial sandwich for the road before changing his dressing. Once the street outside is completely still, we watch Milos disappear in the night with our hopes he will not encounter a German patrol.

*

During the next three days, the mayor works to avoid the worst. German patrols and house searches diminish and the pressure on inhabitants relaxes. Tentatively at first, then with more confidence, people start going outside again. Informal gatherings and discussions resume on Place Notre-Dame.

Surprisingly, not a word of the recent events is reported in *Le Narrateur*, the local paper; but news travel by word-of-mouth. According to one source, the Muslim Croats are part of an SS battalion sent for training in Villefranche. During the night of September 17, they rebelled against insufferable conditions inflicted by the German officers.

Other sources contend the revolt was the result of the soldiers' fear of being sent to the Russian front. Whatever the motivation, the Croats killed four of the five German officers lodging at the Hotel Moderne. The fifth one managed to escape and phoned Rodez to warn the Gestapo, which rushed to Villefranche to suppress the rebellion. An insurgency in the German army had been unheard of. The German commandant threatened Mayor Fontange:

- The population of Villefranche is aiding the rebels, he said. It must pay!

The commandant's reasoning had justified imposing martial law and Fontange had not objected; he was relieved that it prevented, for the moment at least, executing Villefranche residents.

In the meanwhile, many of the Croat rebels had deserted. They disappeared in the city and countryside; managing as best they could without speaking French. The Gestapo descended on those who remained in their barracks, torturing them to name leaders and fugitives. With that information, the Germans pursued the deserters. Those caught were in turn tortured before being executed. Some residents of the *Farrou* district reported seeing Croats forced to walk barefoot, a burlap bag over their head, and poked with the barrel of their guns by Germans.

Some inhabitants described having seen corpses in uniform on the side of a road. Someone in town had seen men loading naked corpses on a truck. A real massacre was reported to have taken place at the *Sainte-Marguerite's* meadow.

Once they began to pursue the Croats in the countryside, the Germans became more lenient in town. The relieved inhabitants prepared to reopen schools, which the Mayor had postponed until October because of recent events.

*

There is a meadow next to *Bel-Air* road, just behind the Promenade du Languedoc where kids often play soccer. It is beyond the limits where I am allowed to meet friends. My uncle and my aunt are afraid I will get into some kind of trouble. When I tell them no one checks IDs of children at play, they reply that I am no longer a child, when I argue that I look younger than my age, they get annoyed and tell me not to argue. I cannot win.

However, I can't stand being cooped up inside. I need to run around with friends and remain active; I need to escape my troubled thoughts, my unhappiness. I therefore ignore the ban.

The field is jammed between two houses and closed at the far end by a row of oak trees and a barn in ruins whose broken down walls are covered in ivy. I linger one day near the barn after a game of soccer, while my friends get ready to go home. I hear a feeble voice calling from the back.

- Simon…

The voice seems to come from inside the barn. I think at first my imagination is playing tricks on me. My friends have already left the field, so I enter the barn, stumbling over fallen stones invaded by weeds.

- Simon!

The weak voice calls again. It is coming from behind a worm-eaten door barely hanging on its hinges. I push the door open.

- Milos!

His face is shriveled and grey, his eyes buried deep and his filthy bandage is still the one made by Marguerite. He leads me to the darkest corner of the barn and explains in gestures that he is starving. Using signs I ask him to stay put and wait for me.

I run home climbing the stairs two at a time. I slip silently in the apartment where my uncle and aunt are napping. Sleep has become for them, a way of escaping worries. I carefully open the pantry door and take everything I can find, sausage, cheese, onions, and bread. I hide it under my shirt and return quickly to *Bel Air* road. On my way I grab a bicycle I find leaning against a wall, and I cross the now-deserted field. Milos comes out of the decrepit barn staggering among the stones and walks towards me. I quietly watch him eat. When he is done, I point to the bicycle and ask to see the map I made for him. I point my finger on *Toulonjac* and explain it is only five kilometers away in the direction of

Carjac. I know a farmer I met there once, buying food with my uncle. Milos gets on the bicycle and I sit on the rack behind.

The country road lined with plane trees is deserted. Once we pass the village of *Graves,* a stream runs alongside us. Milos stops and lays the bicycle down on the grass before lying on his stomach and quenching his thirst slurping the running water. He then opens his bandage and cleans his wound. Thanks to my aunt's admonition, I always have a clean handkerchief in my pocket. I use it to make a new makeshift bandage. I worry because it takes me so long. I am not as skilled as Marguerite.

- We better get going, I say, it's dangerous staying here...

The sun sets on the horizon by the time we reach the farm. I make Milos wait behind a nearby dry stone wall.

A barking dog greets me as I cross the courtyard. I pat him and talk to him while he sniffs my ankles. The farmer stares at me standing on the threshold of his house. He is wearing the inevitable coveralls falling below his knees over black velvet pants of the Aveyron farmers. His large red nose stands above a moustache yellowed by tobacco.

- Hello, I offer in greeting. You recognize me? I am Mr. Carasso's nephew...

He motions for me to come into the dark room that smells of smoke.

- I am not alone, I say.

He looks outside through the open door.

- Who is it? He asks with a worried look.

- A young guy. The Germans are after him.

Suspecting a trap, the farmer stares at me. The militiamen are adept at manipulating people so they betray themselves. After you do, they deliver you to the Germans, then return to loot the house. I continue:

- He is a Croat, a deserter. He is hiding over there, behind the wall. He does not speak a word of French.

With the dog following us, we walk towards the stone wall. The farmer looks around, watching for any possible car approaching. The dog stops and begins barking.

- Shush!

Slipping out of his hiding place, Milos looks like a ghost. The dog starts barking again. The farmer eyes Milos from head to foot with a dismayed look.

- His name is Milos, I say.

- Why do you bring him to me?

- He needs help. Nobody saw us. I need to go back; my uncle is going to yell at me...

- Don't say a word to your uncle about this guy, or else you will hear from me...

- I won't say a word.

- To no one!

- To no one.

- And don't ever come back…

- I won't.

- Now take your bicycle and get out!

I hardly have time for a good-bye wave to Milos. I get on the bike and ride away. Before the first turn, I stop to look back at the farm, in time to see Milos enter the barn adjacent to the house. The trees on the road now cast dark shadows.

*

The Germans leave Villefranche at the end of September, after a military ceremony. The scene makes whoever watches, smile sarcastically, everyone remembers the massacres. The Jewish families who had left in haste are slowly returning, and are once again seen strolling under the arcades of the bastide. They are city people who found it difficult to adjust to rural life. My uncle for one, thinks he was right to stay in town despite the events. He still believes it is best to blend into the local population, to send children to school and go to church regularly.

- When you leave town, everyone notices you are going away.

School starts on the 19th of October. Although the school was thoroughly cleaned we cannot help but recall that the Gestapo tortured rebels in these walls.

Our region suffers less from food deprivation than other provinces; the population is therefore not as prone to agitation, and the majority of citizens are still siding with Marshal Pétain.

Townspeople keep to themselves and out of the way of the Resistance activities.

The morale among Jews lifts a little at the beginning of 1944, when the British radio announces that more than 600 flying fortresses bombed Berlin.

- They have guts these Americans!

As in Italy, a glimmer of faint hope appears as the allies continue their difficult progression towards Rome and the North. Still, no Jew would think of relaxing his vigilance. Everyone remains on his guard and is wary of the man at the bistro, the neighbor, the man in the store who furtively glances your way while serving you; perhaps he hates Jews. Everyone speaks cautiously. A clumsy or tactless phrase can be dangerous. We are all aware that an anonymous letter sent to the prefecture can set off a search, lead to the arrest of an entire family. and their forced departure to an unknown destination.

I toss and turn every night in my bed, and when I finally fall asleep, it is to relive the same nightmare: I am in an apartment; the people with me are not my real parents. A truck passes below in the street; its engine is straining, as if going up a hill. Fear grips me. Will the truck stop in front of our door? I am afraid I will have to get up, get dressed quickly, take a suitcase, and stumble down the stairway where I am taken away… At the moment the truck passes in front of our door, I wake up with a start.

CHAPTER 11

Spring 1944

When a Jewish boy reaches the age of thirteen, he is considered an adult and is expected to observe the commandments of his religion. The Bar Mitzvah ritual is conducted in the synagogue, during a Shabbat service. The boy reads a portion of the Torah and recites the *Shema Israel* prayer acknowledging the unique god of the Jewish people. A celebratory meal and festivities follow the Bar Mitzvah.

Two of us, Jacques Bernstein and I, have reached the requisite age. Our Bar Mitzvah must be clandestine but the idea delights the Jews of Villefranche, even those who are not particularly observant. A Bar Mitzvah is a symbol of life, and in the gloom we have been living in for so long, it offers a glimmer of hope. The Jews of Villefranche will feel like Jews again for the duration of the ceremony.

It is no small matter to organize festivities under the circumstances. But Mr. Segal has a friend, Maurice Singer, the cantor of an important synagogue in Bordeaux who is in hiding at *La Fouillade*, not far from *Villefranche*. Maurice Singer has agreed to come and teach us the rudiments of Hebrew and the chanting of the Torah. Rabbi Meyer, who is in hiding near Toulouse, promises to come celebrate the Shabbat service in Villefranche.

The Bar Mitzvah will take place at Monsieur David's house, on a hill on the road to *Montauban*. From the house at the end of a long drive bordered by plane trees and concealed behind hedges, approaching cars can be seen from a distance, allowing the party to be kept private.

Although the women will not be able to organize the lavish banquet they would have liked, each one will bring what she can from their reserves or from what they can acquire on the black market.

Jacques and I, who see the big day coming with a mixture of imposition and boredom, do not share the excitement that runs through our little congregation. The extra effort required in addition to our schoolwork is a chore for both of us. Monsieur Singer comes once a week from La Fouillade on his bicycle to tutor us in the basics of Hebrew and religion. He teaches us the *Haphtarah* we will read during the service, and we certainly do not make his task easy!

- You must also write a speech to read in front of your families and their guests, he tells us.

- What do we have to say? Asks Jacques.

- You will express your gratitude towards your families.

Each night, my uncle makes me rehearse my *Haphtarah* but as far as the speech is concerned, I am the only one who knows its content.

Those who live far away, such as Rabbi Meyer, arrive the day before and spend the night at Monsieur David's house. We obviously will not read from the Torah rolls usually kept in a synagogue. We will make do with a transcription of the texts in a book.

Monsieur David places a desk to be used as the *Bima* - a makeshift pulpit - in the living room. The book with the Torah transcription lies on a table just behind the desk, centered between two big flower arrangements. Rows of chairs are placed in front for the congregation.

- Here is our clandestine synagogue, shows Monsieur David to Rabbi Meyer upon his arrival.

Guests arrive early. The ladies are dressed up in their best apparel with hats created by the milliners of Villefranche. Men wear suit and tie, and cover their heads with felt hats. The required ten adult men to form a *minian* or quorum are easily exceeded. Jacques, who balked at attending our sessions with the cantor, is beaming when the time comes to chant his *Haphtarah*. My mood is more somber. I cannot help but wish my parents were in the audience and I hold back a lump in my throat.

After the religious service has ended, Jacques returns to the Bima to read his speech. While we wait for him to start, a woman in the audience remarks for all to hear:

- Parece muy bueno. Es ijo de Ashkenazi, se ve en la cara.

- Callate, el va empezar!

- What a handsome boy and obviously from an Ashkenazi family.

- Keep quiet, he is about to start! Says her neighbor.

- My dear parents, begins Jacques. My dear grandmother, dear guests...

He expresses his gratitude towards his family; he tells of his pride at becoming an adult, accepting his future responsibilities, he thanks everyone...

My turn is next. My uncle Salvatore is beaming while my aunt is obviously moved.

- My dear parents...

I strain to control my emotion.

- My dear parents who are not here today, my dear sister: It is principally to you that I address myself today. To you my father, who is laboring in a factory or on a farm, to you maman whose trace I could not find in Drancy, to you Élise. Wherever you are, I hope you are together. May God let my thoughts reach you. I picture you at dinnertime, spending the evening together. I know I am in your thoughts as much as you are in mine. Keep your spirits up; do not despair. Remember that following the flight from Egypt then later in Spain, our ancestors also suffered from persecutions and exile. Yet, we are still here. We bear in us something that refuses to die and I am proud to tell you that I eagerly assume my Jewish heritage.

Dear father, dear mother, dear sister Élise, I would have liked so much for you to hear me read the Torah. As of tomorrow, I will be counted among the ten men who constitute a *minian*. Like you, my dear parents I will try to be worthy of who I am: A Jew among Jews, a Jew among men, and a man among men. My fondest hope is to celebrate your return very soon.

A woman in the audience weeps into her handkerchief, and Fortunée cannot hold back her tears. I thank my uncle and my aunt and I end my talk by a sentence in ladino, the language I refused to speak when I was younger.

- *Benditcho l'Dio, el qué mé décho poner mi Tephillin este dia, y yo agradesco, a mis kéridos parientes y saludo a mi hermana, los que no podian estar aqui en este dia. Tambien yo agradesco al professor Singer, al khakham Meyer, a los de mi familia aqui, y a todos los qué mé enseñaron la ley dé Moshé.*

Blessed be our God who allowed that I conduct my Bar Mitzvah today. I thank my dear parents and I greet my sister, you who cannot be with us on this day. I also thank my professor, Monsieur Singer, Rabbi Meyer, those of my family who are here today and all those who taught me the Law of Moses.

Men and women then come to congratulate me, their eyes shine with emotion.

- *Mazal tov*, Simon.

- God bless you.

And now: Let's celebrate.

A large U-shape table has been set up. Somewhere in the background a phonograph plays a medley of Yiddish and Sephardic songs. The audience hesitates a moment before joining hands to form a circle and launching into an exuberant frantic *hora*. A man forces his way through the dancers, carrying a chair over his head that he sets down in the center. He invites me to sit on the chair and four men lift it in the air while I hold on to the sides. Hands all around clap in rhythm.

*

Diary of Simon Crespi

Sunday May 7 1944

It has been quite a while since the last entry in my diary. I reopen this notebook on the occasion of my Bar Mitzvah, yesterday.

I worked hard to prepare for it, papa and maman, when they return, will be proud to hear how well I did. I insisted on saying a few words in Ladino. It is the least I could do to acknowledge my parents' heritage and express my gratitude.

I held Jocelyne's hand while we danced a wild Hora during the party. She is fourteen and has a beautiful distant gaze. She goes to the same lycée as Sarah. She smiled at me as we danced and I could not take my eyes of her – I was the prince of the day, it was my day…

I hope I did not hurt my uncle's and aunt's feelings as I only thanked them briefly. Perhaps they expected more appreciation from me.

It is a strange sensation to feel I am becoming a man.

I am slipping the text of my speech between these pages.

CHAPTER 12

June 1944

The older kids at the college stop after school at a café to play a game of baby-foot. They shout and curse and drink saccharine-sweetened lemonade. I often meet them to postpone going home to the tedium of homework. I sometimes join in a game but I am not good at it and most of the time I just watch the players.

In fact, what interests me most is the almond-eyed waitress who stands behind the wooden counter. I love the way she ties her apron so it accentuates the curves of her body. Sometime she wears her hair loose, other times in a ponytail. I am under her spell while I sit on a high stool in front of her. I never tire of watching her wiping glasses, and I love her clear voice with that Southern accent. I try to imagine the shape of her breasts. The fact that she is a few years older than me doesn't worry me in the least. As far as I can see, she enjoys my company.

The best times are when we are alone, just the two of us in the café. Her name is Georgette. She is from the *Larzac* region, and she lives on the outskirt of Villefranche. She is nineteen. The fact that she has a fiancé does not discourage me. How could it? I think of her night and day.

- You don't mind me speaking to you? I ask.

- No, it helps pass the time. The days are long and the customers are not very interesting. Her voice sings and remains on the last syllable of each word.

- You don't have the local accent. She remarks.

- I'm from Nice, it's not that far.

- You don't have an accent from Nice either.

- In fact, I was born in Paris.

- Is your father hard on you?

- Hard enough.

I no longer know whether I am talking about my real father or my uncle Salvatore. Embarrassed by the intensity of my stare, Georgette plunges the dirty glass she is holding into warm water.

Soon we get to talk every day. I can see she likes our get-togethers. She tells me our friendship breaks up the dreariness of everyday life. She watches for my arrival after school and is disappointed if I miss a day.

Once she said: - I did not see you yesterday; I wondered what happened.

- My aunt had friends over; she wanted me home right after school.

- You should have told me.

I am just as disappointed when I don't see Georgette. But I am too timid to declare my feelings or even just tell her I miss her.

Once, she has to leave the café earlier than usual to do an errand and she invites me to accompany her part of the way. I am walking in the street with her for the first time, and we stroll as though it were a common occurrence. She smiles at me and I feel great. Her accent enchants me more each day. Her mischievous glance seems to imply a thousand little secrets between us.

*

She goes to the movies with her fiancé every Saturday night, and the following Monday she tells me about the stars she liked. Her favorite actor is Jean Gabin and her favorite singer is Luis Mariano.

- Do you listen to the radio? I ask.

- Just songs.

She never talks about the war, at least not with me. She prefers to talk about herself. She lives alone, on the road to Montauban, in a small apartment with windows overlooking a lake. Her fiancé is from Alsace, she tells me. I imagine he is one of those people displaced in the Dordogne region after the German invasion.

- He works as an administrator, she explains, he is a shipping manager.

- And when he returns home, will you go with him?

- No.

- What will you do, then?

She looks at me. - We will see.

Some of her relatives live in Montauban, but she grew up on a farm nearby. Her parents, younger brothers, and sisters still live there. One memory of her childhood that stands out, she tells me, is the first snow one particular winter. That morning, she says, she awoke to a fine white cover sparkling in the pale sun that covered the *Causse*.

- People said it was God plucking feathers from his angels. Each year we killed a hog. It was a big deal. She waxes on. We waited for the arrival of the slaughterer, whom she calls the *saigneur*, the Blood Letter. Georgette smiles because in French it sounds like the arrival of the *seigneur*: the Lord.

- Do you get the play on words? She asks with a cunning smile.

I would love to talk about my youth, but the same sad images always come to my mind when I think of the rue des Écouffes. It is out of question to talk about my father taken to Beaune-la-Rolande, about the yellow star, of the Vel d'Hiv, about my stay in the camp of Drancy, or about the suffering and humiliations of us Jews. So I say nothing. She continues.

- When someone was hurt, we called in the healing woman. She made dressings with herbs and olive oil and she drew signs in the air while she muttered incantations...

- What did she say?

- It's a secret to chase away the devil she learned from her mother.

- Did you ever hear the words?

Georgette hesitates before reciting softly into my ear.

- Fire of Heaven let go of your heat, just as Judas lost his colors when he betrayed our Lord Jesus-Christ in the grove of olive trees.

Hearing her words, I stiffen. Georgette notices and sighs:

- It must not be said in vain. You make me say foolish things!

- Are you superstitious?

- Not at all! Do you take me for an illiterate? I had my first communion!

*

I am bored at home in the evening. My aunt tells everyone she thinks I have reached the difficult ungrateful age of adolescence. Nobody seems able to define this particular age, but everybody insists it is telling. I just shrug my shoulders and, aloof, I brush off the remarks with a detached stare. Then I return to my homework while my uncle listens to the radio with his ear glued to the loudspeaker.

At night, thoughts of Georgette's body consume me. I try to escape from images burned in my mind by thinking of *The Ripening Seed*, a novel by Colette that I am secretly reading. My life mixes with the dream and Philippe, the main character. Like him, I am living a love story with an older woman dressed in white. By morning, I am tired and struggle to get out of bed. I am bored during class, and all I can think about is seeing Georgette after school.

One day, Georgette's eyes are puffy and red. She had cried the whole morning, after an argument with her fiancé. I hesitate to ask questions. I don't really want to know the details of their disagreement and Georgette does not wish to tell me either. Apparently she is confused and does not know where she stands. I am almost relieved to go home.

*

The "allied invasion," as people call it, seems imminent. Actually, people don't know much about what is going on. They are skeptical of rumors and don't know what to believe.

- We hear so many tall tales, says a priest in the school's courtyard, while someone adds:

- They are going to land on the Channel coast.

- Why should they land there? The coast is much too dangerous with German defenses. On the other hand, they could come up from Italy and enter France through the Savoie Region.

- Is the Channel coast so well defended?

- All the way to the *Finistère*. Don't you read the papers?

- What paper? *The Narrateur*? Is that local rag where you get your information?

*

Nevertheless, the news spreads through town.

- The allies have landed in Normandy!

At first, people greet the information with disbelief.

- If it only were true, says my aunt.

In fact it is exact. The Allies have landed in Normandy. Reliable details begin to emerge. The British radio calls it *Operation Overlord.*

- *Overlord!*

- No one knows what it means, but it sounds hopeful. The word is repeated like a magic incantation that keeps people awake at night.

- One hundred and sixty thousand men, confirms Salvatore. More than thirty thousand vehicles over a seventy-kilometer front…

- Where are they from?

- From England and the United States.

- So, the Germans are leaving? Salvatore bristles.

- Be patient. Normandy is still far away.

If the good news warms our hearts, it does not lessen our anxiety. We still have to deal with a French government that has persecuted the Jews for the last four years. Then there is the Vichy government Militia. Who knows if they will not launch a last big round up? We still feel vulnerable.

- We must not drop our guard, says my uncle. You never know what can happen.

- Can't I at least confide in my best friend? Asks Sarah sulking.

- We are not going to change a thing! We must stay cautious. No gossip. If anyone asks, just say we don't know anything.

The Allies take Cherbourg, but the Germans have destroyed everything and set traps as they withdrew. Then Rome is liberated.

- Let's not celebrate too quickly, warns again Salvatore, to ward off his own jubilation this time.

Outside in the square, people assemble more freely; they form little groups and speculate about developing events. What if the Germans regain the advantage? What if the Allies can't liberate the rest of Italy? In the end, we wait and see. Sharp tongues begin to lash out at the collaborators. Some who had remained silent for four years now loudly demand justice and revenge.

- We must set up special courts of justice, accuses one. That is all these swine deserve.

*

In mid-August we learn that the Allies have landed again, this time on the Mediterranean coast. How long will it take them to reach Villefranche-de-Rouergue? Windowpanes in houses shake as airplanes fly over daily. Bombing intensifies and alerts surge. Men from the resistance paint a big cross of Lorraine on the roof of their black Citroen to fend off the Allied air force.

No one listens any longer to the Vichy propaganda on Radio-Paris. People rely on Radio-Londres to follow the hourly progress of the Allies. A strange atmosphere permeates in town. Everyone goes about their work, but their minds are preoccupied with the drama unfolding around us. The Allied army is coming up the Rhone valley towards Germany. In Villefranche, people dance on the square. We hear that the *resistance* is blowing rail lines to cut off the German armies fleeing north. In Paris, the post office and the police are on strike. Calls for insurrection are heard everywhere. The Vichy radio is now silent, and the government newspapers have stopped publishing. A general mobilization is declared. Fighting takes place in the streets of the capital.

I am longing to see Paris, the Marais district, my rue des Écouffes. If only I could return and be reunited with my parents! Along with other collaborators, Pétain has taken refuge in Germany. General De Gaulle, his enemy in exile, has left England and set foot on French soil in Cherbourg. The armored tanks of Free France General Leclerc are speeding towards Paris.

At last, General De Gaulle parades down the Champs Elysées, hailed by a jubilant crowd.

Jews are still cautious. After all, the Vichy government was French, and French people are not likely to change from one day to the next. Anti-Semitism has not disappeared with Marshal Petain's departure! And who can say the Germans will not turn against us in a last and desperate effort, like a dying animal dragging its victim in its demise? Even though we speak more freely, Jews do not open up entirely. It seems wiser to keep hiding our origins. Our thoughts return to our families sent to Germany. When will they come home? When will we see them again? When will we hug them again?

*

The Germans are in retreat towards Germany, and the Americans enter Chartres! In Villefranche, the municipal brass band marches on the Place Notre-Dame in celebration. A car from the *resistance* with armed *maquisards* perched on the hood leads the band. People rejoice and wave French, English, and American flags. Everyone is smiling. Tonight, there will be dancing under Chinese lanterns.

At home, my aunt cries with relief and happiness. I am confident I soon will see my parents and sister, and normal life will resume. We will remember these last four years as a long nightmare, sometimes saddening us, but not preventing us from living normal lives. The thought that I can take back my name —Crespi — makes my heart beat faster in my chest. I have always been weary of the name Bouchard.

- I hate the name, Bouchard, I tell my uncle.

- Don't curse the name, it protected you.

Still, Simon Bouchard feels like an enemy who separated me from myself and whom I am anxious to leave forever.

*

At about noon on a Saturday, a large crowd forms on Place Notre-Dame. What is this about? Could it be a group of *maquisards* swaggering in town? Curious Villefranchois like me want to see what is happening at the center. I elbow to the front of the dense crowd. I slip between pressed bodies. I hear shouts and insults from the crowd, and women screaming. Pushed forward by the mob, I end up in the front, close to the edge of an empty space shaped like a small bullring. In the center are two *maquisards,* a stool on the ground, and two young women facing away from me. One of the men brandishes a pair of scissors; another roughly grabs one of the women by the hair and twists her head in the direction where I stand. Her face looks distorted with fear and pain. She silently stares at the hand holding the scissors. The man forces her to sit on the stool. The other woman is still standing, her head low, turned away from me. I turn towards the man next to me and ask:

- What have they done?

- They slept with the krauts.

After the woman sits on the stool, her tormenter addresses the crowd.- How about it?

- Yeah! Shave the slut!

All around me people rail against the two victims. The man with the scissors grabs a long lock of the woman's brown hair and cuts it with one stroke. The mob yells its approval. As the man continues shearing, large clumps of hair fall on the polished pebbles that pave the square. The woman does not resist; she remains silent. Soon all that's left on her skull are a few short clumps of hair. She looks grotesque. The job of the man with the scissors over, it is now time for the other woman to sit on the stool.

She is more rebellious and tries to resist. She stares defiantly at the crowd, staring people squarely in the eyes. I suddenly feel dizzy and stiffen in recognition.

- My God! I say out loud. It's Georgette!

She does not appear to have noticed me. How could she, she is beside herself. She sits on the stool on her own. Her hands squarely on her thighs, and sitting erect, she awaits the first cut of the scissor. She maintains her defiant stance for the duration of the cut. Soon her skull is almost bare, with just a few clumps remaining. The conquering *maquisards* have turned her into a distorted creature. Some people spit in her direction and call her names. She submits to the ordeal without weakening, erect as a statue. Her mind seems far away from what is happening here, away from the abuse, and all the while she slowly and intensely surveys the crowd. Her body is here, but her mind is somewhere else.

Suddenly, her eyes meet mine and in one split second I see she recognizes me. With eyes still riveted on mine her guise suddenly alters. She buries her face in her hands and begins to sob.

*

Images of the scene haunt me all night long. After they shaved their heads, the *maquisards* let the two young women go. They had to force their way through the blows and spitting of the mob.

They were not seen anywhere in town for a time. Later, I realized I did not divulge I was a friend of Georgette, nor did I want anyone to know. I only thought about protecting myself. But something inside me told me I should have protected her.

I kept thinking I lacked courage for not speaking or attempting to comfort her. I just stood by and made no effort to help the poor victim. I thought my behavior despicable.

At the same time I wondered about the games Georgette possibly played with me. Was she engaged to an Alsatian, or was it in fact with a German soldier that she went to the movies on Saturday night? Did she lie all along as much as I lied to her? Still, the impression of Georgette I had was not so wrong: She grew up in an isolated part of the countryside and never was concerned by worldwide events. She was just a simple and naïve girl seeking to bring some happiness into her dreary life with dreams she shared with me.

I remained filled with questions and uncertainty. Shouldn't I agree with punishing those who helped and served the Germans? Why do I feel a sense of shame and injustice about what was done to my friend?

During the next few days I occasionally pass in the streets women wearing a scarf over their heads. They look down as they hurry by. I wonder each time whether it is Georgette and I stare at them so intensely they walk away nervously. I am not behaving normally, no doubt the events have troubled me.

I do feel a need to know what happened to Georgette after the ghastly scene, but I don't have the courage to ask the café owner about her. She often talked about her little apartment on the route to Montauban with her window looking onto a lake. I make up my mind to go and see her. I walk the two kilometers of the route to Montauban and reach a red brick house not far from a small pond with ducks swimming in it. Georgette had told me that the honking of ducks would wake her up every morning. I approach the house and knock. Two old people standing close to each other open the door.

- I am looking for a young woman who lives alone near here.

The couple exchanges a knowing look. - It's not here.

- Her house overlooks the lake. I insist.

- You mean the duck pond? What's her name?

- Georgette.

- It's across the road. They slam the door in my face.

Across the road there is another rundown two-story house, and I immediately recognize Georgette's bicycle against a wall. I try to guess which one is Georgette's window. I enter and climb the wobbly stairs rising along a wall with flaking paint. At the top, there are two doors; one is wide open and leads to something like an attic. The other door has no name but seems to be that of an apartment. I knock. No sound inside. I wait, and then knock again.

- Who is it? Asks a voice inside.

If it is Georgette, her voice has changed. - It's me. Simon…

A long silence follows.

- Open up Georgette, I want to talk to you.

I hear shuffling behind the door. The key turns in the lock, and Georgette appears, holding a cigarette between her fingers. Her head is covered with a scarf. Her face looks hard; she looks ten years older.

- What do you want? She asks drily.

Her voice is hoarse, her gaze fierce. I swallow in silence. Georgette has the same defiant expression she had the other day, when she sat on the stool while her tormenter shaved her head.

- I came to tell you... I fumble looking for the right words. I am ill at ease, standing on the landing. Georgette inhales from her cigarette, and stares at me.

- You came to tell me what?

- I wish I had done something for you the other day. I am sorry I did not. The words come out with difficulty, clumsily, but they are said. - What they did to you is not right.

She crosses her arms over her chest, and keeps staring at me. - Is that all?

I shake my head without a word.

- So now you go home, OK? Like her neighbors across the street, she slams the door shut. I stand for a while in front of the door without moving. Finally I go down, the squeaking stairs. Outside, the din of the ducks in the pond adds to my agitation. I head back to the center of town.

*

I arrive home late, that evening. After my visit to Georgette's I needed to think and I walked a long time in the countryside. As soon as I opened the door my uncle demanded to know where I had been dawdling. I answered that he was not my father and that he had no right to ask anything of me. He answered with a slap on my face.

- You ungrateful kid!

I turn away from him, ready to leave, but he is holding my arm and won't let go.

- Let go, you are hurting me!

I hear footsteps coming down from upstairs. My aunt was upstairs with Marguerite. Salvatore slaps me again and shouts that a boy who has completed his Bar Mitzva should show he can act sensibly.

-Wandering outside late at night is not responsible behavior!

- Leave him alone! Urges my aunt stepping into the room.

- He is not a child anymore and must stop acting like one!

I don't want to hear anymore. I escape from my uncle's hold and dash outside. I run towards the old barn in ruin, with tears running down my face. Why isn't my father with me? I would accept anything from him, criticism, or counseling, but I will always reject the authority of Salvatore Carasso!

CHAPTER 13

Autumn 1944

After returning to Paris, I expected my family to appear any day. My uncle's sister let us temporarily use her apartment rue *Camille Desmoulins*. Legal proceedings to recover his properties take all of Salvatore's time. His office building on rue La Fayette and his apartment on nearby rue *d'Hauteville* were occupied during the war. Unscrupulous people assumed that since all Jews died in the camps, the taking over of their possessions and property would go unnoticed. When Jews returned to reclaim their homes and workplaces, those who had unlawfully moved in and had appropriated their properties refused to leave. Throughout France, Jews had to go to court and litigate to get back what was rightfully theirs. It will take Fortunée and Salvatore a whole year before they are able to repossess their property.

*

I am registered at the Lycée Rollin where the attention given to students is remarkably inferior to that given by the Catholic brothers in Villefranche. French people are walking around as though they have a hangover. After enduring the exodus, the occupation, the black market, and the military prisoner camps in Germany; after breaths of hope when the Allies landed in Normandy; after the euphoria of the *Libération* and the uneasy settling of scores between factions; everyday life remains strenuous and hard.

The renovation and reconstruction the country has to undertake must ignore wounds left by deceit and shameful memories. Daily life is an obstacle course. Where can one find food, transportation, and a place to live?

The condition of prisoners of war and returned deportees preoccupies everyone's minds. In any case, what is the difference between prisoners of war and deportees? Weren't my parents prisoners of the Germans? No, people insist, they were deportees. To me, it doesn't matter what they are called. I want to know when they will return.

- You must be patient, Simon.

- Patient? Haven't I waited and been patient already for three years? Isn't the war over?

Added to my confusion are the fears I don't dare express.

*

Jews are Jews again, but they are careful and discreet about their origins. Just in case. They return to the synagogues that are reopening one by one, but cautiously.

I think constantly of my parents and I haunt the streets between the Marais and Bastille, hoping to meet someone I know. In an attempt to distract me, my aunt Fortunée sends me to a vacation camp. The *Chomer Atzaïr*, a Zionist youth movement, organizes the camp. I am not a Zionist, but I agree to go on the trip thinking Fortunée is probably right to send me away. I find myself on a bus, surrounded by a bunch of young people singing in Hebrew. The camp organizers are clear about their goal; it is to forge young Zionists. One day, they say, Palestine will be the homeland where Jews will be able to immigrate and live in peace.

- A Jewish homeland Simon, aren't you looking forward to it?

- All I want is for my parents to return! Nothing else counts for me.

Many of my fellow campers seem to share my feelings. You can read desolation in their gaze. They too saw their parents taken away; they too were in hiding for three years and they await news with a mixture of anguish and hope. In the meantime, they sing Hebrew songs, but their heart is not in it. They have nightmares every night and the counselors have to get up in the dark to calm them.

One day, just as we are finishing lunch in the dining hall, a counselor comes to take one of the young girls and accompany her to the camp director's office. Compelled by unusual curiosity, I follow behind and I peek through the door left ajar and see a well-dressed woman crying. The counselor takes the young girl's hand.- Come, she says, I will help you pack.

A few minutes later as I watch at the window, the young girl enters a taxi, followed by the lady dabbing her eyes with a handkerchief. Perhaps the woman is the girl's mother? I imagine the day when my parents will come and get me. Will they even recognize me? I have changed so much since we last saw each other!

The first thing I do when returning to Paris is to question my aunt.

- Nothing yet, she answers.

Like an obsessed being, I keep returning to rue des Écouffes, rue des Rosiers, rue du Roi de Sicile. There is a new concierge at rue des Écouffes. No one knows what happened to Madame Chevrolier.

- Do you know the Crespi family apartment? I ask the new concierge. The fourth floor left apartment!

- Crespin? Don't know

- Not Crespin, Crespi.

- The apartment of the Crespi family

- Your apartment?

- Yes! Ours! The Crespi family apartment! Where is our furniture? And what about my books?

The woman looks at me as if I were crazy. She seems on the verge of calling the police. I leave without another word and when I reach the street, I cross the rue Saint Antoine. On rue Saint Paul

I learn that Madame Modiano has gone back to the country after all. She left no forwarding address. These fruitless expeditions only depress me further.

*

The start of the year is eventful. The Russian army enters Warsaw and Poland is liberated. Soon after, the first news about concentration camps reaches us. Those who return describe unimaginable horrors. I am convinced such suffering, although horrible, must be exceptional. I am sure my family was sent to a factory or a farm.

Mussolini is shot, together with his mistress. He is hung by his feet, from the rafters of a garage in Milan. American bombers flatten the city of Dresden. Marshal Pétain takes refuge in Switzerland and then surrenders. Camps such as Dachau, where over 32,000 prisoners were interned, are liberated. On April 30th Hitler commits suicide in his Berlin bunker, and the war is officially ended on May 8th. The following November, De Gaulle will become the head of the French provisional government.

A bitter feeling lingers among the Jews. Although, it is true that the French police stood up to the Germans inside Paris during the days of the Libération; indeed, they fought bravely, besieged in the Préfecture building. Their courage was rewarded with the medal of the Libération. Yet no mention is made about the despicable behavior of the same French police during the occupation. French people have already forgotten that it was French gendarmes who were guards in the French camps; that it was the Parisian police officers who pushed the Jews onto the buses going to Drancy and other camps. The French police are honored with medals but nothing is said of their service to the Vichy government. Do a few glorious days in August suffice to obliterate four years of abuse?

Even today, Aunt Fortunée tells me, functionaries at the Prefecture of Police look at her with contempt when she goes there to seek information about my parents. They make her wait for hours. Often they are rude and arrogant, as if supplying information about your family was a burden to them.

- Come back tomorrow.

- But I have been waiting here for hours!

- We're closing.

Her insistence finally yields a bit of news: the mothers, and later the children of Beaune-la-Rolande, were all sent to Drancy, and later to Auschwitz.

- *Auschwitz.* How do you spell it? Where is it? Are there factories in that town?

- I don't know Simon, and she turns away. Did she really tell me all she knows?

One day my aunt asks me to go with her on an errand. While I am getting ready, I overhear my uncle Salvatore reproaching her for taking me along. The errand concerns a visit to the Lutétia Hotel where the returning deportees are first gathered when they return to France, and where the administration keeps records of those that have come home.

- I have already been there a few times, explains Fortunée as we walk towards the métro.

- Have you left a message in case someone might have known them?

- Yes, of course. I would have told you if someone had answered. Then she changes the subject. You should try and be nice with your uncle. He has done a lot for you, you know.

I say nothing. Salvatore would like me to go and work in his store every day after school to learn the business, he says. *His* business! As if I were interested in learning a business! And with him, on top of it! I finally tell my aunt:

- I don't mind being nice, but things would be easier if he left me alone.

- He is trying to help you, Simon.

This is a conversation that leads nowhere. Soon we arrive at the Sèvres-Babylone subway station. The Lutétia is upstairs on Boulevard Raspail. There is a crowd on the sidewalk in front of the hotel. I stay close to my aunt who elbows her way inside. There is complete chaos in the entrance hall. Everyone is looking for someone. Red Cross nurses and boy scouts in uniform hurry about. A deportee appears from time to time, his clothes hanging loosely on his thin frame. His eyes are haggard with the horror they have witnessed and send shivers through me. Lists of names and messages are posted on the walls:

"Have you seen my mother: Sarah Berkowitz? If you have, call Provence 23-45".

Some visitors sob in a corner, others argue. Still others push and demand to get close to the postings. My aunt pushes me towards a list on a wall. We look for the name Victor Crespi but we don't find it, nor that of Fanny or Élise.

- Let's go to the reception desk, mutters Fortunée.

The desk is at the end of the hall. With my hand, I feel the tortoise shell comb in my pants pocket. I always carry it with me, now. It has become my talisman. It's been so long since I saw my mother's face. Almost three years.

- Are there any new lists? Asks Fortunée as she resists the pressure of the crowd behind her.

- Yes, one we just received. We are about to post it...

The crowd seems about to riot as it moves towards the new wall posting. Still, we manage to be among the first to run our fingers over the names.

- Here are the C's, says Fortunée behind me, her hands on my shoulders...

- I don't see Crespi...

- Look for Mechulam...

Mechulam is not there either. We read each column a few times, just to be sure. I notice names of Régine Salomon from the boulevard Voltaire, Victor Goldstein from the rue Oberkampf. There are a few Cohens, some Feders, and some Rosenbaums. A woman next to me just recognized the name of her husband and starts sobbing with joy. In my case, I am crying inside. Fortunée takes my hand.

- Let's go, there is no point in staying here.

- Where is the message you posted earlier?

She takes me to another wall where the note is pinned among a number of others:

"Fortunée Carasso and Simon Crespi are looking for Fanny Crespi, born Mechulam, and her daughter Élise, both arrested and taken to the Vel d'Hiv, then to Beaune-la-Rolande and Drancy in July 1942. We are also searching for Victor Crespi, her husband, arrested in May 1941 and deported from Drancy to an unknown destination."

*

My uncle has made up his mind that I should work in his business. I know I won't like it.

- What am I going to do in your store?

- You'll be the eyes and ears of the boss.

- I am much too young to be taken seriously by your employees, and I am not interested in spying on people.

- It's hard to know what interests you!

- I go to school. Isn't that enough?

- Not with the results you have achieved so far!

My uncle just does not understand me. For him it is simple! When you become a man, you go into business, you make money, and that is it. He cannot conceive that someone might aspire to do anything other than accumulate money and keep it.

My aunt often intervenes in our arguments to calm us down. She understands my feelings and shares my sorrow.

- He would behave differently if his parents were here, she tells my uncle.

- It is not this type of behavior that will make his parents come back! At this stage of the discussion I slam the door and leave.

*

One day my aunt surprises me. She is waiting for me at the lycée at the end of school. She suggests we go in a café.

- Listen Simon, the concentration camps... All the camps are closed by now. Of course there are some deportees left in Germany but they are people without a country, people with no family who have nowhere to go or who for one reason or another cannot go back to their country of origin...

- What are you getting at?

- Your parents lived in France. Victor, Fanny, and Élise are French deportees...

- You don't think they will come back, is that what you are trying to say?

- What I am trying to say is that there is a possibility they will not come back.

- They might have fallen into the hands of the Russians.

- Yes of course, that is a possibility.

- Thousand of deportees are stuck behind the Iron Curtain.

- I know, but… Chances of their return are getting slim. It's a fact. You are a big boy now; I see no reason to hide the truth from you.

- You want to give up, is that it? You have had enough of standing in line at the Prefecture and at the Lutétia?

- I know what you are feeling, Simon. I know how you are suffering. I am just trying to help you understand…

I can't hear her anymore. I stand up, leave the café, and return to what has become a habitual activity. I walk around the streets of Paris.

*

Those friends of the Carassos who came back from the camps and visit us sometimes won't talk about their experience, when I question them. They just say:

- You were lucky Simon, and then change the subject.

Or they say,

- It was hard, it was very hard, but now we are here. All that is in the past, we must talk about happier things, and look towards the future.

I read many accounts of deportees because I want to understand. I can't accept the idea that my family may have suffered such horrors as I have heard described. I once overheard some distressing comments in a crowd coming out of a movie house after seeing a documentary on the camps.

- These are all made up stories! Those who did not return did not want to return. They made a new life somewhere else.

And people keep telling me how lucky I am.

I went through the experience of the Vel d'Hiv and then Beaune-la-Rolande. I felt abandoned and lonely. Even in sleep despair still haunts me. Is that being lucky? My life in Villefranche, its true, was comfortable enough, but we lived with fear and anguish on a daily basis. It does not seem lucky to have suffered as I did and to have barely escaped my torturers. Why shouldn't I complain? Yes, I escaped from being taken to a camp; but I still suffer today, if only because I feel guilty to have escaped the worst.

*

Another time, I am alone in my uncle's office on rue La Fayette with a friend of his, Mr. Epstein. I notice the number on his arm as he checks the time on his watch, and I remark:

- I see you are tattooed.

- Yes, I was two years in Auschwitz.

- Were there women in Auschwitz?

- Oh yes, there were women. They had their own barracks.

- Can you tell me a little bit about life in that camp?

- Oh, you must not raise such questions, young man. It is not a conversation for a young boy to have. We must forget all this.

His attitude infuriates me. I feel that adults all conspire to isolate me. Nobody understands. That very night I see my mother in a dream. She comes toward me, smiling. She seems happy. Suddenly, she turns around peering into space behind her. Now she seems frightened. When she looks back at me, her face is filled with fear. It is a vision I find unbearable, and I choke with sobs. Then she runs away from me. I wake up with a start. I am alone and crying.

*

My aunt gives me a family photo taken before the war. I am so small in the snapshot that my father has to lean forward to hold my hand. Maman is holding Élise's hand. She is wearing a pretty dress with flowers. It must have been a Sunday. The four of us are walking, smiling, and happy, down the Champs Elysees. I slip the photograph in my pocket.

I am on the way to the hotel Lutétia where I decided I would go on my own.

There are fewer people than the last time, when I came with Fortunée. I search the lists on the walls. They seem shorter than they were the other day. I look for the names Crespi and Mechulam. I scrutinize the posted photographs - ID card pictures, group portraits on which one head is circled with a red pen, head shots cut out of family pictures; all ghost-like images that seem to belong to another time. Often, there is a caption at the bottom of the picture: "Deported *from the Phitiviers camp on February 5 1943; corresponded until November 1943".*

Under another picture I read: *"Have you seen my dear husband taken in the round up of August 20 1941 at the metro station Filles du Calvaire? Forward any information to 26 rue Pelée, Paris XIème".* Another says: *"My brother and I are looking for our dear mother taken away at 13 rue des Blancs-Manteaux, on July 17 1942 during the Vel d'Hiv round up. Get in touch with Maurice: at Taitbout 52-47".*

So many faces, so many expressions, so many smiles, so much evidence of disrupted lives. I can't deal with it all. I move away from the boards and walk around the hall. Small groups of people stand here and there. I listen in on conversations:

- I said I was a nurse, says a woman shockingly thin. They send me to the *revier*. It was warmer there than in the barracks...

I move close to the woman and impulsively interrupt her to show my photograph. She leans closer to the snapshot.

- My parents and my sister, I say. Would you have seen them?

A heavy silence sets in. The woman takes the picture between her fingers and gives it back to me almost immediately.

- I don't think so.

I move away swallowing my tears and asking myself whether she really looked at the picture.

CHAPTER 14

1946

I have become passive; I have no energy. I cannot concentrate on my studies, but I am still convinced everything will improve as soon as my parents return. For the time being, I concentrate on gathering information about the camps. Newspapers publish sensational horror stories, but unfortunately, I find few details useful. The photographs portray returned deportees with emaciated bodies and hollow stares that haunt me and give me nightmares.

I cling to statements in the press stressing that the number of returning deportees is far fewer than the departures. To me it means that thousands of people will still come home. It is unfortunate that the Russians have locked up Eastern Europe, including Poland where many of the camps where located. I am certain my family is trapped behind what Churchill calls the Iron Curtain. I expect that agreements between East and West will eventually allow the thousands still detained to return home.

*

My grandmother Esther Mechulam, who was sent back from Drancy to her native Turkey, has returned from Istanbul accompanied by her husband.

They have taken the apartment we are living now and we move to another in the nearby building where my uncle has his store and business. I often visit with my grandparents. Not that we have much to say to each other, but I like their old-fashioned décor, with its oriental carpets and the Turkish food that evokes memories of my earliest years. In a strange way this outlet for my nostalgia helps me remain hopeful. I know my parents would not want me to give in to despair and hopelessness, so I keep telling myself to be patient and try to maintain control over my life.

My biggest problem is that I have no one in whom to confide. Neither my uncle nor my cousin Sarah has much compassion for me. My grandmother bursts into tears, muttering the names of my mother and my sister as soon as she sees me; and I don't want to burden my aunt with my sorrow. People outside the Jewish community don't seem concerned about the way Jews were treated during the war. Nothing has changed, French people say.

- What about us? Don't you think we suffered enough with the war restrictions and our men held prisoners in Germany?

Only the Jews care for the Jews. Sometimes by chance I pass a woman in the street who resembles my mother. My heart starts beating wildly. I stare at the lady. Then I realize that when she returns, maman will have changed. Other times, I think I have seen my father in the métro. I rush to get on that train; I hurry down the aisle to get close to the man, and this perfect stranger looks up at me with surprise.

- I am sorry, I mutter, and I get off at the next station.

Around All Saints day, the radio reports that huge crowds are preparing to visit cemeteries. I realize that if my parents don't return, there will be no grave on which, in the Jewish tradition, I could leave a small pebble to mark my visit. A fit of panic takes hold of me at this thought. But again, I have no one with whom to share these feelings. They come out in nightmares in which I see my parents coming toward me on a sidewalk. The scene resembles the photo taken before the war on the Champs Elysees, except I am not with them, and all three have shaved heads. Maman looks at me from a distance with a strange smile on her face. I wake up with a start in the middle of the night.

What if they never came back? I think out loud, shivering in my sweat soaked pajamas.

*

At the end of the school year I learn that I will not pass into the next grade. My uncle's reaction gives me a glimmer of hope.

- You are just lazy; Simon, and I don't want lazy people in my business.

The vision of having to work for him after my diploma is one more nightmare. I just hope my uncle's threats are serious! He imagines me as a store employee – a job I loathe. A few days later I overhear a discussion between my aunt and uncle discussing me.

- I intend to do for Simon what Fanny would have done if she were here. Says Fortunée in a no nonsense tone. We must help him succeed rather than criticize everything he does, as you do.

- I just don't like thankless and selfish people...

- Are you deaf and blind? Don't you realize he has lost his parents?

- So you think the whole family has to carry Simon Crispi's burden?

After a moment, my uncle adds, - Tell me what you suggest, because as far as I am concerned, I have had it.

- He needs to become independent. I want to register him in a study program in England I heard about. It will be good for him and could change his frame of mind. Ours too. I quietly tip toe away. My only wish is to leave the oppressive environment of this Paris apartment and of France in general.

Diary of Simon Crespi

October 29 1949

So many good things happened since September! Here I am in England, free, for the first time in my life! I am studying economics at the Bradford Technical College, in a charming little town in the center of England. People are nice; life is easy. I am happy.

I am staying in a typical English house; I have my own room, my books, and my things. I keep maman's tortoise shell comb in the drawer of my night table. The landlady leaves me free to come and go as I please. I take a double-decker bus to the college every morning.

Understanding the instructors who speak with a thick Yorkshire accent is a bit of a problem, though. Fortunately, an English girl in my class lets me copy her notes. She is quite pretty! The only problem is she walks with the awkward gait of a cowboy. That puts me off…

Anyway, girls are not in short supply, here. I go to a dancing club near the college to meet them.

I find it so exciting to hold a girl in my arms! One of them is named Sylvia. Like most English girls, she loves French students. She finds my accent – and I quote her - sexy! I could tell when we made love in my room that she had some previous sexual experience. She said she could not believe it was my first time.

Life is almost beautiful since I left Paris…

*

I am aware that my stay in Bradford is only an interlude from my suffering. When I speak to people I say "my parents" without specifying whether I mean my real parents or the Carassos. If only I could be like everyone else! I don't want to mention the events I have endured. It is obvious the war is over for everyone around. People are so eager to turn the page and think of the future! But I can't turn the page. I am not over my suffering. People around me talk about the RAF, the *Resistance,* and the Allies landing. But what of the camps and what happened to the Jews? It is clear people are not well informed on that subject and have no desire to be. For me, the war means French Gendarmes, Vél d'Hiv and Beaune-la-Rolande. Even the Jews I meet in England don't seem to want to discuss the subject…

My aunt sends me a ticket to return to France for the Christmas holidays. I would have preferred to stay in England but I didn't dare mention it. Life here is so much more enjoyable for me. I have my friends, my girlfriends, and I don't have to endure my uncle's criticisms. And then, France remains a land of fear and anguish for me.

*

During these vacations, my old friend Léon from my days at the lycée invites me to attend a party on Boulevard Voltaire. As soon as we arrive, he disappears to greet some friends. I stand in a corner, a glass in hand, feeling uncomfortable as I realize that most of the students here are older than me. How strange! I am not shy in England, but here I am bashful. I am about to leave when Léon comes over accompanied by a slender, pretty woman, her dark eyes enhanced with mascara.

- Olga, says Léon. Olga Rabinovitch. She lives in England, just like you. Olga, this is my friend Simon Crespi… Léon winks at me and concludes before leaving again:

- I will let you get to know each other.

Olga's gaze is intense and sensual. I feel as if she is reading my thoughts. We exchange a few words about England – London, Bradford, the remains of the war. She was born in Lodz. She was eleven when she arrived in France with her parents before the war. I estimate from our conversation that she is seven years older than me. Olga is a woman, not a girl. She now lives in Leeds – not far from Bradford.

- We are just about neighbors, I say.

She agrees with a smile. Dancers are bumping into us, and luckily some seats are liberated on a couch on the other side of the room. I grab two glasses and suggest:

- Would you like to sit down?

- What are you doing in Leeds? I ask as we take a seat.

- I work, she answers evasively. In a fashion store in the center of town, she adds, her eyes peer into mine.

- Do you like it?

- For my clients, France is fashion, she says, drinking a sip of white wine. They don't recognize my accent; they think I am French. She laughs whole-heartedly...

I enjoy her company. My guess is she took an undemanding job to give herself time to recover from the ordeal she must have suffered during the war.

- The music here is deafening. Let's go somewhere quiet to pursue our talk, I suggest.

- Sure. Would you mind getting my coat? She asks.

*

Despite the season, the weather outside is not cold. We walk slowly towards Place de la Bastille, along quiet streets, which were controlled by curfew not that long ago. Olga slides her arm under mine. We stop in a café on the square for a drink of hot rum.

- Are you living with your family? She asks.

- My parents have not yet returned. They were deported.

She knits her brow and her black eyes stare at me, as if my answer surprised her. I change the conversation to Villefranche-de Rouergue. She listens attentively.

- I also lost my parents in deportation, she says.

I am shocked by her remark. It sounds so definitive, and she has said *also*. I avoid raising the point and our discussion shifts to other subjects. Olga is different from my English girlfriends. It is partly because she is older but I suspect this is not the only reason.

- You seem shy, even suspicious, she remarks.

I realize that she has noticed a basic trait of my personality that war events have not modified. But I don't want to revisit the discussion on the deportation.

- Don't you get bored in England?

- I miss Paris, but France carries too many painful memories.

- It's the same for me, I add.

- Leeds is not far from Bradford. You could come visit me, suggests Olga.

We take leave of each other at the métro where we arrive just before the last train. We agree to meet two days later for a stroll along the quays of the Seine.

*

Our rendezvous is at the *Pont Neuf* at 3PM. I arrive early and I see Olga coming towards me in the distance. She looks happy and I don't mind showing I am too. I am not sure how to greet her. Should I offer my hand? Kiss her on the cheek? But she makes the first move, as she did the other night, she slides her arm under mine. We walk towards the Place Dauphine. Everything seems so easy. She mentioned the other evening that she stayed with a friend near *Place Saint-Sulpice* and that the two of them planned to spend a whole morning shopping in the department stores.

- How was your day with your friend? Did you have fun?

- It was great. She just left for the country and I have the apartment all to myself. I am delighted with her response...

We stroll by the second-hand booksellers along the quays where Olga leafs through old books. I tell her how much I enjoy reading and what a comfort it is against loneliness.

- Are you considering writing?

- I keep a diary.

She closes the leather bound book she was looking through.

I begin telling her how my father was arrested but she stops me.

- Not now. Later.

She pursues:

- We did not have a chance to dance the other evening...

- Are you sorry we did not?

- I know a music club in a vaulted cellar near the Palais-Royal. Do you like jazz?

We walk until evening, stopping to eat on rue de la Huchette. We cross the Seine and walk hand in hand towards the Palais-Royal. Couples on the dance floor are lost in a cloud of smoke as they move with frenzy.

- Lets dance the next slow number, whispers Olga in my ear, as if to reassure me.

It is a blues, and we dance cheek to cheek. Olga's skin exudes an exciting perfume. She does not resist when I draw her close to me. My mouth grazes her cheek and her arms circle my shoulders. I feel her fingers caressing the nape of my neck. It is midnight when we leave. Once again, Olga takes my arm. We walk in a long silence.

- Since my friend has left, you can come to my place, she finally says.

*

I spent the night with Olga without calling my aunt and without worrying about what they would think. When I awake, the warm naked body of my lover is snuggled up against me, our legs intertwined under the sheets. Olga is still asleep; her face rests on my chest, her hand is on my shoulder. I am so intent on preserving the moment, I hardly dare breathe. We later share breakfast in bed – café, biscottes, and jam.

- You feel OK? She asks, covering her breasts with the sheet.

Her hair is tousled; a pale smile is on her unmade up face, her thoughts hidden behind her eyes.

- You want to tell me now what happened to your father?

- He was caught in a round up at the Saint-Paul métro station. It was at the beginning of the war. In forty-one. He was interned at the camp of Beaune-la-Rolande, then Drancy, then... Nothing...

- And your mother? Asks Olga in a low voice.

- My mother, my sister, and I... The police arrested us at home. They took us to the Vél d'Hiv before transferring us also to Beaune-la-Rolande. That's where we were separated. My mother and my sister Élise were sent to Drancy ...

- And you remained alone in camp.

- I escaped with a friend. I never was able to get any information about both of them. It was dangerous for a Jew to walk around Drancy. I stayed some time in our apartment in the Marais. But that too was dangerous. A woman helped me get in touch with my aunt and uncle who had escaped to the south. I crossed the demarcation line, and we lived in Nice; but there too, we felt the trap closing in. The rest, you know...

After a while I add:

- I feel I have been waiting for their return... forever. What happened to you?

- We lived in the eleventh arrondissement. On rue *Saint Maur*. It was a Thursday morning; there was no school that day. I was with my father, my mother, and little sister. Neighbors came by to warn us the police were searching homes. We realized the whole neighborhood was surrounded. Daddy started packing a suitcase. He thought they only arrested men. We heard noise in the stairway. Rising to the top floor, the police systematically came down knocking on every door. My father opened the door to two police officers and told them: "I am ready". They had a list with all our names: Maman, my sister, me. Five minutes later we climbed on a bus.

I hold Olga tightly against me. We remain silent. Then she falls asleep and eventually I do as well. We wake up around noon to share a second breakfast. We make love. Naked, Olga gets up and goes to the bathroom; after a while she comes out, still naked. She snuggles against me, smelling of soap. I caress her hair. I never felt so good.

- Are you getting dressed or are we spending the day in bed?

- I'll get dressed.

- Where are we going?

- Rue La Fayette. You are coming with me.

She waits in a café while I go up to the apartment. My uncle is out, just as I hoped. My aunt is alone in the living room. She is not happy, but I know she understands.

- I came to tell you not to worry about me. I am going right back out. Someone is waiting for me…

- Next time tell us when you are not coming home.

- I promise I will.

*

We are inseparable. I love walking through Paris with Olga on my arm. We wander through the bookstores. When we feel the urge to make love, we rush home to her friend's who had the good idea to remain in the country. Most of the time we ignore days and time.

But Olga has to return to England for work. I accompany her to the Gare du Nord. On the platform, I hold her in my arms until the last minute. After the train leaves, I suddenly feel cold. I wrap my scarf tightly around my neck, raise the collar of my coat and walk away, hands in my pockets.

My own return to England is only in ten days. I bury myself in my books on rue La Fayette, but my thoughts are in Leeds. I spend every minute wondering what I am doing alone in Paris. One morning, while I am alone in the apartment, I call Olga on the phone. Her voice is far away.

- How are you doing? I ask.

The discussion is difficult, full of silences. It feels as though Olga is keeping her distance. Am I imagining it?

- Maybe you can't talk because of people in the store…

- No, I am alone.

Panic seizes me as soon as I hang up. Could it be over already? Was I fooling myself about our relationship? Olga might be thinking I am too young for her, or maybe there is someone else. An Englishman, a mature and well-established man in Leeds or London…Unable to bear the wave of agonizing possibilities that confront me, I grab my coat and scarf. I run into Fortunée and Sarah on the landing.

- Where are you going? Asks my aunt.

I scramble down the stairs without even attempting an answer. I spend the rest of the day walking through Paris that I suddenly hate.

*

As soon as I get back to Bradford I call Olga. She seems happy to hear from me this time, even though there are people in the store. She has just enough time to invite me to join her in Leeds for the weekend. When I step down from the train she is on the platform. She is not at all distant, but I need to understand what went on:

- What happened the other day on the phone? You did not want to speak to me. Am I wrong?

-- Don't make a big deal of it! I was just upset... I was in a bad mood. That's all. And she closes the discussion with a kiss.

We walk to her flat, a charming studio located on a quiet street, some ten minutes from the center. We jump immediately into bed where I kiss her madly. In a hurry to undress her, my hands slide under her clothes. Although she pretends to resist me, I can tell she enjoys my impatience.

Olga has prepared a little dinner and arranged a charming table with a bottle of Bordeaux awaiting us. We eat without bothering to get dressed, keeping an amusing and superficial conversation before returning to bed. Sleep eventually overtakes our nested bodies pressed together.

Olga's gentle sobs wetting my shoulder wake me in the middle of the night. I take her in my arms; I kiss her hair and whisper in her ear.

- Tell me...

She continues to cry, and then dries her eyes with the sheet.

- We arrived in France in 1937. We came from Lodz, near the German border. My father was a furrier. My sister and I were registered in the public school. We learned French very quickly. Our parents still spoke Polish at home.

She stops talking and sobs again.

- How sure are you that your parents are dead? I ask.

Her body stiffens.

- You can't understand, she says irritably.

A cold draft settles in the room in the silence established between us. I pull the blanket over our bodies.

- Olga's attitude troubles me. I know how difficult it is to stir painful memories. But why can't she accept I am still waiting for my family's return? So many people were deported. It would be impossible for all of them to be dead. I have read numerous documents on the subject that support my point of view. The word *"probably"* is recurrent in testimonials and reports, clearly indicating nothing precise is known. I am convinced a great number of deportees are still trapped behind the iron curtain.

*

We now spend all our weekends together in Leeds. I am beginning to understand Olga's mood swings. Deep down, she is a cheerful person, but the experience of the camps has left a wound that will not heal. Sometimes she opens her heart a little and talks about her suffering, but the memories are terribly painful. Now and then her face darkens, and I know then where her thoughts are. I urge her to talk to me, but most of the time she refuses.

- I don't want to relive these moments, she says.

- To speak is not to relive.

- You were lucky, so you don't understand.

Again! I hate to be told I was lucky. When she says that, an argument is never far away and arguments lead to hurtful words. We both try to stop quarrelling and slowly, Olga recovers her charming smile. Once again she lets herself go in my arms. Our lovemaking is at times violent, at times tender. But too often, sadness enters right after making love, and Olga cries again in the dark.

*

When June and the nice weather settle in, Olga borrows a car for a weekend to Gretna Greene. The little town in the south of Scotland is well known for romantic, quick weddings. We are both in a good mood as we drive, joking about marriage. Why not get married? Why not have a secret wedding? Olga laughs heartily at my joke. But should marriage be a joke? She is not quite sure about that, and neither am I. I have been driving for about an hour when Olga's face suddenly darkens. Her gaze is static, fixed in the distance. When I try to engage her in conversation, she does

not answer. We drive two long hours in almost complete silence.
We made a reservation at the Cross Key, a traditional inn.

- If only the walls could speak, I say closing the door of our room.
I wonder how many honeymoons were spent in this room.

She turns away as I try to take her in my arms. Hopelessness
has taken over. I try to comfort her, but it's in vain. She tells me
she wants to rest; she wants to be alone for a while. I go down to
dinner alone. The dining room is bursting with couples who came
from London for a romantic weekend.

The next morning is bright and sunny. Olga agrees to join me for
a walk. We leave the town and stroll in the countryside. Her hand
in mine is cold. Olga is silent. As we are walking along a country
path, she suddenly sits down on a large stone, she stiffens, and
without crying, she stares at the ground, darkly. I am distraught.

- Tell me what's wrong.

She shrugs her shoulders, with a desperate look. Her cheeks are
as pale as if she were sick. She starts speaking softly, her voice
barely audible.

- We were in a camp at *Vught*. You don't know the place. It's in
Holland, at the border with Germany. It is not a very well known
camp, not as big as others, but still equipped with a traveling
crematorium. A crematorium on wheels, if you can imagine…

Words are coming out of her mouth with difficulty. I kneel in
front of her and take her hands in mine to warm them.

-- The camp was two kilometers away from a factory, she continues.
They made us work on machines. We made parts for airplane

engines. We had to get up at 4:30 AM, before daylight. After roll call, we left for the factory where they made us work for 12 hours.

She is silent again. Her forehead creases, her gaze is lost in visions of the past; she trembles, remembering suffering and fear. - The Canadians liberated us. You saw the pity in their eyes. We no longer looked like human beings. We were wrecks. They told us we were free. We could not understand what that meant. I had a girlfriend in camp. She had just died in my arms a few hours before the Canadians arrived. And I was free...

Olga sighs. She stops talking. Around us, birds flutter in the bushes.

*

When we get back to town, I ask her whether she would prefer to go home and finish the weekend in Leeds. Truth is I would rather take her home and return to Bradford. I suddenly feel the need to be on my own, to think, to consider. My room, my books, and my studies are a refuge from anguish of the past. For an instant I dream of happier times with my carefree and lively girl friends in Bradford.

- So, I ask, what do we do? As we enter our room.

- I don't know, she says. I would like to rest.

I go down to the bar, order a drink, leaf through newspapers without reading them. I thought I had found a measure of peace in England, but since this woman entered my life, the anguish of war has once again reappeared and torments me. A deep anger surfaces. It seems that Olga holds the answers to questions I need answered so that I can understand the fate of my relatives. She either cannot or does not want to share her awareness with me. We return to Leeds at the end of the afternoon.

*

Since that day, our relationship has been altered. I dread the heavy atmosphere of my weekend visits to Leeds. First the quarrels, then the tears, finally reconciliation in bed. One Friday when Olga seems more relaxed and in a better mood than usual, I start again to ask questions about the camps. She immediately loses her temper. Her face turns red, and her voice shrieks:

- What do you want to know, after all? That I shaved the heads of those who would be dead an hour later? That I pulled gold teeth from bodies before they went to the ovens? That just a week after my arrival in camp I found my parents suitcase on a pile of luggage of those who went to the ovens?

-- All camps were not extermination camps! I am unable to resist muttering.

Howling, this time, she adds:

- They are dead Simon! Your parents are dead! They will not come back! You will not see them again! They went up in smoke the day they arrived in the camp! I have seen it happen thousands of times! She abruptly turns away.

I get up and go to sit in the kitchen; and take my head in my hands. I hear Olga going to the bathroom and closing the door. I am still stunned by her screams. My mind is a blank; I cannot absorb what I just heard. Minutes pass. I realize no sound is coming out of the bathroom. Intuitively I go to the door and knock. No answer. I turn the knob. Olga has locked herself inside.

- Olga!

I put my ear to the door. I think I hear a moan or heavy breathing.

- Olga!

I knock on the door again.

- Open up or I will break down the door!

I back up two steps, ready to push with my shoulder, but the key turns in the lock and the door opens. Olga is half naked, her hair disheveled, her face ravaged, her eyes empty. She looks drunk…

- What did you do?

An empty pillbox lies on the bathroom floor. Olga steps forward. Her eyelids close heavily. She staggers. I rush to catch her just as she slumps in my arms.

*

- Barbiturate, explains a doctor at the hospital.

The ambulance arrived a few minutes after I called.

- We pumped her stomach, continues the doctor. She took quite a few tablets, and on an empty stomach.

- And now?

--She is asleep…

- But...

- She is no longer in danger.

- When will I be able to see her?

- She will wake up in a few hours.

*

Diary of Simon Crespi

Night has fallen. I am writing these notes for my diary in Olga's apartment. They will keep her at least one more day in the hospital.

I was next to her when she woke up. At first she did not recognize me. Her eyes were still full of nightmares. Then she tried a little smile before turning her head away. I took her hand and I noticed she had fallen asleep again. The nurse suggested I leave. They say Olga is no longer in danger, but a psychiatrist has to see her tomorrow. He will decide what will be next. He may recommend a stay in a rehab center. I feel so guilty for what has happened.

*

The next day, the psychiatrist who has examined her invites me into his office.

- Here is how things stand. We can let her out as long as she stays with someone who will take care of her and watch her for the next few days. She must not remain alone during that time. If this cannot be arranged she will go in a rehabilitation house for a while.

- She will be in good hands with me, I say. You can count on me. May I see her now?

- Of course.

The doctor seems satisfied with my answers. He takes me back to the hospital's main ward. I walk along the corridor, knock, and open the door. I sit down next to Olga who begins sobbing as soon as she sees me, begging:

- Don't let them send me to a psychiatric hospital.

- Don't worry; we're going back to your place. Today.

That night, after turning off the lights, I move close to Olga's warm body. She doesn't push me away. I take her in my arms and we make love quietly, without a word or even a sigh. Then we each turn away and fall asleep.

Olga is on sick leave from work for a week. I will stay with her until she is fully recovered, then I will leave. She knows it, although we don't talk about it. In fact, we don't talk about anything anymore. Olga recovers in the next few days, but we avoid all meaningful discussion.

There are so many things I need to clear up. I knew I was vulnerable, but Olga is even more vulnerable than me. While our break up has been postponed, it now seems unavoidable. Her last words before she attempted suicide still haunt me. "They went up in smoke!" I promise myself to analyze, them later, when I am alone, when I feel calmer and them later, when I am alone, when I feel calmer and more able to sort through the tangle of my thoughts.

Olga is tidying up her flat. She says my books, and my things in general have a tendency to take over her space. I notice that she has said *her* space. I help her tidy up.

*

Then, one day Olga sees me off at the train station. We decide to stay in touch, but we both know there is little chance we will see each other again. Are we friends or not? I cannot say. I don't want to talk about it any more than she does. I have learned there are two Olgas. One wants to be happy; the other is incapable of it.

The train stops in front of the platform with a shrill mechanical grinding noise.

On my return to Paris I search for David Berlinsky. But neither he nor his family has left any trace...

EPILOGUE

1985

One episode comes back to me as I am about to end this book. At the end of that college year in Bradford, I decided to continue my studies in the United States. I know the Carasso family received the news with relief. Although my aunt cared a lot for me, she could see that my return to her family would be an endless source of conflict with Salvatore.

I hugged everyone good-bye and boarded the Queen Mary ocean liner sailing to New York. One night, when I could not sleep during the crossing, I went up on deck and leaned on the handrail. I watched the ocean reflect the glow of a moon, low above the waves. Familiar faces scrolled through my mind—Olga, my friend David, my grandmother Mechulam, my uncle, my aunt, my cousins, my missing parents, and my sister. I was about to start a new life.

I put a hand in my pocket and felt maman's tortoise shell comb. I had vowed to keep this talisman until her return, but Olga's words echoed in my head. "They are dead, Simon! Your parents are dead! You will never see them again! They went up in smoke the day of their arrival in camp! I have seen that happen thousands of times!"

I took the comb out of my pocket and fingered it for a while. I was undertaking a new life... I brought the tortoise shell comb to my lips with my eyes closed, I kissed it and then threw it in the ocean where it instantly disappeared.

*

I spent the rest of my life in America. My two marriages ended in divorce. My first wife was born in France; like me she hid during the war in a small village with her family. The parents of my second wife are holocaust survivors. This is what former deportees are called today.

One day I learned of a group of holocaust survivors that met regularly in town. I decided to attend their meetings. We were originally only eight men and women, all natives of various European countries. We shared having survived Nazism in camps, in hiding, or by fleeing. We dedicated ourselves to perpetuating the memory of Holocaust victims and the legacy of the survivors by telling their stories, engaging in Shoah education, and holding conferences.

We felt the need to share experiences that many of us had kept secret for years. The meetings were beneficial. The opportunity to recount painful memories to others who had experienced comparable ones, eased the persistent sorrow.

Sarah Rosenfeld, one of the women I met at these reunions, owned a book *"The Memorial of the Deportation of French Jews,"* published in France by Serge Klarsfeld. The book's source material was registers prepared by the meticulous Germans. It listed each of the transports that left France, the names of each individual on the transport, and the date of each departure. Sarah offered to let me consult the book, but I hesitated. I feared reawakening a painful, perhaps unbearable experience.

Eventually, I gathered my nerve and asked Sarah:

- I would like to examine your book.

- Are you sure? She asked.

- The harm was done long ago, and as if sharing a confidence I added in a low voice:

- You know, I really never mourned my departed relatives. In the end, I still keep hoping for a miracle…

That was the way I felt, despite the fact that I had thrown the tortoise shell comb into the sea on the Queen Mary, and that it rested at the bottom of the ocean as the eternal link uniting me with maman.

- Go into my office, Sarah said, look at it quietly and stay as long as you need to.

I remained a long time looking through the large format book that lay on Sarah Rosenfeld's desk. My emotions swept over me like a tidal wave and I was no longer myself, I was no longer in America; I was back in Europe. I was no longer a man; I was a child again.

I began turning the pages. My father was arrested in May 1941. The first transport mentioned in the book was March 27, 1942. I ran my trembling fingers over the alphabetized list of names reproduced from typewritten lists. Through eyes blurred by tears I reached the section of names starting with a C, and there I found my father's name.

CRESPI Victor   5. 7.05   SALONIQUE

Oh my God...

Tears now ran freely from my eyes. I remember biting my finger hard. Why did I open that book? I kept repeating to myself. But it was too late to turn back. I kept turning the pages. I went over the list of the other transports. When I reached the 27th transport I read:

CRESPI Fanny   8.10.10   ISTANBUL
CRESPI Élise   6. 6.28   PARIS

It was all there. I had the answer I had been looking for, for over forty years. The truth seemed so simple, a few names on a list. I read the names of my relatives over a number of times.

It took a great effort to close the book. I never felt so close to my father, my mother, and my sister than at the moment when their names appeared to me in that book. I asked Sarah to let me photocopy the pages with the names of my relatives. I later framed these pages and hung them on a wall in a corner of my living room. Finally, I could start mourning my family

Printed in the United States
by Booxmasterd

Printed in the United States
By Bookmasters